***"Nice to see you again, Lieutenant," Roc drawled.***

"Liar."

Stunned, Roc stared at Dr. Samantha Andrews. "Excuse me?"

Sam met and held his surprised gaze. "You're a liar, Captain Gunnison. And don't try and sweet-talk me, because it won't work. I call a spade a spade."

Lips tightening, Roc stared at her. "Okay, Doctor, have it your way. I was just trying to be social."

"Yeah, right. I saw the look you gave me. I know where I stand with you on this mission."

He glared down at her. "We need to talk. But not here. And not now. Once we get to Area Five, you and I are going to chat. Alone."

Giving him a cutting smile, Sam said, "Fine with me, Captain. Because frankly, you're the *last* man on earth I'd ever want to have with me on a mission."

Dear Reader,

Things are cooling down outside—at least here in the Northeast—but inside this month's six Silhouette Intimate Moments titles the heat is still on high. After too long an absence, bestselling author Dallas Schulze is back to complete her beloved miniseries A FAMILY CIRCLE with *Lovers and Other Strangers*. Shannon Deveraux has come home to Serenity and lost her heart to travelin' man Reece Morgan.

Our ROMANCING THE CROWN continuity is almost over, so join award winner Ingrid Weaver in *Under the King's Command*. I think you'll find Navy SEAL hero Sam Coburn irresistible. Ever-exciting Lindsay McKenna concludes her cross-line miniseries, MORGAN'S MERCENARIES: ULTIMATE RESCUE, with *Protecting His Own*. You'll be breathless from the first page to the last. Linda Castillo's *A Cry in the Night* features another of her "High Country Heroes," while relative newcomer Catherine Mann presents the second of her WINGMEN WARRIORS, in *Taking Cover*. Finally, welcome historical author Debra Lee Brown to the line with *On Thin Ice*, a romantic adventure set against an Alaskan background.

Enjoy them all, and come back again next month, when the roller-coaster ride of love and excitement continues right here in Silhouette Intimate Moments, home of the best romance reading around.

Yours,

Leslie J. Wainger
Executive Senior Editor

# LINDSAY McKENNA

## Protecting His Own

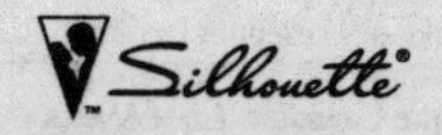


INTIMATE MOMENTS™

Published by Silhouette Books

**America's Publisher of Contemporary Romance**

ISBN 0-373-27255-3

PROTECTING HIS OWN



This edition published by arrangement with Harlequin Books S.A.



Visit Silhouette at www.eHarlequin.com

**Printed in U.S.A.**

## Books by Lindsay McKenna

Silhouette Intimate Moments

*Love Me Before Dawn* #44
ΔΔ*Protecting His Own* #1184

Silhouette Special Edition

*Captive of Fate* #82
**Heart of the Eagle* #338
**A Measure of Love* #377
**Solitaire* #397
*Heart of the Tiger* #434
†*A Question of Honor* #529
†*No Surrender* #535
†*Return of a Hero* #541
*Come Gentle the Dawn* #568
†*Dawn of Valor* #649
***No Quarter Given* #667
***The Gauntlet* #673
***Under Fire* #679
††*Ride the Tiger* #721
††*One Man's War* #727
††*Off Limits* #733
‡*Heart of the Wolf* #818
‡*The Rogue* #824
‡*Commando* #830
***Point of Departure* #853
°*Shadows and Light* #878
°*Dangerous Alliance* #884
°*Countdown* #890
‡‡*Morgan's Wife* #986
‡‡*Morgan's Son* #992
‡‡*Morgan's Rescue* #998
‡‡*Morgan's Marriage* #1005
*White Wolf* #1135
◊*Wild Mustang Woman* #1166
◊*Stallion Tamer* #1173
◊*The Cougar* #1179
Δ*Heart of the Hunter* #1214
Δ*Hunter's Woman* #1255
Δ*Hunter's Pride* #1274
§*Man of Passion* #1334
§*A Man Alone* #1357
§*Man with a Mission* #1376
◊◊*Woman of Innocence* #1442
ΔΔ*The Heart Beneath* #1486

Silhouette Romance

‡*The Will To Love* #1618

Silhouette Desire

*Chase the Clouds* #75
*Wilderness Passion* #134
*Too Near the Fire* #165
*Texas Wildcat* #184
*Red Tail* #208
Δ*The Untamed Hunter* #1262
‡*Ride the Thunder* #1459

Silhouette Shadows

*Hangar 13* #27

Silhouette Books

*Silhouette Christmas Stories* 1990
"Always and Forever"
*Lovers Dark and Dangerous* 1994
"Seeing Is Believing"
*Morgan's Mercenaries:*
*Heart of the Jaguar* 1999
*Morgan's Mercenaries:*
*Heart of the Warrior* 2000
*Morgan's Mercenaries:*
*Heart of Stone* 2001

Harlequin Historicals

*Sun Woman* #71
*Lord of Shadowhawk* #108
*King of Swords* #125
*Brave Heart* #171

*Kincaid trilogy
†Love and Glory
**Women of Glory
††Moments of Glory Trilogy
‡Morgan's Mercenaries
°Men of Courage
‡‡Morgan's Mercenaries: Love and Danger
◊Cowboys of the Southwest
ΔMorgan's Mercenaries: The Hunters
§Morgan's Mercenaries: Maverick Hearts
◊◊Morgan's Mercenaries: Destiny's Women
ΔΔMorgan's Mercenaries: Ultimate Rescue

---

## *LINDSAY McKENNA*

A homeopathic educator, Lindsay teaches at the Desert Institute of Classical Homeopathy in Phoenix, Arizona. When she isn't teaching alternative medicine, she is writing books about love. She feels love is the single greatest healer in the world and hopes that her books touch her readers' hearts.

To Lynda Curnyn, my editor, who works so hard
on my behalf and always makes my day.

# *Chapter 1*

*February 2: 0700*

"How do you get oil and water to mix?" Morgan Trayhern asked out loud as he stood looking out the window of his office at Camp Reed. The marine base near Los Angeles had been operating twenty-four hours a day, seven days a week since an earthquake registering 8.9 on the Richter scale, had hit the Orange County area on New Year's Eve. The devastation had left millions of people without food, water or medicine. Only this base had the air facility and personnel to even begin to try and save lives in that destroyed region. As an ex-marine and the head of Perseus, a covert agency that provided top-secret assistance to the government, Morgan had signed on to help with the recovery efforts. It hadn't been easy.

And with this next problem on his plate, his job had gotten a bit tougher.

Tucking his hands into the back pockets of his jeans, Morgan scowled. How was he going to get two very strong, bullheaded people to work as a team out in area 5 without killing one another? Morgan studied the faint pink color along the desert horizon, the sight of the new dawn filling him with hope.

The airport, a mile below the hill where the headquarters and logistics buildings sat, hummed like a stirred-up beehive. Fifty helicopters, mostly Sea Stallions and UH-1N Hueys, were lined up for takeoff—the backbone of the relief fleet. They had all been loaded the night before, and today two pilots would man each one, to fly goods into assigned areas. The flights would continue nonstop all day. Hardworking marine crews were also unloading huge Air Force cargo planes coming in regularly from points east. It was backbreaking work.

Absently, Morgan adjusted the collar on his red Polo shirt. Even though it was winter in Southern California, with temperatures dropping down to the thirties and forties at night, he wore short-sleeved shirts most of the time. His wife, Laura, always teased him about being so warm-blooded.

Turning, Morgan sighed, glancing around the tiny room and taking in the standard-issue green metal desk, the maps tacked to every inch of wall so he could plan and organize the flights. The radio on his desk was connected with each of the supply and rescue camps they'd already established in the devastated area. Each channel was designated for a specific region. It was also connected to the brain of the operation, in HQ, where the generals convened to create workable strategies along with federal and local government officials.

"Knock, knock?"

Morgan lifted his head. He smiled when he saw Dr. Samantha Andrews peek her head around the corner of his partially opened door. Seemed he was going to have that oil and water problem sooner rather than later. "Good morning, Sam. Come on in." He lifted his hand.

"Thanks, Morgan. How's Laura? I haven't seen her since her last official checkup with me, a week ago. How's her ankle doing?"

"She's now on crutches. She hated that wheelchair, but she also hated being in bed with her leg suspended. I think the surgery you performed was successful."

Frowning, Sam muttered, "Yes and no. When she got that blood clot later, that was a bump in the road to her recovery. I'm just glad we were able to fly in the drugs to get rid of it, since drugs of any kind are on short supply around here due to the earthquake crisis."

Morgan nodded. "Well, like I said, she's happy being on crutches. She was so elated when you gave them to her last week, and thrilled to be able to send the wheelchair back to Supply."

"It will be eight weeks total before she can put real pressure on that ankle and the pins in it," Sam said. "Hopefully, we can get her out of here by that time, back to Montana, and she can begin physical therapy at that point, to bring it back to almost full use."

Lifting a pot from the coffee dispenser, Morgan held a cup in Sam's direction as she stepped into the room. "Coffee?"

Laughing huskily, she said, "You need to ask a navy person if they want *coffee?*"

Chuckling, Morgan poured her a cup. "Right now, Laura is keeping busy by helping the pediatric ward take care of the babies. My wife is especially fond of Baby Jane Fielding, the little girl we found buried in the rubble while I was still out there in the field looking for Laura."

"Ah yes, that cute little tyke," Sam murmured, smiling. "Well, at least Laura has something to do. That's important for her right now." She came over and extended her long, thin hands toward the white ceramic cup he held out. "Coffee..." she sighed. "Nectar of the gods and goddesses...."

"Marines like java, too."

"Yeah, marines aren't far behind on that one," she said genially as she watched Morgan pour himself a cup.

"Even ex-marines like me never lose the habit. It's ingrained, I think."

Laughing, Sam slid her hands around the thick cup and lifted it to her lips. "Understandable. The navy pays marines their checks twice a month, so they're a part of us whether they like to admit it or not."

"There's the rub," Morgan said. "Marines like to think they're a stand-alone service, like the army and Air Force."

Sam took a chair in front of Morgan's desk, rearranging her white lab coat and the stethoscope hanging around her neck. "Yeah," she said wryly, "I know. I run into that attitude all the time. Marines are too proud to admit they're a part of something else. I think they forgot the concept of teamwork a long time ago."

"Maybe so," Morgan murmured as he sat down in the squeaky desk chair. "But the esprit de corps of the marines is known around the world and it's very real."

Sam sipped the coffee gratefully. She'd just gotten off a twelve-hour tour of duty, and it was 0700. She had twelve hours of rest coming to her before she went back on duty in the emergency room of the base hospital. "No question about that. It's just that marines have a *real* problem working with anyone but their own kind. You used to be one. You know that."

Grunting, Morgan nodded. "No question, at times, that it gets in the way of good teamwork with others," he said, studying the young woman before him speculatively. Sam's shoulder-length red hair curled about her thin, proud shoulders, a bright contrast to the white lab coat she wore over her standard navy issue light blue, long-sleeved blouse and dark blue slacks. Despite his concerns about *her* ability to work with others, Morgan knew Sam was a damn good surgeon. She had saved his wife's badly injured ankle after Laura had been dug out of the rubble of the hotel they'd been staying in. If not for the doctor's knowing hands in surgery, Morgan knew his wife might have lost her whole foot.

In fact, Sam, the head of E.R. for the navy hospital on Camp Reed, had insisted upon performing the surgery herself when she'd heard that Laura was married to the famous Morgan Trayhern. Morgan was forever grateful for Sam stepping in. Especially since the M.D. had already put in fourteen hours in E.R. that day, trying to help the hundreds of patients flowing through the doors in the wake of the earthquake. The hospital was on triage standing, and when Morgan had flown in with Laura, he had wondered if they'd get any help at all.

He remembered seeing Sam in the busy passageway just inside the double doors of the hospital when he'd arrived with Laura, who had been carried in on a stretcher by two marines. With her bright red-gold hair, Sam had been hard to miss beneath the fluorescent lights. The hallway was jammed and crowded. Morgan had heard the moans, the cries, had seen the obvious shock on the faces of dozens of people sitting on the floor, lying on gurneys, or standing and holding their bloody wounds, waiting for medical help.

Laura had been in deep shock herself, Morgan knew. Making his way through the crowd, he'd grabbed hold of Sam's bloody white lab coat to get her attention. Automatically, he'd sensed she was in charge, because of the way she gave orders to the corpswaves and corpsmen, as well as the nurses. Her voice was cool, calm and authoritative. When she spoke, people settled down and listened. It was obvious Sam Andrews knew how to get things done, and that was the type of person Morgan wanted helping his wife.

When he'd grabbed her sleeve, Sam had stopped, turned her head, and then stared at him in surprise. Morgan had introduced himself, though he'd seen recognition in her eyes. For once, his legendary reputation had paid off. To Sam's credit, she'd dived through the crowd to examine Laura's mangled extremity, and then had called two orderlies over to take Laura up to an operation theater for immediate surgery prep.

Morgan would never forget the intense look of compassion in Sam's eyes as she'd turned back to him. Gripping his hand briefly, she'd promised him that she would perform the surgery on Laura herself, and that everything was going to be fine. He'd nearly broken down and cried then. The genuine understanding in her eyes of what he was going through after nearly losing his wife in the hotel collapse had touched him deeply. Sam was a noble person, with such integrity and grit that Morgan had sworn he'd somehow repay her. Right now, he was going to do that, but he wasn't sure she'd be thankful.

Leaning back in his chair, he said, ''Sam, I'm pulling you from the ranks to help me. You're the head of E.R. for good reason, and I need someone with your brains, moxie and abilities. Right now, we have an epidemic starting to flare up in the L.A. basin.''

Nodding, Sam sobered. ''Yeah, I know. It's inevitable, Morgan. The basin has no good local sources of water. I knew it would happen. A lot of people are gonna die if we can't get someone in there to help, and soon. I know thousands of people are leaving the affected area and our agencies are trying to take them in, but they're overwhelmed, too.''

''No disagreement. We have info that roughly a hundred thousand people have walked out of the area seeking help. But there are still those in the area who need medical attention. That's why you're here, Sam.''

She sat up and crossed her legs, resting the coffee cup on her knee. ''Oh?''

''Yeah.'' Morgan eased upward and placed his own cup on the desk in front of him. ''Starting tomorrow morning I want you to go into area 5 with a Recon team to protect you, and set up three sites for medevacs—medical evacuation areas—where people can get help for the dysentery, typhoid, food poisoning and other acute medical emergencies that are cropping up. Many people can't walk ten or twenty miles to get out of the area, either because they are injured too badly or ill, elderly, or they are parents with children who might be more at risk on the road. These centers are being put into each area to take care of the people who are left behind. Plus, critically injured people have to be flown out ASAP because our road system is completely destroyed. We need you to formulate a medical system in one area, make it work, refine it if necessary, and then take that model to the other areas. You would be the advance medical team going in, setting up things for the regular teams.'' He looked into her narrowing green eyes. Morgan could see she was very interested in the project. That was good. Maybe that would make up for the part he knew she probably wouldn't like. ''You think outside the box, Sam. I saw that when Laura was brought in and we were standing there in the passageway of the E.R., waiting for medical help. I watched as you assessed a lot of different triage situations, set things in motion and catalyzed everyone around you. You're efficient. You grasp the whole of a problem, but you get the details right, as well.''

''Thanks,'' Sam murmured, pleased. ''Maybe you could suggest to the higher-ups to write that on my next six-month fitness report,'' she said with a chuckle. Twice a year every person in the service was rated. The members on the fitness report determined whether or not a person would get promoted. A good report in one's personnel jacket guaranteed it. A bad one could keep a person stuck in a job for years. It was a brutal, inflexible system, and many times, politics got involved. In these cases a career could be sandbagged and go to hell in a hurry, just because a superior didn't like someone.

"Don't worry," Morgan promised her fervently, "after I get done talking to your superiors you're going to get such a glowing report that you'll jump from lieutenant commander straight to commander."

Sam grinned mischievously. "*That* I have to see." She warmed to the genuine sincerity in Morgan's eyes. "I'm interested in this mission. That is why you called me in, right? To head up an advance medical team to create medevacs?"

"Yes. But..."

"Uh-oh..."

"Yeah," Morgan said, trying to soften his expression, "there's more to this mission than just you going in with key personnel, a map and ideas, Sam. As you know, we have a survivalist group running around out there. You've heard about them, right? The Diablos?"

"Yes. They murdered two marine helicopter pilots a couple of weeks ago, didn't they?"

"Unfortunately, yes."

"That puts them on my list."

"Mine, too." Opening his hands, he added, "And that's why I'm sending in a Recon team with you. Things aren't safe out there, Sam. These survivalists hit and run. We don't have enough marine personnel available to cover the L.A. basin and hunt them down. They move from one area to another, although it does look as if they have a base of operations. We just haven't located it yet."

"Too little manpower to do so," Sam agreed. She placed her coffee cup on the desk and clasped her hands on her knee. "Okay, so I handpick a small team of people to, first, find good sites for these three med-evac tent areas, right?"

"Right."

"And this Recon team is my big, bad guard dog, protecting me and my people while we reconnoiter the area to find what locations work best for helo landings and takeoffs for patients needing hospital care here at Camp Reed?"

"Yes, but we're widening our scope of hospitals, since the navy CH-53E Super Stallions we just got on board have a helluva lot longer range and carry more fuel. We'll be flying patients to hospitals north and east of Los Angeles, as far as San Francisco."

"Well, that's good news. We're totally overwhelmed here and can't do more than we are presently."

"You know that more than anyone, Sam," Morgan said grimly. "I'm surprised you've done as much as you have. You're a magician."

Sam smiled. "Look, I know this is a picky point, but I *am* in charge of this new operation, right? *All* of it?"

Moving uncomfortably, Morgan held her flat stare. He knew what was coming. "Sam...you'll need to share the power and decision-making process with the captain who heads up the Recon team."

"What, exactly, does that mean?"

His stomach clenched. From the short time he'd known her, Morgan knew Sam was a gung-ho, take-charge and take-no-prisoners kind of woman. She was a natural leader, a damn fine one. His own experience told him that Sam would balk at the idea of someone of the same rank being "boss" over her. She wouldn't take kindly to the situation.

"It means," he said gently, "that there may be times when Captain Gunnison may have the final decision instead of you, Sam. It would be in the area of safety," he said, trying to reassure her. "I want you and your team safe. He and his men are trained for that. You're going to have to work *with* him and vice versa. You might not be happy about it, but you're going to have to base your decisions about the medevac areas and so on on his perceptions of the dangers."

Morgan saw her rear back, surprise on her face. Her green eyes widened enormously and then narrowed to slits. Trying to avoid a blowup, he said, "I know this isn't what you want, Sam. But under the circumstances, I can't, in all good conscience, turn you loose out in the field with those survivalists roaming around like a pack of wolves. It's a volatile, dangerous situation. The *last* thing I need is you to have wounded or dead. I'm looking to you to create the medical model for each of these areas. The epidemic is already flourishing out there. A lot of people are dying. Medevac stations should have been set up weeks ago, but I had to battle the top brass to get this plan in the works."

"Tell me I heard wrong, Morgan. You said Captain Gunnison?"

"Yes. Why? Do you know one another?" Morgan guessed the answer to that by the look on her face, and his gut clenched.

"Do I know him?" she drawled. She threw her hands upward. "Do I know this arrogant, know-it-all, I'm-right-and-you're-wrong marine? Oh, brother, do I! One of his men got hurt in a Recon mission here at Camp Reed about six months ago, and he was the biggest pain in the arse in Emergency. I happened to be on duty when the guy was flown in, with Gunnison at his side. Talk about a mother hen, Morgan. Gunnison was in my face, demanding that his man be taken care of immediately, ahead of other emergency cases that were a helluva lot more severe and life-threatening.''

''And he got into an argument with you on it?'' Morgan could see where this was going. He'd been right: these two were oil and water, and would never mix. But he was so strapped for personnel. What he couldn't tell Sam was that Gunnison, the executive officer of the Recon company stationed at Reed, was the last man available to pull for this five-man team. Everyone else was assigned to another area. Morgan was stuck. He hadn't known about this earlier confrontation between her and Gunnison. He hadn't anticipated this kind of reaction from Sam. Damn.

''Argument?'' Sam said lightly, derision in her husky tone. ''Let's put it this way, Morgan—I was nose-to-nose with this arrogant SOB out in the passageway. I told him I was in charge of E.R., not him. He had the balls to say it didn't matter, that his man's injury took priority.'' Sam laughed sharply and shook her head. ''When Gunnison wants something, he'll move heaven and hell to get it. When I refused to treat his man right away, he went over my head—stormed out of E.R. and went to my direct superior, Commander Talkins. Fortunately, Talkins didn't side with him, and put him in his place. But Gunnison called over to his company commander, Major Branson, to raise hell and have pressure put on me to deal with his marine's injury.''

''Oh, boy...'' Morgan murmured.

"Yeah, no kidding. And you're assigning this guy to *me* and my team? Morgan, I'm sorry, but I don't ever want to deal with that dude again. He's bull-headed. He won't listen to reason. I can just see the kinds of hell I'll go through out there with him. Besides, he'll see it as a way to get even with me for not making his marine's injury a top priority, and he'll stick it to me. I know his type. I don't need the hassle. Just let me go out there and do my job, okay? *That* I can do. And well." Besides, the death of her fiancé, Captain Brad Holter, who had been a Marine Cobra helo pilot, was enough for Sam to deal with. Since her loss two years ago, she avoided marines. Having to work closely with Gunnison wasn't going to be easy, emotionally, for her. He would remind her all over again of the magnitude of her loss.

Rubbing his chin, Morgan sat back, trying to think. The noise outside his door intruded. People rushed up and down the passageway, always in a hurry. Radios crackled and voices spoke in haste. Everyone at Logistics was under pressure; the tension was palpable.

"Okay, Sam, I'm going to level with you," he said finally, sitting up and pinning her with his gaze. "We have *no* other Recon teams left. They're all out in the field, providing protection in the other areas. Area 5 has none. It does have a marine fire team, but that's not enough, since it looks as if the Diablos, the survivalist gang, are a major problem in that area. For all we know, they may have their base there. There's no hard evidence of it, but it appears to be a possibility."

"Okay," Sam murmured, "so you're telling me I'm stuck with Gunnison, right? He's the *last* man on earth I'd want to deal with on this mission, yet he's my partner in this?''

''I'm afraid so,'' Morgan said apologetically. ''If I could, I'd give you another team, Sam. Honest to God, I would. But this is beyond my scope to change. I think, right now, that we need to focus on what's really important here—setting up medical sites to handle this emerging epidemic. Somehow, you and he are going to have to overlook past insults and injuries, take the higher ground here and get along.''

Quirking her lips, Sam said, ''I can do it. But can he? Honestly, Morgan, he's a trip. He thinks he's God on earth. His men worship the ground he walks on. Gunnison thinks that everything he says ought to become law and then some. This guy does *not* know how to compromise or even delegate.''

''I hear you,'' Morgan said unhappily. ''Look, here's what I can do, because I have you written in for a helo flight tomorrow morning at 0600 with him and his team. I can call Gunnison in, read him the riot act, give him a paternal talk about getting along with you and letting past history go for the sake of saving people's lives.''

''Good luck,'' Sam murmured. ''Oh, hell, Morgan, I understand you're caught between a rock and a hard place. My E.R. has been in that position since the earthquake occurred. Let me go gather my team, okay? Can I get a delivery of medical supplies, to bring with me to fight the epidemic?''

''Thanks, Sam. You're special. You really are. I'm going to try and get Captain Gunnison to realize that about you. Sure, get your list of supplies together and bring it over to me. I'll contact the loadmaster down at the airfield and make sure you get what you want on board that chopper later today. It'll be a Sea Stallion, by the way, so it can hold extra cargo as well as people."

"Fine," she sighed. Shaking her head, she gave him a wry look. "Never a dull moment, is there?"

"Not in an emergency of this magnitude," Morgan agreed quietly. "But you're the right person for this mission, which we're calling Operation Rescue. You access area 5. You find three locations for medevacs. You have Captain Gunnison call in the coordinates to me, and I'll make them happen within twenty-four hours, to give those poor folks some intervention. Maybe then," he sighed, "we can nip some of this epidemic before they start raging."

"Humph," Sam groused, standing. "Bad water's the reason for many of these health problems. I know the helos are flying in as many cases of water as they can. But there are too many people out there, Morgan, and not enough clean water. They're going to drink questionable stuff rather than die, and that brings on cholera, typhus and a whole host of other uglies."

"You're preaching to the choir," he said, smiling. Getting up, he thrust his hand across the desk. Sam's grip was warm and firm. "Thanks. For everything. I'll talk to Gunnison today."

Wrinkling her nose, she released his hand and growled, "Oh, yeah, that's like telling a pit bull not to bite. Good luck, Morgan. You're gonna need it with that stiff-necked marine."

# *Chapter 2*

*February 2: 1500*

Captain Roc Gunnison scowled, opening and closing his right hand as he sat in his executive officer's cubicle at the Recon company barracks. Morgan Trayhern had just left and Roc still had a bitter taste in his mouth from his meeting with the venerable ex-marine and head of Perseus. Glaring at the bulkheads, which were covered with photos chronicling his four years at Annapolis, his rise through the ranks of the Marine Corps and the awards he'd received for innovation within the reconnaissance arm of it, he quirked his lips.

Before he had time to ponder the situation, Sergeant Buck Simmons entered and came to attention. The twenty-six-year-old redhead was a hell of a noncom and Roc was glad to have him as a member of his five-men Recon unit.

"You wanted to see me, Captain?"

"Yes. At ease, Buck. We've got a mission." Roc saw surprise followed by an almost feral gleam of pleasure in Buck's eyes.

"Really, sir?"

Smiling grimly, Roc said, "I know you've been antsy, Buck, and wanting to take a ride outta this place."

"Yes, sir, I would!"

"Well, you're getting your wish, but I don't know..." He stopped short. As an officer, Roc couldn't let on to the politics of the situation. The enlisted people under his wing couldn't know that he was seething with anger over being stuck with Dr. Andrews on this mission. "Anyway," Roc growled, lifting his head, "get the team prepared to saddle up at 0530. We're taking a Sea Stallion into area 5."

"Are we going after Diablo?" Buck leaned forward, his lips curling back to reveal his teeth, like a wolf anticipating jumping a quarry.

"Kind of..." Roc muttered. But not really. He wanted to say, *We're playing baby-sitter to that pain-in-the-arse doctor we had a run-in with six months ago,* but he didn't. "We're going to be protecting a group of medical people coming in to canvass the area and set up three medevac stations. The epidemic is breaking out all across the basin, as you probably know. We're going in to make sure the Diablos don't get to the medevacs before the people can get help."

Frowning, his thin red brows bunching, Buck rubbed his chin. "Are we going to be *baby-sitters,* sir?" The words came out with a distinct distaste.

Roc's grin was twisted. "Now, Sergeant...we do what we're ordered to do. This is an important logistical step in getting the people of the L.A. basin the help they need. We'll be playing a key role in makin' it happen.'' Roc saw Buck's green eyes narrow.

''Well, sir, maybe after baby-sittin' duties, we can kind of nose around for Diablo on our off-hours?''

Roc's grin widened. ''All things bein' equal, Sergeant, yeah, we *might* be able to do that if circumstances dictate. But for now, get the team squared away today and ready to push off at 0530—at pad Bravo at the airport tomorrow.''

Coming to attention, Buck said, ''Yes, sir!'' He did an about-face and quickly left the cramped office.

Moving to the map of the quake zone, showing the entire southern Los Angeles area divided up into quadrants by Logistics, Roc studied area 5. But his mind wandered back to that redheaded witch of a woman doctor he was going to have to tangle with—again.

''What the hell kind of karma do I have?'' he muttered out loud, turning back to his desk.

''Sir?''

Turning with surprise, Roc saw Lance Corporal Ted Barstow, also young and also part of his team, standing expectantly in the doorway. ''Yes, Barstow?''

''Sorry, sir. I didn't mean to startle you,'' he said. ''Er...Sergeant Simmons sent me up to ask if you want demolitions loaded with our equipment. He said this was a milk run, not a real mission. We're babysitting?''

Wryly, Roc smiled to himself. He leaned against the edge of his green metal desk. ''We're protecting. And yes, load *everything.* We're going in as a Recon team prepared for any and all possibilities.'' He saw

Barstow's triangular face light up with enthusiasm. Barstow was their demo expert, the guy who set the claymore mines and anything else he could get his hands on to blow up the enemy. Barstow was like a mad scientist, always fiddling with chemicals to see what would happen. A couple of times he'd had his hair and eyebrows singed, playing around with volatile concoctions. What Barstow should do was go to college and take classes, but the Oregon native didn't take to schooling. He had grown up in the Cascade Mountains, was an outdoors kid who hunted for food for his family's table. After barely getting his high school diploma, he'd joined the Marine Corps and had found his niche in the Recon marines.

"That's great, Cap'n! I'll get on it, sir!" Barstow turned and trotted down the hall, his boots thunking on the wooden floor and creating a loud echo in the nearly empty barracks.

Roc smiled again, his spirits momentarily lifted by Barstow's visit. The kid was sharp, and eager. Everyone on his team was like that, and so was he. Gathering up the papers on his desk, he put them in his out basket. It was time to get moving. Roc was glad to be heading into the field at last. He'd been feeling restless and antsy as this earthquake mission got off the ground. All around him, Camp Reed hummed with activity. It was the hub of a great web that stretched in every direction, bringing in supplies to save lives.

Major Carson, his commanding officer, had needed Roc here at the base to help coordinate the Recon teams that were already out in the quake zone. Roc had been in charge of planning and logistics for the teams. Now it was his turn to go out in the field, which was what he lived for. Working in an office wasn't his idea of fun. It was a special hell.

Stepping into the hall, he headed to his locker, where he kept his M-16 rifle, pack, flak jacket and helmet. He would oversee the preparations for tomorrow morning's liftoff. All their gear would be brought to a central location to be loaded on a Humvee for transport today. And, he wanted to acquaint himself with the airport facility so there would be no screwups. Glancing at his watch, he saw it was nearly time for them to take the Humvee over to the airport. Buck would make sure their team was at the pickup point, Roc was sure. That's how eager they all were to cut loose from this place and do what they did best: field operative work.

As he pulled the flak vest over his desert utilities and pressed it shut, Roc felt his heart squeeze in anticipation of the coming confrontation. Dr. Andrews was no weak sister. She was formidable, as he'd found out when Private First Class Louis West, a nineteen-year-old on his team, had injured his leg during an exercise. Roc had never run into such a strong, bullheaded woman. And she hadn't budged from her position. He'd lost that first battle with her, and his ego still smarted.

"I won't lose this time," he growled, settling his helmet on his head. Allowing the straps to hang free, he adjusted the goggles perched atop the camouflage-colored headgear, then reached for his pack. If Andrews thought she was going to tell him what to do in the field, she had another think coming.

The truth was, Roc would much rather send his team out on a scouting and reconnaissance mission, to try and locate the Diablos. There wasn't a marine on the base who hadn't heard how the gang had ruthlessly murdered two pilots weeks earlier. In his heart, Roc longed to go after them. No one killed marines and got away with it. No way. Even though his wasn't designated a hunter-killer team, Roc dreamed of finding the survivalist gang and settling the score once and for all.

As he hoisted his sixty-pound pack onto his shoulders, settling it in place on his rangy frame, a thrill shot through him. Fieldwork. It was something he loved. He'd trade indoor time for outdoor any day of the week. Despite the fact that he'd have to put up with sourpuss Andrews, the day was looking brighter already.

*February 3: 0600*

Sam gathered her team on the landing pad next to where the Sea Stallion sat ready to go. The two marine pilots were already in the cockpit, going through pre-flight procedures before the blades started to turn. The airport was a noisy cacophony of screams, shrieks and whistles from fixed-wing aircraft, the thump, thump, thumps of rotorcraft. It was 0600. They were slated to take off in fifteen minutes.

"Jonesy, have we got all the supplies on board?" she called to her corpsman, Jones Baker, a twenty-two-year-old African-American.

"Yes, ma'am, we're good to go!" Jonesy flipped her a thumbs-up.

Sam smiled, noting the excitement and eagerness in Jonesy's brown eyes. He was one of her best corpsmen, and had worked with her in E.R. for two years. Nothing rattled the Harlem, New York native. Nothing. He'd grown up on the city streets and knew how to survive anything. When things got hot, heavy and intense in E.R., Sam could always count on this young man to keep a cool head and calm presence.

Though a gangly six foot tall, Jones had the hands of a concert pianist. Sam had talked to him early about taking premed classes at a nearby college, and had told him she felt he'd make a great doctor. Jonesy had taken her belief in him to heart. He was now in his second year, a straight-A student. When he wasn't working in his navy functions, she'd always find him with a book open, studying relentlessly. Often he came to her with questions, and they'd discuss medical points and symptoms. The world needed more people like Jonesy—self-motivated, smart, and hungry to better themselves. Sam was glad he was along on this mission.

"I've got all the IVs boxed up, Dr. Andrews," Lieutenant Lin Shan announced, approaching the open cargo door of the helicopter, near where Sam stood.

"Great, Lin. Think we've got enough?" She looked down at the surgical nurse, her right-hand woman in the operating room. Lin was Chinese-American, her parents having escaped from their own country under political duress. Born in San Francisco, the twenty-seven-year-old nurse was five foot two inches tall, thin as a reed and beautiful. Today, her dark, almond-shaped eyes shone with excitement. Like the rest of Sam's team, Lin was dressed in dark blue slacks, a pale blue, long-sleeved shirt, a flak vest, mandatory protection for the upper body, and wearing a dark blue navy baseball cap with Camp Reed Hospital, USN, embroidered in gold across the front.

"We've got three hundred IVs," Lin said with a grin. "As many as the loadmaster would let me load on board. I tried to get more, but that would make us exceed the weight limit. The head guy told me if I wanted more, some of us would have to stay behind. I didn't think you'd like that."

Sam nodded. "Not on this trip, at least," she said with a laugh. "Good job, Lin. Go ahead and board. I'll be in shortly."

Holding her clipboard in her hands, Sam looked around for her other cohorts. Corpswave Ernestine Larrazolo, whose parents came from Nicaragua, hurried around the chopper, an expectant look on her face. "You got all the dressings, antibiotics on board, Ernie?" Sam asked.

"Yes, ma'am, all that they'd let me stow away on this bird."

Sam smiled. "I hear you, Ernie." A corpswave first class, Ernie was priceless, in her opinion. She spoke Spanish, which was a big help, and she was quick and efficient in emergencies. Sam knew that Ernie didn't want to leave her husband, Jose, and their two young children, but she understood the importance of this mission. Five foot three inches tall, with a stocky build, Ernie was not only strong physically, but had a big warm heart, as well. Sam had picked her for several reasons. Ernie had come out of the barrio of Los Angeles and knew the area and its people. Sam suspected that, on this mission, they'd run into many Hispanics who were in the States illegally. She wanted Ernie there as an interpreter as well as a nurturing mother figure. No one was a better mama in the E.R. than Ernie. She was able to put her chunky arms around a crying child, or settle her dark brown hands on a man in pain, and soothe child or adult with her touch and soft voice.

"Climb on board," Sam said as she checked off the supplies that Ernie had been responsible for getting on the helo.

"You betcha." Ernie eagerly clambered up the lip of the chopper, with a helping hand from Jonesy, and into the cargo bay.

Sam smiled to herself as she signed off the supply sheet and handed it to the marine loadmaster, Sergeant Dunway. "Thanks," she told him. It was cold, so she slipped her dark blue wool gloves back onto her chilly fingers. Cold was not something Sam liked. The morning was frosty, near freezing, she guessed, for she could see the white vapor coming out of her mouth as she spoke.

"Thanks, ma'am," Dunway said, tucking the order into the breast pocket of his desert-colored jacket. "This bird is loaded to the gum stumps." He turned and looked at an approaching Humvee. "And if I don't miss my guess, here's the rest of the weight load—the Recon team."

Heart pounding briefly, Sam stood at the opening and watched the heavy vehicle approach at high speed. As it drew up to within thirty feet of the Sea Stallion, she could see Captain Roc Gunnison in the passenger seat—the last man on earth she ever wanted to work with. Lips tightening, Sam tried to gird herself as she stared at her through the window of the Humvee. There was no welcome in those hard eyes.

Trying to appear nonchalant, which was tough for Sam, since she usually wore her emotions on her face, she watched as the door to the Hummer opened. Out stepped her nemesis, and her heart thumped again.

Only not from dread. What was it, then? Stymied, Sam took a deep breath, studying his hard, unyielding profile as he turned and allowed his team to climb out.

Roc Gunnison was thirty-two years old, a seasoned marine vet. Highly decorated, he had seen action, she understood, not only in Somalia, but in Kosovo. Lanky and broad shouldered, he appeared strong, capable and athletic in his desert cammos. There was something confident and sure about his every movement. His black hair was close cropped and barely visible beneath the helmet on his head. Those eagle-like blue eyes, the color of the Montana sky she'd been born under, always got to her. Once, as a teenager, she'd rescued a bald eagle that had been shot by a hunter, its wing broken, and had carried it back home to her father, who was a veterinarian. Sam had never forgotten the hours she'd spent watching that eagle recuperate in the huge, airy cage outside her father's office. More than anything, she'd loved the way the eagle looked, the alertness in its eyes, which never missed a thing. Roc Gunnison had that same alert quality.

As he swung his head in her direction, Sam's heart thundered briefly. Their eyes met and locked. Frozen beneath his assessing gaze, Sam felt naked and vulnerable. Under any other circumstance, she'd find him handsome, with his square face and craggy, good looks made rugged by many hours out in the elements. Sam never liked pretty boys; instead, she was fascinated by faces of experience and character. Unfortunately, Gunnison's face fit that profile. She found herself staring almost hungrily at him now. Remembering how revealing her face could be when she was entangled in an emotional situation, she did her best to keep her expression deadpan as his gazed raked over her.

Maybe the chaos she felt inside was simply a result of the times. The events. The pressure of the crisis situation she had been living and working in, she thought, as he stared belligerently across the vehicle at her. She saw his mouth thin, the corners turning down as his black, thick brows drew into a V of obvious displeasure. A part of her knew that Gunnison had already formed an opinion about her, and he wasn't happy with her presence on this mission. Why couldn't he be more compassionate? More understanding? What had happened in the E.R. six months ago should be over and done with. Somehow, Sam had hoped for a less nasty reception from the captain. Obviously, he wasn't one to let bygones be bygones. A part of her wanted to cry at that discovery.

Roc couldn't tear his gaze from Dr. Andrews. She stood near the helicopter in her U.S. Navy regulation clothing, her desert-colored flak jacket hiding the upper part of her five-foot-seven-inch frame. She was large boned, and despite the mannish clothing she had to wear, he could see she was curvy. He glared at her, trying to let her know silently that he wasn't going to brook any arguments on this mission. Eighty percent of all communication was on a nonverbal level, Roc knew. He hoped that by nailing her with a lethal, I'm-not-going-to-take-any-crap-from-you look, she'd get the message, loud and clear.

The early morning breeze lifted some strands of her red hair, which gleamed with threads of gold. Her thick, shoulder-length locks, framed her oval face, the color emphasizing her large green eyes, which glittered with intelligence. Roc didn't fool himself; this wasn't just any woman. She was sharp and articulate, and could be lethal with that cutting mouth of hers. And speaking of mouths... He groaned inwardly. Why did Andrews have to have such a soft, full mouth? Now, as he stared at her across the distance, he saw her lips part slightly. That was his undoing, dammit. He didn't want to like her, but he couldn't help but admire her clean, fine-boned features. She looked like a Grecian statue he'd seen in Athens as a kid on a vacation with his well-to-do parents. And with that blanket of copper freckles dotting her high cheekbones and nose, she looked more like a teenager than a medical doctor.

He scowled even more deeply. Andrews was not fashion-model pretty, but she had an arresting and interesting face, Roc had to admit. He saw the gentleness in her mouth, the bear-trap intelligence in those huge green eyes that gave away her every feeling. And that red hair was a warning to anyone not to cross her, because she was a warrior at heart.

Snorting, Roc ordered his men into the helicopter. After thanking the driver for bringing them to the landing pad, he shut the door of the Humvee. Girding himself emotionally, he hefted his pack in his left hand, the M-16 in his right, and stepped around the vehicle. The hum of the Sea Stallion's engine began. In a few minutes, the rotors would begin to turn. As he walked toward the helo, Roc saw Andrews still standing there, her gloved hands crossed in front of her body. He felt her tension, saw it in those huge green eyes.

As he approached, she looked up, defiance clearly written on her face.

"Nice to meet you again, Lieutenant," he drawled, as he proceeded to toss his pack into the cargo bay of the helo.

"Liar."

Stunned, Roc paused and turned to take a second look at her. "Excuse me?"

Sam met and held his surprised gaze. "You're a liar, Captain Gunnison. Don't try and sweet-talk me, because it won't work. I call a spade a spade."

So much for her soft mouth and eyes. Lips tightening, he stared at her. "Okay, Lieutenant, have it your way. I was just trying to be social."

"Yeah, right. I saw the look you gave me. It said it all. Fine. I know where I stand with you on this mission." Sam could get away with being honest because everyone else was in the chopper, unable to hear them. She was glad to see she'd caught Gunnison off guard. She had to keep her wits about her so he wouldn't box her in. She was just as much in charge of this mission as he was, and she wasn't about to allow the Recon to intimidate her, as she knew he'd been trying to do with that frosty look he'd given her earlier.

Facing the chopper, Roc hefted his pack up into the hands of his sergeant. Then he turned and, his hands on his hips, glared down at her. "We need to talk. But not here. And not now. Once we get to area 5, you and I are going to have a chat, out of earshot of everyone."

Giving him a cutting smile, Sam said, "Fine with me, Captain. But you might as well know now that you're the last man on earth I'd ever want to have with me on a mission."

With that lob of a grenade, Sam brushed past him

and leaped up into the cargo bay of the helicopter. She found her nylon seat against the bulkhead and sat down. Looking up, she watched as Gunnison, frowning now, climbed lithely into the hold and sat on the opposite side with his men. The loadmaster slid the door shut and it locked.

Sam couldn't steady her fluttering heart. She felt like she'd been in combat, adrenaline was pumping so hard through her veins. If Gunnison thought she was a weakling and he could run over her or intimidate her with just a look, he was badly mistaken. Judging from the frustration she saw on his face as he strapped in, Sam knew he'd gotten her message, loud and clear. She smiled to herself. This was her mission. People needed her and her team's help. Gunnison was going to play second fiddle—or else.

# *Chapter 3*

*February 3: 0615*

Once they had taken off from Camp Reed and were en route to area 5, Roc decided to tip the balance of power between Dr. Andrews and himself. After taking off his helmet, he donned a headset, unstrapped his seat belt and stood up. Pinning her with his gaze, he walked across the shaking and rattling green metal deck. Her eyes widened as he reached up, his finger brushing her thick red hair and grabbed the set of earphones that hung nearby.

She wore nothing on her head, so he simply took a step back and lowered the headset over her ears. The noise in the Sea Stallion was so bad no one could hear another without putting on the protective earphones that hooked them up to intercabin communication.

"Get up," he told her, "and follow me."

Stunned at his aggressive and unexpected move, Sam stood. Grabbing at the overhead nylon webbing for stability, she followed him as he walked, legs apart for balance, toward the cockpit. Her heart was hammering. The captain's unexpected move toward her was a surprise. What was he up to? She'd seen him studying her from the other side of the helicopter, his eyes a flat blue color, intent upon her. Sam squirmed inwardly but she was damned if she was going to let him know how uncomfortable he made her feel. When his fingers had accidentally brushed her hair, she'd gasped. Contact with Gunnison wasn't in the game as far as she was concerned. But at just the right moment, the helo had pitched slightly to port and he'd swayed forward, off balance for a moment. Nevertheless, her scalp tingled.

Sam kept her distance as she followed Gunnison. Even in the cool morning air, there was some turbulence and the helicopter wasn't all that stable beneath her booted feet. When he reached the open door to the cockpit, he jabbed a finger at the window near the dark green panel behind the pilot's seat. "Get down on your hands and knees and look out that window," Gunnison growled. "You need to get a gander of area 5 from the air. If you're looking for possible sites and locations for your medevac models, it would help to see the terrain from up here first."

It made sense. Why hadn't Sam thought of this? Stung by his foresight, his understanding of her mission, she gripped the nylon webbing tightly. She really didn't want to get that close to Gunnison, but he stood with his back to the bulkhead, only inches from where she'd have to kneel to look out the window.

Sam didn't relish the idea. Dressed in his military camouflage gear, Gunnison appeared even larger and more intimidating than usual. The look on his face was grim.

"Yeah...okay," she muttered defiantly. She'd just started to step forward when the Sea Stallion pitched unexpectedly. Sam let out a little cry as she found herself knocked off her feet.

Hands, strong and caring, grabbed for her. A second later she found her face pressed against Gunnison's chest as he planted his feet far apart to take her full weight. Oh! The mortification of it all!

Sam made a strangled sound and instantly pushed away from Gunnison's chest. He was laughing at her; she saw his blue eyes gleaming with humor. His mouth, however, was still a thin, disapproving slash as he helped her regain her footing. His hand remained firmly on her arm as she quickly knelt down and gripped the metal bars on either side of the window for support and balance. She felt heat flooding her neck and face. Oh, God, she was blushing! Fortunately, Gunnison couldn't see her schoolgirl reaction.

Or so she hoped. As she looked out the window, her heart pounding, her pulse erratic, she felt his bulk settle directly behind her. Jerking her head to glance over her right shoulder, she saw him kneel down on one leg, his body barely an inch from her back. What was he doing? Intimidating her? She watched as he settled the mike of his headset close to his lips.

"Look to your left. That's area 5 coming up in a hurry." Roc leaned over her right shoulder, his left hand brushing her hair again as he pointed. He felt her tense as he loomed over her. The slight turbulence of the helicopter kept both of them off-kilter. Every time the helicopter bobbled, he would accidentally brush her shoulder or back, though he'd immediately compensate and pull away.

The look on her face was one of anger and frustration. Did she think he liked this any more than she did? That he was doing it on purpose? Was she going to be able to rise above personal dislike of him and focus on their real objective? Knowing that both their headsets were tuned to a private intercom channel, he said, "Look, Doc, settle down, will you? Focus on the objective, the sites. Take a look down there instead of staring at me like I'm attacking you."

Gasping again, Sam glared up at him. Then, jerking her attention to the yellow-brown earth five thousand feet below, she tried to steady her chaotic breathing. Gunnison was so damn male, and very intimidating. He knew it, too, the bastard. He was doing this on purpose. Sam could see the glimmer of laughter in his narrowed eyes as he snapped at her.

"What am I looking at?" she demanded tightly.

Roc pulled a folded map from a jacket pocket and passed it to her so she could study it.

Sam gripped the dirty, well-used map. The chopper was bobbling again. She felt Gunnison tense behind her, straightening his left leg and bracing his boot against the bulkhead. To his credit, he was trying not to brush against her, but the turbulence made it impossible.

His face was so close to hers as he leaned forward and traced his index finger over the map that Sam felt trapped. Suffocated. He was so tall, almost larger than life as he framed her body with his.

She winced as he spoke. "This is area 5. There are

a couple visual markers to indicate the boundaries, and I'll point them out to you. Out there, at three o'clock, is a radio tower. See it?''

Sam tried to concentrate, but she could smell his masculine scent, feel his moist breath near her right cheek. Blinking, she followed his index finger as he pressed it against the window.

''Uh, yeah, I see it.''

''Okay. Good. That's your northern boundary marker. Once we fly past, you're in area 5, so everything below is your turf. That's what you want to eyeball. You want to look at terrain, the possibilities for helicopters getting in and out, how far each potential site is from suburban housing and so on.''

In a perverse way, Roc enjoyed the unexpected closeness to the doctor. She smelled of lilacs, and he wondered if it was from her shampoo or if she wore perfume. At this range he could see every freckle on her cheek. Her nostrils flared and he wondered if that was a sign of her displeasure at him being so close. Her eyes were a beautiful color, he discovered—like an evergreen forest. The pupils were huge and black, and if he read her gaze properly, she didn't like him bending over her. *Tough.* He had a job to do.

''Now,'' he said, ''here's the south marker, one of the few microwave towers still standing.'' He jabbed his finger down at the map she held unsteadily in her left hand. ''We'll see it in a second. I gave the pilot orders to fly on south of the tower so you could see your whole area.''

*How smart of him.* Sam chided herself for being so immature. In reality, Gunnison was just doing his job—far better than she was at the moment. Trumped by his ability to focus on the task before them instead of the pettiness between them, she felt humiliated. Right now, Gunnison was being a lot more professional than she was. It was Sam holding a grudge from six months ago, not him.

As a trained medical doctor, she had learned a long time ago to disconnect her feelings while working. She had learned not to take things personally. But sometimes, depending upon circumstances, that was hard to do.

Right now, Gunnison was pushing every emotional button she owned. He had taken the high road in all of this and she…well, it wasn't pretty. She was behaving like a fifteen-year-old girl who had been jilted.

Sam tried not to think what he must think of her. Sending him a swift glance, she saw his eyes thaw for just a moment. In that split second, she glimpsed the man, not the marine on duty. But it happened so fast she thought she was imagining it. Jerking her head back toward the window, she concentrated on finding that microwave tower.

"Yes…I see it," she muttered finally.

"Good. Now—" Roc swung his finger in an arc "—start checking out this area. The eastern boundary is nothing but desert and sagebrush." He pulled his left hand back and looked at the dials on his watch. "In two minutes, we're gonna hit that boundary—I'll tell you when we fly over it. Then you'll have three sides of area 5 in view. The pilot is going to fly to the western boundary and then turn back to the landing zone, which basically sits in the middle of it. There's a destroyed shopping mall there. That's in the heart of the area you want to consider."

"Yeah…okay. Thanks…" Sam scowled. She didn't sound very grateful. It was a good idea to peruse the area from the air. This way, she could get an idea of where she might want her three medevac site models created. Trying to steady her heartbeat, which became faster and more erratic each time Gunnison accidentally brushed against her, she stared out the window.

This was her first chance to look at the actual devastation caused by the giant quake. For the last five weeks she'd been handling the huge number of casualties from it, but she'd had little concept of the massive damage the earthquake had wrought on the L.A. basin. Mother Nature, when she was pissed off, could really stick it to them, Sam thought sadly. Holding the map in her left hand, she focused all her concentration on the job before her. As she spotted the second tower, she heard Gunnison tell her they'd just flown across the eastern boundary.

Below her, Sam saw rolling hills of sagebrush and cactus flowing down toward the first block of red-roofed homes, which seemed to be carved from the land. After that, suburbs spread everywhere, like a colourful quilt covering the earth as far as she could see. As they flew on, Sam could see the utter devastation that the monster quake had wrought. Few homes were standing. Most were flattened totally. Red-tiled roofs were scattered helter-skelter across winter-brown lawns. Fences between homes were broken and splintered, trees knocked down like toothpicks. Sam noticed groups of people huddled around campfires here and there. In the early morning air, the number of thin black plumes of smoke showed her just how many campfires there were. Hundreds of them. Her throat tightened.

"Oh, God...I didn't realize...I just didn't know how bad this really was...."

Roc heard the tears in her husky tone and was unexpectedly moved. As he stared over her right shoulder, trying to ignore the strands of her hair tickling the side of his jaw, he growled, "I didn't, either. This is my first time over the area, too. It looks like all hell has broken loose."

Nodding jerkily, Sam felt tears come to her eyes. Rapidly, she blinked them away. Roc's voice was low and filled with emotion. That surprised her. Before, his voice had been hard and flat—sounding like a robot's. Well, he had feelings after all. Maybe she'd been wrong about him. Maybe he did have a heart.

She focused again on the devastation below, trying to absorb it emotionally. As they flew on toward the western boundary the magnitude of the tragedy became even more painful to her. The poor were obviously suffering the same as the well-heeled; just as many campfires dotted the barrios as the wealthier suburbs, with even more people huddled around them, trying to get warm. How quickly humans could be thrown back into stone-age survival mechanisms, Sam realized.

"Okay, the pilot is going to make his last turn at the western boundary," Roc told her. He'd watched as Dr. Andrew's expression had gone from anxiety to obvious pain and suffering while she watched the devastation unfold before them. When she turned, her gaze meeting his when he spoke, he saw tears in her eyes.

It hit him in the heart like nothing ever had. His only experience with her had been when she'd faced him down about his injured man, like a harpy eagle unleashed. Now he was seeing a completely different side to her, and it touched him deeply. Unexpectedly. Scowling, Roc tried to protect himself from her vulnerability. It was impossible.

Sam quickly looked away. She hadn't wanted Gunnison to see her with tears in her eyes. Dammit! Why couldn't she be tough and distance herself from this kind of thing? Her professors at medical school certainly would be able to. Blinking again, she jerked her head toward the window once more in hopes that Gunnison wouldn't say anything. She half expected him to make fun of her, or deride her as he had in the E.R. that day six months ago. Tensing, she felt him shift behind her.

''Okay, you got the picture,'' he was telling her in a gruff tone. ''Let's get back to our seats. This chopper is gonna land pretty soon.''

Sam felt him stand up behind her, and she waited until he stepped away.

''I can make it back on my own.'' To her own ears her voice sounded brittle and tinny. She swallowed hard, trying desperately to squelch her tears before she had to turn around and face her people and his men. As an officer, Sam couldn't be seen crying. Not ever. Especially not in front of enlisted people. They had a job to do, and her crying like a baby didn't exactly instill faith in her leadership. Bowing her head for a moment, she remained on her knees, trying to gather her shattered emotions.

Unexpectedly, she felt Gunnison move to her right side. Looking up, she realized he was creating a physical barrier between her and their crew, most of whom were probably watching them. And then it hit her what he was really doing: protecting her from being seen in this condition by her people and his. As she looked up at him, amazed that he'd do that for her, as a fellow officer, she met and held his gleaming blue gaze. There was curiosity in his expression, and something else Sam couldn't decipher.

"Take your time, Doc," he told her, his voice husky. "I've seen this level of suffering over in Somalia and Kosovo. It takes some getting used to." And he managed a twisted one-cornered smile that let her know he understood what she was going through.

Choking, Sam bowed her head and shut her eyes tightly. It took everything she had to force down her unraveling emotions. Afraid to talk for fear of bursting into tears of sympathy for those suffering so badly below them, she simply nodded to let him know she'd heard him.

Finally, after what seemed interminable minutes, Sam took a long, unsteady breath. There. Her emotions were tamped way down deep once more. Giving Gunnison a quick glance, she whispered, "Thanks... I'm okay now. You can step back."

Roc nodded and did as she instructed, though his protective instincts were running full bore. He knew Dr. Andrews needed a human touch. To be held. To be told everything would be okay. But he knew better than to take her in his arms. Besides, his experience in Kosovo and Somalia had taught him that sometimes things didn't always turn out okay and that the situation below was truly chaotic.

As he stepped back to give her room to get to her feet, he watched her closely. Even though Andrews was dressed in the mannish navy uniform, her bulky flak jacket hiding her womanly assets, she was incredibly graceful, like a ballerina to him. He wanted to ignore her femininity, but found himself absorbing her into his heart like a starving animal instead. That disgusted him, because Roc knew her to be a red-haired witch of the worst sort and his nemesis on this mission, despite the emotions he had just witnessed.

As Sam carefully made her way back to her seat and sank into it, Roc continued to stand, just in case she lost her footing again. The good doctor wasn't used to walking on the heaving deck of a helo as he was.

Once she was seated and strapped in, Roc moved forward. "My map?" he said, extending his hand.

"Oh!" Sam quickly held it out to him as he bent over her, one hand on the overhead strap to keep from falling. The instant their fingertips met, she had the crazy urge to jerk away. But she didn't. That would look childish to her people, who were watching them with curiosity.

"Thanks," she managed to reply in a strangled tone. As she looked up into his darkened eyes, she saw his mouth twitch wryly.

"You're welcome, Dr. Andrews."

Feeling inept and completely out of her league, Sam turned away, looking anywhere other than at Gunnison, who sat down right across from her. She heard the engine change and felt the chopper begin to sink earthward. Swallowing repeatedly, Sam tried to gather her thoughts. What was going on? Was it seeing the awful devastation that had her so shaken up? Was she in shock?

She didn't want to give Gunnison credit for any sympathy. The man made her feel like an awkward teenage girl who had a crush on the star football player.

How ridiculous! Jerking off the earphones, Sam dropped them in her lap. She didn't want to talk to Gunnison. He took off his earphones, too, his face once again inscrutable.

*He's just doing his job,* Sam told herself. *Calm down, will you? He's got you rattled. He probably did it on purpose, just to keep you off balance. Get your stuff together, woman. Don't let him intimidate you.*

Sam continued to berate herself with that litany until they landed. Outside, dust rose in thick yellow clouds around the helicopter, almost obliterating the marine in the distance who held a pair of orange flags in his hands that signaled where they were to land.

Though it seemed like forever to Sam, a few minutes later the engines were shut off and the rotors stopped turning. When the blades came to a halt, the loadmaster on the flight unlocked the sliding door and hauled it open. As the dust filtered in, Sam saw a small group of people standing well beyond the range of the blades, waiting with anxious looks on their faces. She watched as Gunnison got up and ordered his team to move out. She waited until the five-man Recon team disembarked. Then she unstrapped her seat belt and looked at her own team.

"Okay, we're here," she told them. "Let's go."

As she stood on the lip of the cargo bay, ready to jump down, a hand appeared: Gunnison's large, heavily scarred palm and fingers. Mesmerized by the sight, she noted that his fingers were long and strong looking, his nails blunt cut. Under any other circumstances she'd have found his hands beautiful to look at. As she hesitated there, unsure of whether to accept his offer of help as he stood looking up at her, her mind was filled with the sudden unexpected image of his fingers trailing over her flesh.

Discombobulated by her tumbling thoughts, Sam reached out automatically and took his hand, gripping it as she eased down off the lip of the helo to the dusty ground. Quirking her lips, she barely looked at him as she jerked her hand out of his. Moving quickly away from him, she headed toward a male marine lieutenant and a woman in a deputy's uniform beside him, who looked like the leaders of the group.

''Dr. Andrews?''

Sam halted in front of the marine, who was dressed similarly to Gunnison and his team. ''Yes, that's me.''

He smiled. ''I'm Lieutenant Quinn Grayson. Welcome to area 5.'' He saluted her.

Sam returned the salute. ''Thanks, Lieutenant.'' She turned her attention to the woman at his side. ''And you must be Deputy Chelton?''

''Yes, I am, Doctor. Call me Kerry. We don't stand on formality around here,'' she replied, as she offered her hand.

Sam instantly liked the young woman. ''Me, either. Call me Sam,'' she said, shaking her hand warmly.

''Thanks, I will. We're here to help you all we can.'' She looked up at Grayson. ''The lieutenant will take you to your tents. They just came in yesterday, and have been erected near ours. We're looking like a tent city at this point.'' Rubbing her hands together, Kerry added, ''I'm sure you're just as cold as we are. Winter mornings can be chilly even in Southern California. We've got hot coffee, hot chocolate and a warm stove waiting for you over at our main tent, which is where we plot and plan for area 5.''

"Great!" Sam exclaimed. "I'm freezing. The hot coffee sounds too good to be true." She turned to her team. "Ready?"

They chorused in agreement, their smiles eager.

Sam saw Gunnison remaining behind with his men and the loadmaster on the flight. Frowning, she said, "Kerry, can you take my team over there? I've got to coordinate the off-loading of our supplies."

"I can help," Lieutenant Grayson said, stepping forward. "Let me direct them, ma'am. You go get warm with your team. Kerry will show you where you're going."

Sam hesitated. It would be a relief to let Grayson deal with Gunnison and his men. "Okay, Lieutenant, you've got a deal. Ask Captain Gunnison to join us when he's done?"

Quinn nodded. "Of course, ma'am. It'll take only a few minutes to get your supplies into our storage tent, which is guarded twenty-four hours a day against theft. I'll pass on your request to him."

*Good.* Sam turned and smiled at Kerry. She seemed warm and gentle for someone who worked in police enforcement. Noting that Kerry moved slowly and with a limp, Sam came up beside her.

"Are you okay, Kerry? You're limping."

"I'm fine. I took a bullet in the thigh a while back. Quinn—I mean, Lieutenant Grayson—saved my life. We got into a shootout with the Diablo gang about two miles from here." She pointed in a northerly direction.

Sam eyed the younger woman, automatically going into doctor mode. "I see…. Are you in pain?"

Shrugging, Kerry said, "Sometimes. I take aspirin and that helps a lot." Then she flashed her a smile.

"Lieutenant Grayson just rigged up a bathtub he found and brought to our washroom facility." She pointed to a tent to their right. "He's a master at finding stuff and putting it together. When my leg starts aching, I get into a hot bath and sit there for ten minutes, and the pain goes away."

"What a creative guy!" Sam exclaimed. "But if your aches get to be too much, you let me know. I got some pain meds with me in that shipment the guys are unloading right now."

"I will. Thanks, Doc—I mean, Sam."

Sam smiled at her before turning her attention to the huge camouflage-colored tent that loomed before them. Fifteen tents had been erected in three rows. A small American flag flew atop the largest tent, and someone had hand scribbled HQ with a black marker over the top flap, which was shut. Kerry stepped forward and unzipped it, holding the flap open.

"Come on in. Welcome to HQ for area 5." She motioned the group inside.

Sam was the first to duck under the opening and step on to unpainted plywood floor, where her boots thunked hollowly with each footstep. At the opposite end of the tent was a redwood picnic table with a bench on either side. Nearby, an electric heater was throwing out a lot of welcoming warmth. On one side of the tent was a makeshift coffee bar. On top of a half-destroyed buffet counter that someone must have salvaged from the wreckage and brought in was a coffeemaker and a number of ceramic cups, some of them chipped or missing handles. There was a name written in black marker on each one. The coffee smelled fresh and inviting, Sam thought as she stood near the back and watched her team trundle in.

"Have a seat," she told them, and gestured to the picnic table.

Kerry zipped the tent flap shut and turned around. "Our ace hound dog, Private Orvil Perkins, has located about twelve new coffee mugs. If you each tell me your name I'll write it on your mug and that will be yours while you're with us."

Sam smiled and held her hands toward the electric heater, enjoying the warmth. Outside, she could hear the chugging sound of a generator, which supplied electricity for the heater to work.

"This is really nice of you, Kerry," Sam said, as the deputy made her way around the table to the coffee area.

"Actually, it was Quinn's—I mean, Lieutenant Grayson's idea. He knew a couple of days ago that your teams were coming in, so he set to work on trying to make this transition as easy as possible. The one thing he said you would all need is coffee."

Applause rose around the table. Sam joined in. There were smiles of delight on every face as Kerry began to ask names and write them on the cups. Sam got into the act by pouring fresh coffee and passing it out to her team. Within minutes, she felt a camaraderie that made her heart swell with pride. Kerry was the epitome of compassion as far as Sam was concerned. She was kind, thoughtful and sensitive—just the sort of person Sam wanted to work with.

As Sam stood there near the stove and watched her team eagerly drink their coffee and chat with the amiable Kerry Chelton, she felt a strong trickle of hope. She also felt pride that the people of area 5, despite all the devastation, could go to this kind of trouble to try and make her and her team feel welcome. Even in hell there was kindness, she was discovering.

All her enthusiasm and good feelings plunged, however, when the tent flap opened and Captain Gunnison came in, standing to the side to allow his grim-faced men to enter. Grayson was the last to come in, zipping the door shut behind him.

At once the energy of the place changed dramatically, making Sam sigh inwardly.

Grayson did the talking, explaining how things worked to the Recon team. When Gunnison looked up, he settled his gaze briefly on Sam. Her hands tightened around her mug as their eyes met.

''Your supplies are off-loaded, safe and sound,'' he told her gruffly, heading with Grayson toward the coffee dispenser.

''Good. Thank you, Captain.'' Sam cringed inwardly. Her voice was clipped and distant, and hearing it, her entire team lifted their heads as if in unison, collective surprise written on their faces. She sounded so…hard. They never saw this side of her.

Scowling, Sam sipped the scalding coffee, almost burning her tongue. *Damn.* At all costs, she had to cover up her dislike of Gunnison. But it wasn't going to be easy…

# *Chapter 4*

*February 3: 0730*

An hour later, Roc sat across the table from Sam. He'd sent his team to go set up their logistics center, and Sam had given Lieutenant Lin Shan orders to oversee the setting up of a makeshift medevac tent facility here at the landing zone. Kerry and Lieutenant Grayson had gone also, to provide expertise and information.

Sam was antsy and refused to look directly at Gunnison as he spread out a terrain map between them on the rough surface of the picnic table. One naked lightbulb hung over the table to provide illumination, but the sun was shining on the canvas wall, making the space brighter.

''Maybe we need to have a heart-to-heart talk, Doctor,'' Roc began, in a low tone no one passing near the tent could hear. Roc was well aware that tents didn't have solid walls. Voices carried very well to sentries posted outside, or to people walking by. And he didn't want what he had to say to her overheard by anyone.

Sam lifted her chin. She met and held the captain's hard, merciless blue eyes. Her stomach felt as if a massive hand had grabbed it and was squeezing painfully. "Look," she said, holding up her hands, "I was out of line earlier. I owe you an apology, okay? It won't happen again."

Furrowing his forehead with a frown, Roc stared at her. He was mesmerized by her long, lean hands. They were the hands of a healer. Hands, he realized obliquely, that he'd like to have graze his flesh. Would her touch be as tender, as warm as he imagined? Disconcerted by his errant thoughts, which had nothing to do with the business at hand, he quirked his mouth.

"You were probably just upset by what you saw out the chopper window," he said reasonably.

Sitting back, Sam digested his comment. He looked dark, almost threatening, with deep shadows thrown across his impassive features by the light overhead. Gunnison had discarded his helmet and pack and sat in his desert camouflage utilities, his tan web belt around his waist, a pistol at his side. There was nothing tame or polite about him, Sam decided. He was dangerous. In all ways. To her.

Moistening her lips, she said in a low voice, "You're right, I wasn't prepared for what I saw. I had no idea...." She shrugged helplessly. "My world has been confined to nice, clean hospitals."

He managed a sour smile. ''Yeah, that's what I figured by the look on your face up there.''

Placing her hands on the map, Sam nodded. ''I didn't know what to expect. Not what I saw, that's for sure.'' Still on guard, because she didn't trust Gunnison due to their explosive and vitriolic past, she searched his face. There was a slight thawing in his blue eyes as he sat there, his broad shoulders thrown back, his chin lifted with a steel-clad assurance that made her wonder if *he'd* ever made mistakes in his life. That's what Sam didn't like about him—his arrogance and implacable confidence.

''I saw this level of suffering over in Somalia. Then Kosovo,'' he answered, opening his hand as he looked down at the map before him.

''You don't seem affected by it.'' Sam cringed inwardly. There was censure in her voice. When he looked up at her, his eyes had narrowed.

''We have responsibilities, Doctor. Duties. I can't sit out there like a baby and cry for the world. People suffer. They die. I'd like to think that we can play a key part in stopping that from happening. Don't you?''

Stung by his simple black-and-white perspective, his frank comment, Sam gritted her teeth. ''Anyone ever accuse you of being a burr under someone's saddle?''

A lazy grin stretched across his mouth. ''Now and then. Like six months ago, maybe?'' He saw her green eyes flash with anger, and watched her lift her head to an imperious angle. ''You think I've forgotten our introduction to one another?''

''No. And neither have I.'' Sam gripped her hands

together until her fingertips whitened. She didn't like his grin; it said he wasn't really taking her seriously.

"I can tell," he answered dryly. "You won that round, though. You should be feeling pretty cocky at this point."

Nostrils flaring, Sam leaned forward, her voice brittle with tension. "Captain, I don't see anything as a win or a loss in my E.R. I just didn't like having to face down a belligerent know-it-all like you."

"Out in public, even," he replied smoothly. Roc saw her cheeks burn a rose color. It made her narrowed green eyes even more beautiful. Her thick hair tumbled across her shoulders as she leaned forward. Hair he wanted to touch, to slide his fingers through to find out if it felt as soft and sensuous as he thought it might.

"You were the one who made *that* happen," she whispered harshly, her voice shaking.

"I don't take no for an answer, Doctor. Especially when it involves one of my men."

"When your man came in, our E.R. was full of a lot of other cases that were a helluva lot more life threatening than his. *That* was what you didn't want to hear."

Shrugging, Roc studied her tight features and flashing eyes. "Yeah, you made that clear, too. But he was bleeding."

"You're a paramedic. You know that direct pressure on that leg wound of his would have sufficed under the circumstances."

"I knew that," he agreed mildly. She looked absolutely beautiful when she was angry. "But he was my responsibility. A part of my team."

"You know what?" Sam whispered hotly. "You're

a mother hen. You protect your own. To hell with anyone else who might need help—your people come first. I know your type, Captain. Well, that doesn't wash in my E.R. Not now, not in the future.'' Sam jabbed a finger down at the map. ''Tomorrow we'll be out in the field, and I'm sure we'll be doing medical work wherever we go. You're under *my* command out there, and I hope you realize that. I won't stand for you questioning my authority like you did in my E.R.''

''That's what you're worried about?'' He smiled slightly.

She reared back and glared at him. ''You think this is some kind of joke, don't you?''

''No. I just need to know where you're coming from, that's all, Doctor. My first responsibility is to make sure your team is protected by me and my men. After we get a perimeter defense set up, if you want my help as a paramedic in your makeshift clinic, I'll be happy to assist you and take direction. I can push an IV just as quickly and efficiently as anyone else on your team.''

She disliked his smug attitude. But at least he wasn't smiling now; he was serious. Some of her anger dissolved. ''Yes, I am concerned about your manners, Captain, if you want the truth. I don't want to be out there in the field, under the pressure I know that's coming, and then have to arm wrestle you because you think you know what's best.''

Shifting his hands, Roc said gently, ''Ramp down, good doctor. I'm not your enemy. I'm here to support you in any way I can so long as I get my responsibilities taken care of first. After that, I'm all yours as a paramedic. I see myself as an addendum to your team. I'll take orders from you without questioning or challenging them. Okay?'' He searched her widening eyes. Roc saw the wariness in Sam's face, saw her waffling over his sincerely spoken words.

''You mean that?'' There was a tremor in Sam's voice. This man just reached inside her and got to her. How did he do that? He was so damned overconfident. She wanted to dislike him, but right now the persuasive tone in his voice was like cooling balm to the fiery anger she felt. For the first time, Sam was seeing the captain's ability to persuade or dissuade. She began to understand why his men idolized him. He was very good at manipulating them with his voice, his expression. He was not the dummy she'd first taken him to be, she realized, measuring Gunnison with her gaze.

''Of course I do. We're on the same side. At least we were the last time I looked. You're navy, I'm marine, but we work together, right? We're not enemies.'' Roc pointed toward the zippered door to the tent. ''Our real enemy, the Diablo gang, is out there. Our other enemy is the epidemic. We've got our hands full, Doctor. I don't need to fight with you, on a third front, do I?''

''Unless one of your men gets injured,'' Sam growled.

Chuckling, Roc smiled at her. ''Guilty as charged. I'll give them orders to stay clear of injuries, okay? That way, we'll have our agreed-upon truce in place and we can each do what we do best, without interference from each other.''

Sam couldn't return his smile, but grudgingly agreed. ''Yeah...okay...''

''I think you're a little shook, is all,'' he added gently. ''Give yourself some breathing space on this mission. This is an ugly situation, no two ways about it. We're hemmed in with danger from Diablo. They can strike unexpectedly, so we have to keep our guard up all the time. You have to focus on your medical efforts to help the people. I'll do everything in my power to keep you all safe, so don't let that be a worry to you. Recons are good at what we do. Frankly, I'd like to get my hands on the leader of Diablo. Nothing would make me happier."

Sam sighed audibly and relaxed her shoulders. "Okay, Captain Gunnison, truce. I need one. You're right, I'm shocked by what I've seen. I haven't been in third world countries like you and I know this situation is gonna hit me hard."

"It will be worse out there," Roc warned her gravely. "These are *our* people, Doctor. This is our country. Our kids are the ones suffering and dying." He leveled a stare at her. "This isn't going to be easy. You're going to be in a triage situation all the time, with very little wiggle room to do anything for those who are going to die, anyway. What do you tell the parents? They're going to be distraught. They'll be angry and in your face because you put their child aside for another who might make it with aggressive medical intervention. I'd say you've got your work cut out for you."

"You're right," Sam whispered. "It's bothering me already...."

Rubbing his jaw, Roc saw the last of the anger dissolve from her eyes. "Want some advice?"

She looked at him and nodded. "Yeah. Voice of experience?"

"You could say that. In Somalia, the kids always got to me. They're cute little ragamuffins with huge eyes and bright, hopeful smiles. They followed us around like excited puppies. And they were starving. They were full of worms and parasites. They were gaunt. Yet just giving them a hug, a piece of candy, a smile, made them happy. The advice is—do what you can and you have to be satisfied. You cry in private.''

Sam found it tough to believe that Roc Gunnison had a heart, but as she sat there, their knees nearly touching beneath the table, she heard the undisguised warmth in his baritone voice and saw his eyes thaw with fond memories. Maybe he wasn't the ogre she'd met in E.R., after all. He was complex, Sam decided, and right now, she had to focus on the mission—not him. Still, there was a part of her that was intrigued, and she wanted to know more about the man who wore that Marine Corps uniform. The realization surprised her.

''Okay, I hear you.''

''Let's look at this map, shall we? I'll help you piece together what you saw from the air a little while ago, and we'll discuss some possible sites that we should look at.''

Nodding, Sam said, ''Yeah, I'd appreciate that. Reading maps is not my thing. I know it's yours.''

''Map and compass work,'' Roc agreed with a slight smile.

Meeting his gaze, Sam felt hope. Maybe this would work, after all....

---

*February 3: 0930*

Sam hadn't realized two hours had flown by. She'd been so focused on Gunnison's terrain evaluations she'd lost track of time. It was only when Lieutenant Shan came into the tent that Sam realized how long they'd been working.

"Doctor, we've got several tents set up over here." She gestured with her right hand. "Word's gotten out that a medical team is here, and already about thirty families are waiting in line with sick kids or elderly that need immediate medical help. Do you want to come and show us what we should do?"

Sam was on her feet in an instant. "Yes, Lin." She looked at Gunnison who was studying her through half-closed eyes. His gaze sent a shiver through her; and the feeling wasn't a bad one. Unable to stay and thoroughly analyze that sensation, Sam grabbed her dark blue knit cap and settled it on her head.

"Put your flak jacket on, Doctor," Gunnison drawled, pointing to the dark blue flak jacket hanging on a hook behind her. "You go nowhere without it on. Just get used to wearing it, like the good friend it is."

Frowning, Sam nodded. "Yeah…thanks." She threw it on, grabbed her dark blue navy pea coat made of thick, warm wool, and her baseball cap, then followed Lin out of the tent.

The sun was bright. The temperature at 0930 was in the low fifties, the wind brisk and chilling. Looking around the small tent city, Sam could see a line of people waiting patiently near the medical tents that had just been put up.

"What's the mood of the people?" Sam asked as she shortened her stride to match her nurse's.

"Desperate," Lin said sadly. "There are a lot of kids. Many babies."

"You got the IVs set up?"

"Yes, we do. Jonesy has ten IV carts set up. We're as ready as we can be."

"Okay…good."

"I put Ernie on the admissions desk."

"Excellent."

"She's not happy about that."

"I don't imagine she is, but we need someone bilingual on the desk because we need these people's names, addresses and so on."

"Even if their house is rubble?"

"Yes." Sam's heartbeat picked up as they approached. She tried to abort the emotions that hit her. These people, Americans, looked like gaunt prisoners from some foreign country. Their clothes were dirty, unkempt, their faces filled with desperation. Many of the fathers held sick children in their arms, wrapped in blankets to keep them warm. The faces of the mothers mirrored the same anxiety.

Swallowing hard, Sam glanced down at the lieutenant. "This is not going to be easy, Lin."

"No kidding. My heart's breaking already, Doctor."

"Yeah…" Sam stepped into the main tent. Ernie sat at a "desk" that was really several wooden fruit crates placed next to each other. She had her admissions forms and pen in hand. There was a heater spewing out warm air, but because one side of the tent was open, it didn't do much good. Still, it was better than nothing. Sam checked on Jonesy, who had ten metal chairs set up in a row with an IV drip next to each. They were going to need a lot of intravenous fluids to replace lost electrolytes in the children who had dysentery or diarrhea from drinking bad water.

Without fluid replacement, an infant could die within a day. Sam felt an urgency thrumming through her as she took off her dark blue jacket and pulled on the white lab coat Lin handed to her. Wrapping her stethoscope around her neck, Sam looked over at her people.

"Okay, let's roll. Ernie, start admittance procedures. We're good to go...."

*February 3: 2300*

Roc looked at his watch. It was 2300—11:00 p.m. He huddled deeper in his jacket against the evening chill. For once the flak vest, always a pain to wear because of the way it chafed his flesh, was doing some good; it was keeping him warm. Leaving the HQ tent, he ambled toward the medical complex, where an ever-growing line of people waited. Kerry had told him midday that word was flying like wildfire around the area that a medical team had arrived, and people were walking miles with sick infants and children, hoping to get the urgent medical care they needed.

In his hand Roc had a thermos of hot, fresh coffee and two cups. He'd been busy all day working with Lieutenant Grayson, plotting and planning strategy in order to understand the dynamics of Diablo. Grayson had direct experience with them, and Gunnison needed his valuable input. He liked the young officer a lot. Grayson was thorough, quick and knowledgeable.

The garish lights around the tent complex threw deep shadows across the dusty, chewed up asphalt under Roc's black military boots. With his M-16 rifle slung over his left shoulder, Roc was careful where he stepped on the uneven ground. There was no such thing as "safe" around here. Not with Diablo roaming the area. The gang was unpredictable, a loose cannon. Two days earlier, they'd attacked the military complex, but had been thrown back by Grayson's team in a brief, vicious firefight. The tent city was growing and held a lot of supplies. It was obvious the gang members were testing the camp's defenses to see if they could break in and get the goods. They hadn't managed to, but their attempt served as a warning that no place was safe.

Mulling over potential strategies and scenarios, Roc headed toward the main tent. He hadn't seen Dr. Andrews since morning. Kerry Chelton had come to him at 2100 and mentioned that the medical team was still working nonstop. They hadn't eaten all day. Was Samantha Andrews a workaholic? he wondered. Did she drive her people into exhaustion? Of course, looking at the line of people, the desperation clearly written on their dirty faces, Roc understood why the doctor would do just that. He would, too.

Ducking into the main tent, Roc halted and took a look around. The place was filled with noise and mayhem. Children were screaming and crying. One mother was trying to soothe her toddler as a medic put an IV into his tiny arm. Roc knew that hurt. Another mom knelt by her upset child, trying to soothe and quiet her. Several elderly folks, wrapped in blankets given out by the medical team to try and keep them warm in the dropping temperature, sat quietly, their eyes closed.

Roc spotted Sam across the tent, bent over an infant on a makeshift table. The Hispanic parents, both young and anxious looking, hovered on either side of her. Sam's face was bleached out and exhausted looking. She was placing the stethoscope on the infant's chest. The child couldn't be more than three months old. Grimly, Roc headed toward them.

Sam didn't know Spanish. She listened to the young parents, both in tears, as they rattled along in that language, but she didn't know what they were saying. Even more frustrating, she could barely pick up a heartbeat on the infant. Wanting to call Ernie over, but knowing she was deluged by people trying to get on the admissions list, Sam took a deep breath. She couldn't ask her to just get up, leave her job and come over. What was she going to do?

"Doc? You look like you could use an interpreter."

Swinging her head to the right, she stared in surprise. Captain Roc Gunnison stood there, larger than life, smiling down at her. He held a thermos and two cups in his hands. Hot coffee? she wondered numbly.

"Uh...yes. Do you know Spanish?"

"I do." Setting down the thermos, Roc turned to the parents and began asking them about their infant.

Once again Sam gently felt for the baby's pulse. It was weak and fluttering. Still, hope flowed through her, along with gratitude as Roc stood at her side. He was fluent in Spanish, she realized. She saw the relieved looks on the parents' faces as he talked with them. They eagerly responded.

Roc turned and smiled at her. "The baby's name is Eduardo. He's three months old. His mother, Maria," he continued, gesturing toward the woman, "ran out of breast milk because there's not enough water to drink to produce milk."

"Oh..." Sam said. "That's good news. Then all these symptoms are about dehydration and not something worse."

"Right on, good doctor." Roc eyed her closely, noting the shadows in her eyes. It was obvious she cared deeply. She kept her hands around the baby, helping to keep it warm beneath the new, soft pink blanket that had been given to the parents earlier. "I think an IV of Ringer's solution would be just the thing for this little one."

"You're right," Sam said. She smiled at the parents.

"I'll take the baby over to Jonesy for the IV," Roc announced calmly. "You sit here and take a break. There's hot, fresh coffee in this thermos. Pour yourself a cup."

Before she could respond, Roc scooped up the infant as if he'd been a father all his life, placing the baby in the crook of one massive arm. He told the parents in Spanish to follow him. The looks of relief shining in their eyes made Sam feel good.

As she sat down on the table, cup of coffee in hand, she watched Gunnison hand Jonesy the infant. The captain surprised her. She'd never expected him to show up over here. Nor had she expected his thoughtfulness in bringing her or her team hot coffee. Damn, but the man was complex. Gratefully sipping the coffee, Sam sighed and shut her eyes. She realized she was tired and running out of stamina. Her normally tireless crew needed to rest, too, she knew. They'd been working for hours.

And yet, as she looked out the open tent flap, she saw at least forty more people standing in line. How could she tell them to go away? That she and her crew needed sleep? Sam was torn. Her mind was stretched and strained from grueling hours of work in a cold environment. What she'd give for a hot shower! And then she felt guilty because these people—Americans one and all—had no hope of such a luxury. She would feel guilty showering over in Kerry's tent. Sam knew she would.

Roc came back to where Sam was sitting on the table. Stopping near her left shoulder, he turned and faced her, his back to the awaiting crowd.

"How are you doing, Doc?"

"Better, now."

"Like my prescription?" he asked with a grin as he gestured to the coffee cup she held.

Shaking her head, she muttered, "I don't know about you, Captain. You're one surprise after another."

"Not all bad, I hope?"

Sipping the coffee, Sam didn't answer. Her gaze went past him to the crowd. "I don't know what to do."

Roc nodded. "Yeah, I know. I knew this would catch you off guard. They won't go away. They'll stay here all night."

With a grimace, Sam whispered, "I've got to call Morgan Trayhern. He's *got* to get a relief medical team in here. How can we leave them?"

"I've already put in a call to him on this," Roc told her quietly. He saw the surprise in her expression. "You were busy. Kerry said you were overwhelmed in here. I made the call on your behalf."

Sam should have been angry at his going over her head, but under the circumstances, she was grateful. "That's okay. What did Morgan say?"

Roc shook his head and scowled. ''He's working on it. There's a lot of civilian doctors volunteering. The problem is getting medical stations set up so we can bring them in. A doc is no good without medical supplies, so we can't get the cart before the horse. You know how overworked the navy people are at the Camp Reed hospital.''

''Too well. We've been working sixteen hours a day, nonstop, taking time only to grab some food and sleep, and we're back at it. And we've been getting some relief from civilian volunteer doctors. The problem is these civilian docs aren't familiar with the way the medical military works, so it's a sharp learning curve.''

''Exactly. Morgan says he can't spare anyone else. But—'' Roc smiled down at her ''—he's working on another angle. He's in touch with the San Diego Naval Hospital, and he *thinks* he can get a Super Stallion crew to fly up another four-person medical team, with even more medical supplies for us, more IVs. It could be as soon as tomorrow if all goes according to his plans.''

''Wonderful!'' Sam whispered, her voice suddenly wobbly.

''Morgan Trayhern is a magician,'' Roc said, admiration in his voice. He saw the sudden glistening of unshed tears in Sam's eyes. More than likely they were tears of relief. ''He's doing everything he can for us under the circumstances.''

Looking down at her coffee cup, Sam choked back her tears. Somehow, just having Roc Gunnison at her shoulder, his tall form shading her from the glaring lightbulbs strung across the tent ceiling, above them, made her feel better. He inspired her with his ingenuity and his grasp of the situation.

"Yes...he is," she murmured. "And I'm grateful you called him, Captain. Thank you."

His grin widened. "You mean you aren't going to go toe-to-toe with me on breaking chain-of-command and stepping onto your turf over this?"

At his gentle teasing, Sam pursed her lips wryly. "No, I'm not."

Pressing his hand over his chest, Roc said, "My heart be still. The truce really is working—so far."

"Don't let it go to your head, cowboy," Sam said, her lips finally twisting in a smile. Roc deserved a pat on the back for his creative problem solving. Sam was wary, though; if she gave him an inch, would he take a mile? She was afraid he'd take over and that wasn't about to happen.

Chastised, he lost his smile. "I won't, don't worry, Doctor." Roc looked at his watch. "Want more advice?"

"Yeah, give it to me," Sam said, finishing the coffee with relish.

"Close up shop. I'll order Lieutenant Grayson to give these people our supply of blankets, and have them sign their names on a roster so that they don't lose their place in line. I'll have him instruct them to come back at 0800 tomorrow morning."

"Sounds good," Sam whispered. "My team is wrung out. We're all used up for today."

"Yeah, and you haven't seen anything yet," Roc warned her gravely.

# *Chapter 5*

*February 4: 0530*

"Roc?" Kerry Chelton called as she approached him outside his tent the next morning. It was barely dawn, but the line of light on the eastern horizon promised better things in an hour or two, she hoped. Just in case it didn't warm up, Kerry was bundled up, a wool muffler wrapped warmly around her neck and chin. Her hands were buried deep in the pockets of the marine jacket Lieutenant Grayson had given her.

Roc had just finished giving his sergeant orders to get the team ready for a three-mile march to the first potential medevac site north of the landing zone. "'Morning, Kerry," he said, turning to her.

She smiled up at him. "Ah, I see. 'Morning' instead of '*good* morning.' You're just like Quinn."

Grinning lopsidedly, Roc adjusted his flak vest and pulled his heavy jacket closed over it. "I'm a realist," he corrected. "I'll wait to see what the day brings."

"Quinn said it was quiet last night. So that's good."

"Yes."

"Listen, Dr. Andrews doesn't seem to be up and moving around yet. I was wondering if I should go over to her tent or—"

"No, I'll do it." Roc wondered why the hell he'd said that.

Kerry's eyes grew merry. "Considering how you two don't seem to be getting along, I was willing to do the duty. I think she worked too hard yesterday and needs the sleep. I gave her an alarm clock. She probably slept through it." Looking at her watch, Kerry added, "And Quinn said you wanted to be out of here within thirty minutes."

"Well," Roc murmured, slinging his M-16 across his left shoulder, "that isn't going to happen if the doc isn't up yet."

"No, I don't think so. I do have a suggestion...."

Roc appreciated Kerry's unobtrusive style of handling a delicate situation. "I'm all ears."

Motioning to the chow tent, she said, "I'll betcha a hot cup of coffee under her nose will wake her up."

"I can learn a lot from you, Kerry. Stick around." He nodded his thanks and headed off for the chow tent.

The February morning was quite chilly. Looking to the right, Roc could see his team assembling outside the HQ tent. They'd already eaten and were ready to saddle up. Looking to his left, toward where the doctor's tent sat at the end of a row of similar structures, Roc felt his heart melt a little.

Judging from Sam's face last night, she'd worked way too long yesterday. Roc understood why. Going to the chow tent, he got a cup of coffee in a chipped white ceramic mug and headed to her tent. At the entrance, he called her name. "Dr. Andrews?"

No answer.

"Sam? You awake in there?"

No answer.

Setting the cup down near his boot, Roc unzipped the tent opening. Picking up the cup once more, he slipped inside. When he'd allowed his eyes to adjust to the dimness, he saw a cot on the left side of the space, with a bundle of covers over a scrunched-up body. An unwilling grin pulled at his mouth. Setting his rifle down, he zipped the tent back up to stop the warm air generated by the electrical heater from escaping.

There was a lightbulb overhead and he switched it on. The naked glare illuminated the cozy space. Roc turned and saw a mass of unruly red hair sticking out from the covers. She'd pulled the thick wool blankets across her face to keep warm. Something tugged at his heart again as he moved toward Sam.

There was something childlike in the way Sam was sleeping on her side, that topknot of red hair in stark contrast to the marine-green blankets covering her. Leaning over, Roc placed his hand on her shoulder and gave it a firm, gentle shake. "Sam? Hey, wake up."

She groaned.

Smiling, he lifted his hand away and stood there watching her move slowly. Though the covers had been pulled away from her face, her eyes were still closed. Roc hadn't realized how thick and long her lashes were until just now. He stood above her, his hands resting on his hips. She had a sprinkling of freckles across her cheeks and nose that made her look more like a schoolgirl than a mature woman. Fighting a desire to lean over and caress that soft cheek to see if it really felt like smooth velvet, Roc simply stood there, absorbing her beauty.

A voice chided him for being here. It was an invasion of her privacy. But his heart said, *Forget it, stay.* So he did.

As Sam's lashes fluttered upward to reveal drowsy green eyes, Roc couldn't help but smile. He sat down on the cot across the way. Holding the cup of coffee near her face, he said, "Time to wake up, Doc. You've overslept. I've brought you some coffee to jump-start your day."

"Wh-what? Huh?" Groggy, Sam rose up on one elbow. She had been so cold last night that she'd slept in her uniform to keep warm. The only thing she'd shed was her combat boots. Blinking sleepily, she saw Roc staring back at her, one corner of his mouth pulled upward. That was a smile, she supposed, as her gaze settled on the proffered cup of coffee he was patiently holding out in her direction. Rubbing her face, she groaned. "Uhhh...what time—"

"Zero-five-thirty."

"Oh, jeez, I overslept!" she exclaimed, throwing off the covers and awkwardly sitting up. The tent floor was dirt, and when her sock-covered feet hit it, she quickly lifted them up once more and sat cross-legged on the cot.

''Here,'' Roc offered quietly, ''hot coffee. This was Kerry's idea and it's a good one.''

Murmuring a husky thank-you, Sam eagerly took the cup. The moment her fingers touched his, she felt that same wild tingle arc through them. Giving him a quizzical look, Sam brought the lip of the cup to her mouth and sipped gratefully.

''Mmm...''

As she tipped her head back, closed her eyes and made that purring sound in her throat, Roc decided she was truly beautiful, in a wild, untamed way. Her thick, slightly curly hair made an unruly halo about her head. Again he was struck by the desire to get up, thread his fingers through that red-and-gold mass and kiss those soft, parted lips of hers.

Shocked at the direction his thoughts were taking, Roc scowled. Before he could get up, Sam opened her eyes and gave him the sweetest smile he'd ever received.

''You know what?'' she said, her voice raspy with sleep. ''You are truly an angel in disguise. Thanks for the coffee. I owe you one....''

Forcing himself to his feet, Roc suddenly felt hemmed in, as if the tent were growing smaller by the moment. This was Dr. Samantha Andrews without all her armor in place. What he saw thrilled him and scared him. She was incredibly attractive and vulnerable right now, not the hard-nosed medical doctor he'd confronted before.

''Forget it,'' he told her gruffly, bending to pick up his weapon. ''Can you make HQ in thirty minutes? My men and your team are already saddled up and almost ready to go. And the good news is that the other medical team from San Diego is going to be here at 0800 to take care of these people on the list."

Stung by his sudden gruffness, Sam cringed inwardly. For a brief moment, she'd seen Roc's face come alive with interest and surprise. Those icy blue eyes had thawed and she'd felt an undeniable warmth aimed toward her. She'd felt his protective aura embrace her, too.

Shaking her head, Sam wondered if she was crazy. No, she just wasn't good at waking up all of a sudden. She never had been. It took two cups of coffee and at least an hour for her to get rolling.

"Yeah…I'll make it, Captain. Thanks for bringing the coffee. And I'm glad Morgan was able to free up that team. My day is starting off great."

Unzipping the tent opening, Roc grunted and slipped out. Why had he gone in there in the first place? He should have let Kerry do it. She'd offered. Unhappy with himself, he said tersely, "Okay, Doctor. Thirty minutes. We'll be waiting." And he zipped the tent back up, turned and left.

*February 4: 0600*

Sam hurried to the HQ tent exactly thirty minutes later. She was winded, having run a comb through her hair, brushed her teeth and thrown on a fresh blouse. Everyone was already there, standing around and chatting. Roc was off to one side, his brows drawn down in silent censure over her tardiness. As she hurried up to the group, Sam realized he had a right to feel that way.

"Good morning," she called out breathlessly.

There was a chorus of jovial responses.

Sam smiled and said, "I'm late and I'm sorry. It won't happen again." Everyone looked forgiving except the captain. She turned to Roc. "Okay, Captain, lead the charge. I'm good to go."

Nodding, Roc barked at Lance Corporal Ted Barstow to take point, or lead the procession.

Barstow nodded, hefted his weighty pack and slung his M-16 over his shoulder, keeping it handy. Immediately, the twenty-one-year-old Oregon native moved out in a northerly direction, map and compass in hand.

Roc turned to the group. "Doctor, the ball's in my court now. We're going to proceed like this. You will instruct one of your people to follow Corporal Barstow no closer than fifty feet. We'll keep that distance between us for the entire trek. That way, if we meet up with any snipers, they can't nail us as a group. Staying spread apart gives us an advantage that way. Understand?"

"Of course," Sam murmured. "Jonesy? You go first. Then me—"

"No, Doctor. You'll stay at the rear of this column with me and my radioman."

"Oh...okay." Sam shrugged. "Ernie, you're next. And then Lin." She smiled at them. "And I'll bring up the rear with Captain Gunnison."

The other two marines joined the straggling group at the distance dictated by Roc. Sam stood and watched everyone move out at a good, striding pace. Then she picked up her pack, which weighed around forty pounds, and struggled with it until Roc came over and lifted it so she could get her arms through the shoulder straps.

"Thanks," she said. Turning, she saw the radioman, PFC Lorenzo Gonzalez, moving out. "I guess it's our turn?"

"Yeah," Roc said. He'd seen her expression change wonderfully when he'd come over to help her. She was such a softie underneath that bristling pit bull demeanor, he was discovering.

Strands of her hair were trapped beneath her shoulder strap. "Hold on," he murmured, walking up to her after slinging his rifle across his left shoulder. "Your hair...." He slid his fingers beneath the strap and gently pulled the thick strands free.

Her hair was silky. Strong, like her. Even in the gray light of dawn, Roc could see the gold threads gleaming. When he looked up, his hand a bare inch from her cheek, he saw her green eyes grow huge with surprise. And then some other undefined emotion flitted through them. What it was, Roc wasn't sure. Feeling awkward and uncertain all of a sudden, he quickly pulled his hand away, as if burned.

"Time to go," he growled.

"Uh, yeah," Sam muttered, frowning. Roc's touch had been strong, yet gentle. Her scalp tingled pleasantly where he'd touched her hair. The look in his eyes...well, it had reminded Sam of a hunter who had his sights fixed on a target. Gulping nervously, she stepped away from his powerful presence. Right now, in his uniform, with his rifle in his hands, and wearing that helmet, he looked positively dangerous.

And he was, Sam decided as she turned, her gloved hands holding the straps of the heavy pack she carried, which bit into her shoulders. Roc Gunnison, she was discovering, was dangerous to her in ways she'd not counted on. That made her even more scared of him.

Roc moved with a fluid stride and easily caught up with Sam's jerky one. She wasn't used to wearing a pack, he could tell. The ground was uneven, the light still poor. Though the eastern sky was becoming lighter by the minute, deep shadows darkened the huge mall parking lot, which had been chewed up and spit out by the devastating earthquake, leaving nothing but rubble. Shadowing Samantha Andrews, he watched as she fumbled, tripped and finally got her balance and rhythm for the trek ahead. When she was marching steadily, Roc moved to her side. Far ahead, he could see his point man leading, with everyone else moving at a reasonable pace and keeping the necessary distance between them.

Sam turned her head, and smiled at him. "I have a new appreciation for what marines do." She jerked a thumb toward the pack she was carrying.

It was tough to be serious with her when she gave him that girlish smile. He could see the enthusiasm for adventure in her large, expressive eyes. Grudgingly, he smiled.

"Yeah, we operate under a lot of physical demands, as well as mental ones."

The morning was cool and invigorating. Sam was beginning to come alive now that she'd been up almost an hour and her sluggish metabolism had picked up. Glancing toward the eastern horizon, she saw the light turning a pink color, the sky above brightening by the minute from a deep, dark blue to a diluted aquamarine. "What's 'point' mean?" Sam asked, referring to the order she'd heard him give Barstow earlier.

"Point is a man who's put out at the head of a column to nose around like a wolf. He's our first warning that there's trouble around.'' Roc gestured ahead toward where Corporal Barstow was walking alertly, swiveling his head constantly from side to side, then looking down to see where he was placing his booted feet on the rubble. ''Barstow is from the Cascade Mountains of Oregon. A hill boy. He grew up hunting and trapping with his father, so he's got a keen eye, good ears and plenty of brains between them.''

''I see him looking around,'' Sam said. ''What's he hunting for? Diablo?''

''Yes, but also trip wires.''

''Mines?''

''Yep. Even though there's been no report of Diablo setting up trip wires for claymore, or rockets hidden beneath the dirt that we might step on and blow ourselves up with, we can't take any chances. For us, this is hostile territory, and we take *nothing* for granted.''

''Especially us,'' Sam teased, grinning. She took a close look at Roc. She knew he'd recently shaved because she could see where he'd nicked himself along the hard line of his jaw. His profile was tough looking. Sam knew without a doubt that she wouldn't want to run into him in a back-alley fight. She'd already had the experience in her E.R., and she knew how much of a warrior he could be.

''Yes, especially you.''

''We're your precious cargo.''

Snorting, Roc saw that she was teasing him. ''Is this what a cup of coffee does for you, Doctor?''

''What?''

''This early morning teasing?''

''I suppose. You don't like it?''

"Naw, I didn't say that...." Roc didn't want to let on how much he liked this side of her. She was like a bubbly teenage girl, full of enthusiasm, full of life. He liked it immensely.

"I guess I should don my serious doctor mask."

"No...don't do that. Not if it means we're going to do battle again," he said, referring to the very first time he'd encountered her in doctor mode.

"No kidding," she joked.

"I like peace, not war."

"Really?" To Sam he seemed girded for war.

"Yeah. I'm a peaceful person at heart."

"I'd never have figured that one out."

"No, you wouldn't have because of our past experience in the E.R. that day."

"Right about that."

"My mother always said there was hope for the hopeless."

"Oh? You mean us? Instead of being two pit bulls circling one another, we might actually come to respect each other? Maybe even—*gasp*—like one another?"

Roc managed a strangled sound, part laughter and part groan. "You're fast on your feet, Doctor."

"Thanks to you. To that coffee. This is your fault, you know?"

He met her smiling eyes. "I like your bedside manner, Doc. It becomes you. Remind me to wake you up tomorrow morning."

Laughing liltingly, Sam slid her fingers beneath her pack straps and readjusted them again. She was glad their group only had three miles to go. Looking at Roc's frowning face, she felt her heart expand euphorically. The sensation took her breath away for a moment. What *was* there about sourpuss Captain Gunning that made her feel as nervous as a schoolgirl? Sam couldn't figure it out. Yet here she was, teasing him, being light and happy with a marine whose head she had been ready to rip off only yesterday. Was it the fact that he'd come, woken her up and given her that lifesaving cup of coffee? That had been really thoughtful of him. He'd surprised her with his sensitivity.

They walked along in silence for nearly thirty minutes. Gunnison consulted the map constantly and had his GPS—global positioning device—in his hand to make sure they were going where they were supposed to. Sam watched him when he called Gonzalez back and made a radio call to the point marine. There was a brief conversation, then Gunnison put the phone back on the pack the private first class was carrying and gave him orders to move ahead once more.

The terrain around them had changed shortly after they'd left the destroyed shopping mall. Sam had seen people straggling back to the clinic tent to line up as before. She knew the medical team from San Diego would be able to help those people today. Sam vacillated between the weight of the immense responsibility before her and the near euphoria she felt taking this trek with Roc Gunnison.

Unable to explain why she felt so giddy this morning when she shouldn't, really, Sam bowed her head, her hair falling like a screen on either side of her face, and marched at a steady pace. Finally, her curiosity got the best of her.

"Where do you come from, Captain Gunnison?"

"From?" He looked up from his map briefly. "Where was I born? Is that what you mean?"

"Yeah. That."

"I was born in Portland, Maine."

"Ah, that fits."

"Really? What does?"

"Your sense of individualism. You know how Maine people are seen—as hardy, independent and tough."

"I'll take that as a compliment."

"I would."

He grinned. "What about you? Where do you hail from?"

"White Bear Lake, Minnesota. I'm a cold-country girl."

"That's why you knew how to wrap up like a mummy last night, with only the top of your head exposed," Roc said.

Chortling, Sam said, "Oh, yeah, me and cold. I know how to dress for it and sleep in it. My dad used to take us ice fishing up at Lake Milac, which is north of where we lived. I used to sit for hours in an unheated shed out on the ice, my pole dangling in the water, hoping some poor northern pike would come by and nibble on it."

"You're an outdoor type, eh?" Roc hungrily absorbed this information about her. Right now, her cheeks were a glowing red from the temperature and her exertion. He wanted to focus his attention on her but he didn't dare. The suburban neighborhoods on either side of them, the houses in shambles, the small groups of people huddled around campfires, also claimed his attention. Diablo were known to fade into the landscape, assume the same kind of clothing innocent civilians wore, and it would be hard for him to separate friend from enemy. It was just as it had been in Somalia; one never knew who might be hiding a handgun under his clothing. So Roc kept his gaze constantly moving and stayed on high alert. Sam seemed unaware of the possibilities, but then, she was a medical doctor, not a trained field specialist.

"I love the outdoors," she said with a sigh. She again readjusted the pack, which was becoming burdensome. After thirty minutes her shoulders were beginning to ache. She wished that she was in better physical condition for this. She didn't want Gunnison to think she was unable to carry her share of the load.

"I do, too," he murmured.

"You grew up in Maine hunting and fishing, I bet."

"You're on target," Roc said. He saw people from the suburbs they passed lifting their heads and studying them intently as the two teams made their way down the broken asphalt street between the homes. Roc could see even from that distance the bedraggled state these civilians were in. There was no water available for them to wash with. Their clothes were filthy. Few homes were left standing. In most cases, the roofs had cracked and fallen, flattening the walls, so that people were unable to get in to salvage anything of value, such as blankets, clothing or food. He felt sorry for them.

Focusing on the conversation once more, he said, "My uncle took me out in the woods on weekends."

"What about your father?" Sam asked.

"My dad owns a computer company," Roc said gruffly. "He was flying around the world on business most of the time. His brother, my uncle, helped him run the corporation from Portland. On weekends, my uncle would take me and his two sons into the mountains.''

Glancing up, Sam saw the line of Roc's mouth hardening. She heard emotion behind his last statement. ''Wow. A geek for a dad. That's pretty cool.''

His mouth twisted. ''Yeah, my father's a geek, that's for sure.''

''So you rarely saw him?''

''I didn't see as much of him as I wanted.''

''That must have been tough.''

Roc liked her ability to sympathize. ''Yeah, as a kid, I didn't understand it very much. My mother... well, she didn't handle it well, either.''

''Oh?'' Sam felt a change in Roc. Again she saw his mouth tighten.

''My mother was always very...weak. Weak-willed, maybe, is a better word. She cried a lot. She was depressed because he was gone so much. He'd fly in for a day or two, come home late at night, be gone early the next morning. Eventually, over the years, her depression got worse.''

''Are you an only child?''

''Yeah. I guess after they had me, they figured one was more than enough.''

''Did your mom ever seek medical treatment for her depression?''

Roc shrugged. ''With the money my father made, and still makes, she was able to have the best medical intervention the world has to offer.''

''And?''

Shaking his head, he muttered, ''She's still depressed.''

''And he's still flying around the world?''

"Yep. Not much changes, does it?"

Hearing the wistful note in his voice, Sam met and held his stormy gaze. "I'm really sorry, Captain. That doesn't sound like much of a childhood for you. I've treated a lot of patients for depression and I've seen how it affects the rest of the family, especially the children involved."

"Now, don't get that sorry look on your face for me, Doc. I survived."

"Yes, you did. But knowing what you went through helps me understand you, too."

Though he arched an eyebrow, Roc said nothing. He'd probably divulged too much of that vulnerable part of himself, he decided. Still, the soft look in Sam's green eyes nearly undid him. There was more, much more to her than he'd ever thought. She was the diametric opposite of his mother. In fact, she wasn't anything like the women he'd had the sorry luck to have had relationships with. Heart thumping once in his chest, as if to underscore that realization, Roc felt disgruntled around the red-haired doctor. He wanted to conveniently place her in a box and label her as a spitfire. Instead, she was surprising the hell out of him, and he wasn't sure of anything anymore except that his silly heart was expanding in his chest with a joy he'd never before experienced.

Roc didn't know what to do with it, or how to handle it. Dr. Samantha Andrews was an enigma to him, upsetting his established view of women and the world. She was like no other woman he had ever met....

# Chapter 6

*February 4: 0700*

Sam couldn't keep her burning curiosity about Gunnison at bay. As they walked briskly along the rubble-strewn streets, through suburbs wrecked beyond belief, she decided to get nosy.

''Do you have any kids of your own?'' That was pretty nervy, she thought, seeing him give her a surprised glance. Holding up her hand, she grinned apologetically. ''If I'm getting too personal, tell me to butt out.''

Shrugging, Roc shifted the rifle from his left hand to his right. ''No...I'm not married. No rug rats.''

''Ah, yes, the quaint nickname marines give their children.''

''Aren't they, though?''

''Absolutely not! Kids are precious. Like little uncut gems. You get to watch them be born, watch life hone them, shape them, then you get to see them grow up. You watch their facets develop, until they shine in the world.''

''Not all of 'em are diamonds,'' Roc told her dryly, holding her dancing gaze. He liked talking to Sam. She was engaging and animated today, the doctor's facade nowhere in sight. Her thick hair bounced with each of her short strides as she strove to keep up the pace he was setting. The sun was climbing higher now, often striking her hair and making golden highlights in the fiery strands. ''So, you have kids?'' he asked, after clearing his throat.

''Me?'' Sam sighed and opened her hands. ''No…''

''You sound wistful. Like you wished you had them.'' He saw her brows scrunch and she tore her gaze from his. He sensed that he'd hit a sore spot, and the realization made him scowl. When she finally looked back at him, her smile was gone and there was a turgid darkness to her large eyes.

''I love kids. All of them. When I was made chief of E.R. a year ago, special efforts were made at our E.R. at Camp Reed to have a room just for children. We had it painted bright colors, with book characters that all kids read about, a teddy bear with green scrubs on… They love it.''

''I imagine it helps lower their anxiety, too,'' Roc noted somewhat distractedly. Coming up on their right, he spotted several people around a large fire. They were cooking a meager breakfast, from what he could see. Immediately he was on full alert. Diablo was known to infiltrate the populace, he knew, assume their clothing and stance. According to Quinn

Grayson, that had happened to him and Kerry Chelton; they'd come upon what looked like a typical group of civilians. Only gang members hiding behind them had opened fire. The situation had turned ugly, and Kerry had been wounded twice by bullets.

Roc's heart squeezed with sudden terror as he held Sam's thoughtful gaze. Under no circumstance did he want her or any of her team harmed. It was his responsibility to keep them safe.

"Yes, the kids love that room," Sam said wistfully.

"I do a lot of off-duty clinic work around here," Roc told her, relaxing slightly as he became convinced that the group cooking breakfast looked non-threatening. Everyone around the fire was too busy hovering over the small amount of food the skillet held over the flames. It smelled like beans to him. Judging from the thinness of their faces, Roc knew they weren't receiving supplies of food from the area 5 HQ. Every can of tinned goods they came across would be a treasure at this point. Could mean the difference between living and dying. He would be glad when the medevac facilities were established, because they would automatically become food and water distribution centers, as well.

"So, you never wanted to get married?" Sam asked. "Because of your mother's depression?" She knew it was another highly personal question, but something was egging her on to find the real human underneath that hard marine exterior. She saw his mouth hitch upward.

"Is this twenty questions?"

"It can be if you want it to be."

"Well," Roc murmured, "how about if I answer one of yours, and then you answer one of mine?"

Sam laughed softly. "Okay, I'll bite. Me first, though."

"Of course." He moved the heavy pack on his shoulders, then said, "Let's just say the women I seem to attract are a lot like my mother."

"Depressed?"

"That's two questions."

"Oh...yes, you're right. Okay, your turn."

He grinned wolfishly. "What do you do to relax? I haven't seen you do that yet."

Sam rolled her eyes. "Oh, that. I'm a triple type A. I never stop working."

"Why?"

"That's two. It's my turn."

"You're right." He grinned. She had a nice smile. Even more, he liked her full lips. The sunlight struck momentarily, illuminating Sam's entire profile and making a halo of her fiery hair. She was beautiful in an arresting way, and Roc found himself staring at her in fascination.

"What's your favorite hobby?" she asked him. Then suddenly, she tripped. His hand shot out, gripping her left arm as he steadied her.

"Thanks...I'm a klutz in this stuff." Laughing a little breathlessly as she felt the strength and firmness of his hand on her arm, Sam added, "I guess I'm used to moving around on polished tile floors, not chewed-up asphalt streets."

Reluctantly, Roc allowed his gloved hand to slip from her arm. Seeing the flush of pink across her cheeks, he realized she was embarrassed by her stumbling. "That's my job—to take care of you. Otherwise I'd feel useless."

Chuckling, Sam gripped the straps and readjusted

her load once more. "You're far from useless, Captain."

"Can we be less formal in situations like this?" he asked. "Would you call me Roc when we're out of earshot of our people?" Searching her eyes, he saw Sam's flush deepen, if that was possible. Her gaze skittered away from his and she looked flustered. Had he overstepped his boundaries with her? Militarily, they were the same rank, even though they were from different services. It wasn't unusual in such a situation, when alone or behind closed doors, to refer to one another by their first names. So why was Sam reacting like this?

"I realize you don't like me," he said, trying to help her out of his faux pas.

"Oh, no!" Sam exclaimed quickly. She raised her hands. "I never said I didn't like you. Did I?"

"You never said it, but it sure showed."

Pursing her lips, she shrugged and wagged her head. "You don't exactly endear yourself to others when you get in their face and start demanding things, Captain…er…"

"Call me Roc," he insisted once again.

"Like Rock of Gibraltar?" she teased. Sam realized that he was genuinely trying to create a connection with her that would override their past. More than likely he was doing so because they had to work closely with one another over the next week, and he wanted a more neutral atmosphere between them so they could get their mission accomplished. That made sense.

"Sometimes my men refer to me like that. Roc is fine."

"You strike me as utterly solid. Like a canyon wall

rising a thousand feet straight up, made of granite.'' Giving him a smile as she spoke, because she didn't want him to think she was insulting him, Sam saw redness tinge his cheeks. Was he blushing? It was cold out and the early morning sun hadn't made an appreciable difference in the temperature yet. He *had* to be blushing! Well, of all things. Thrilled that she'd gotten to him, Sam tried to rein in her assertiveness.

''So I'm a rock wall to you?''

''Well...kinda. There's nothing *wrong* with that.''

''Can I call you Samantha?''

''Er...sure. But my friends usually call me Sam. Either will do....''

''Sam's kinda masculine sounding.''

''I get kinda masculine when I need to be.''

''No kidding.''

Laughing softly, Sam saw his mouth thaw. Even more, she saw warmth in his eyes for the first time. ''Okay, my reputation precedes me.''

''You earned it the hard way. You confronted me.''

''You weren't the first, nor will you be the last. Sometimes a woman has to stand strong and speak up. Speak the truth, no matter what.''

''Well, you certainly took me on and did just that.''

She heard the dry humor in his tone. ''Thank you. I think.''

''You're welcome.''

''I don't think you like strong, independent women, Roc. Do you?''

''I have a tendency to draw women like my mother, as I said,'' he admitted.

''Oh,'' Sam murmured, ''that's why I was such a shock to your poor system.''

Chuckling darkly, Roc saw her grin. He was really

enjoying seeing the playful, teasing side of her. There was so much to this woman. Far more than he'd realized. ''That's putting it mildly. You flatlined me.''

Flatline was a medical term that meant a person's heart had stopped beating. She chortled. ''Oh, now who's embellishing things? You gave as good as you got. Judging from the murder in your eyes aimed at me in that E.R. that day, I shoulda been DOA—dead on arrival!''

''Now who's embellishing?'' As he laughed with her, Roc felt his chest expand with an unfamiliar sensation of warmth, followed by a heady joy. What was happening? He was in a devastated area, surrounded by millions of people in dire straits, and he was laughing with this woman. A woman whom he'd thought had no heart, just a steel trap mind, who wanted things her way or else. How wrong he'd been.

''You're a fifteen-thousand-pound Daisy Cutter bomb, Samantha.'' He saw her brows rise in surprise. ''You know that baby they drop by parachute from a C-130 at high altitude, which explodes three feet above the ground, killing everything for six hundred yards around it? That's what I thought you were. A real destroyer.''

''Wow...and I only compared you to a rock wall. Whew!'' Frowning, Sam searched his face, which was far more readable at the moment. She was starved to know him better, because she saw he wasn't the ogre she'd first thought. ''Sometimes, as a doctor, I'm the last line of defense. You're a paramedic, so this isn't news to you. You work with these types of situations all the time.''

''Yes, I do. I just never had the experience I had with you.''

"Because I was a woman medical doctor and not a male? That made it different?" She was searching to understand his reaction to her.

"Yeah, I guess that was part of it."

"And would you have come up and demanded the same things if I'd been a male doctor?"

Roc pursed his lips. He thought about that for a minute as they walked shoulder to shoulder in silence. Ahead, the residential area ended, revealing a small hill, maybe five hundred feet higher than the present terrain, that was flattened on top. According to the map he'd studied last night, there should be another shopping mall on that hill.

"You're probably right. If it had been a male doctor, I probably wouldn't have gotten in his face like I did in yours."

"And you got into mine why?" Sam asked. She eyed the changing landscape as they walked. Ahead of them, the houses ended at the foot of a hill, the top of which had been bulldozed flat. It seemed to be a construction site, from what she could make of it. There were cracks on the slopes in the compacted yellow dirt, due no doubt to the earthquake. Except for that, it looked like an excellent spot for a medevac unit to be built.

Roc glanced at her. "I don't know. I saw you across the E.R. It was your red hair, I guess, that got my attention. You looked competent. You seemed to be in charge and I was desperate. He'd lost a lot of blood with that leg wound, and I was afraid he'd need a transfusion and go into deeper shock than he already was if he didn't get it pronto." Roc scratched his jaw and gave her a searching look. "Maybe it was your face that made me think I could count on you. There was something about you, with the red hair and those freckles.''

Sam touched her cheek. ''My freckles?''

''Yeah,'' Roc said uncomfortably. ''You looked, well, I guess...trustworthy. You reminded me of a young girl, full of life, of fire, and I felt like you could help my man. So that's why I headed for you.''

''There was a male doctor in E.R. that day, too. Did you see him?''

''Yeah, I did.'' Roc grinned sourly. ''He didn't inspire me like you did.'' Slinging the M-16 over his other shoulder, he added, ''I don't know. Maybe because you were a woman I felt he would get better treatment. Quicker attention.''

''I see...so on some level you trust a woman in the midst of an emergency more than a man?''

Her insight was as startling as it was unnerving to Roc. ''You aren't afraid to shoot from the hip, are you?''

Grinning, Sam said, ''Is there any other way? I prefer the truth over the other possibilities. Don't you?''

''You don't play games.''

''No. Never did. Gets people in trouble when they do that, don't you think?'' She gave him a probing look.

''The women in my life were the opposite of you. All they did was play games,'' Gunnison muttered. ''The wounded-bird-with-the-broken-wing routine.''

''So, you headed for me because I was maternal.''

''Probably, looking back on it.''

''And when you hit a brick wall and I told you we were in a triage situation and to put your man out in the passageway to wait for help, it destroyed your expectation of me as a woman healer?"

Nodding, Roc said, "Yeah, that about sums it up."

"You realize now I was right to make the decision I did?" Sam held her breath. If Roc held a grudge, she'd find out shortly. Watching his face, she saw him scowl.

He swung his head toward her, he met and held her serious green gaze. "Yeah, you were right. I was wrong."

Releasing that held breath of air, Sam jerked her gaze from his. Relief pounded through her chest. "Thanks for being honest, Roc. It becomes you."

"You're the woman who likes honesty. I was just following your bullheaded charge in that direction."

Her lips pulled upward. "So now you see me as bullheaded."

"Sure I do. You can't be in charge and not be."

"Well, you're just as bad as I am in that department."

Roc pointed to the black embroidered captain's bars sewn on the shoulder of his desert-cammo jacket. "Yep, and here's all the authority I need to be that way."

Her heart lifting unexpectedly, Sam looked up and saw the point marine, Corporal Barstow, halt at the base of the small hill and turn toward them.

"Duty calls us both now," she told Gunnison. "It looks like we've arrived at our destination."

Roc nodded. "Yeah. This is the area I'd chosen. You remember seeing it from the air the other day?"

"Yes," Sam said. She watched her people gather with the marine contingent. Starting forward again, she picked up her pace, excitement thrumming through her. Roc strode easily at her shoulder. Suddenly, the pack she wore seemed lighter. "It looks perfect, Roc."

Warming to the way she used his first name—in a hushed tone only he could hear—he grinned. "Thanks! A compliment this time, not an insult..."

Chuckling, Sam met his blue gaze. "Captain, I think in the last hour we've been able to put the past behind us. I'd even predict that the only way we have to go from here is up. Wouldn't you say so?"

Her teasing was direct and unmerciful, but Roc had the good grace to take it in stride. "You're right, good doctor."

Sam could see the enthusiasm written on the faces of her group as she approached them.

"This is perfect!" Lieutenant Shan said excitedly. "Look how flat it is for tents, Dr. Andrews!"

Roc nodded to his men as he halted in front of the huddled group. The sun was higher now, the sky a light blue color and cloudless—another beautiful day in Southern California. Judging from the looks on his men's faces, they liked being out in the field as much as he did.

"Listen up," Roc called, to get the group's attention. "We need to climb this hill and check out the top, as well as the neighborhood. From up there, Dr. Andrews and I will study the map and see if this site will do. Sergeant, I want you to take the team and start assessing how many cracks have appeared in this hill due to quake activity."

Sergeant Simmons nodded. "Yes, sir. You want me to mark their location by latitude and longitude?"

"Yes, I do. Measure the length and depth of each one. We need to feed this info back to Logistics and have the engineers eyeball it. This section—'' he pointed to the left flank of the hill ''—will likely have at least one, maybe two helo pads built on it. We can't have the whole slope start sliding down when a helo delivering tons of supplies tries to land on it.''

''Got you, sir,'' Simmons said. He promptly raised his hand and called the rest of the team to follow him. ''We'll get started in the north, and work our way right around the base of the hill.''

Nodding, Roc said, ''Excellent plan, Sergeant. See me when you've got it completed. Keep your eyes and ears open for Diablo, too.''

''Don't worry, sir, they're top of the agenda.'' Simmons grinned.

Roc smiled briefly and waved them off. Then he turned to Sam and her team, who stood by expectantly.

''Doctor, do you want to check this out as a potential medevac site?''

''We sure do,'' Sam said enthusiastically. She smiled slightly. ''You're very smart, Captain.''

Lifting his head, he studied her. ''Oh?''

''I'd have never thought about those cracks in the hill being problematic.''

''You stick to saving people's lives, Doctor. I'll stick to what I know best.''

The medical team chortled at his dry teasing. Roc saw Samantha's face turn crimson, but he knew that she took his jesting in stride.

''Still,'' Sam said, ''I'm impressed. I can see I'm going to learn a lot from you.''

''Everyone can learn something from the marines, Doctor.''

Again the group laughed. It was a good sound to

hear, under the circumstances. Roc knew the age-old rivalry between the navy and Marine Corps was a good-natured one. And faced with this unmitigated disaster, they all needed a lift. After hiking through that hell in the suburbs, seeing victims of all ages barely hanging on, and knowing that epidemics were going to kill many of them if medical help didn't get in here fast, they all needed a moment of relief.

Roc didn't say it, but just seeing the gold flecks in Samantha's eyes as she stared at him lifted his spirits. Sam made him happy. That was a new and startling revelation. As he opened his map and refolded it to show this area, he stopped smiling and pinned her with a serious look.

"You and your team ready to look at this site with me?"

"Of course, Captain. Lead the way." She gestured gracefully toward the hill.

As Roc took a scrambling leap up the dried, hard-packed yellow dirt, which was mostly clay with some sand mixed in, he smiled to himself. Maybe this mission wasn't going to be the hell he'd feared it might be. Maybe Dr. Samantha Andrews had a pair of hidden wings, and a halo beneath that blazing red hair that he hadn't been aware of until now....

# *Chapter 7*

*February 4: 0815*

It wasn't long before the curious residents nearby started trailing over to the site. Roc had given Sam the assignment of walking the square, flattened hilltop and drawing a rough sketch of where the medevac should be set up.

As the sun warmed her and the air lost its chill, she stood with a clipboard in her gloved hands and began to draw where each tent would sit. The rest of her group were helping Roc's men measure the fissures in the hill. Happiness threaded through Sam as she stood alone amid the activity.

Hearing voices below, Sam lifted her head. She saw Roc pause at the edge of the hill, his rifle in hand, ready to be fired at a moment's notice. Alarmed, Sam started toward him. He was wearing the helmet, but had set down his pack. With its bulky weight off his back, she could see that he was in damn good physical condition beneath the camouflage utilities he wore. Around his sand-colored web belt were grenades, a black leather holster with a pistol in it, and two canteens.

Approaching him from behind, she decided to call out and let him know she was coming. Under no circumstances did she want to scare him or make him think she might be an enemy. Everyone was jumpy because of the ever-present threat of Diablo, and Sam knew better than to come up unannounced.

"Captain Gunnison?"

Hearing Sam's strong, clear voice behind him, Roc partially turned away from the two men standing below him. "It's okay, Lieutenant." He'd heard the question in her tone.

Sam came to a halt nearby. Below were two silver-haired men, their faces lined and weathered. Each was dressed in civilian clothes—dark-colored jackets and slacks.

"Trouble?" she asked in a low tone.

"No."

"Good. Who are they?"

"Their names are Frank and Jack, and they are retired civil engineers who have come to volunteer their services. I was just explaining to them that we have to gather information on this hill as a possible medevac site. They're going to help my men with measuring the cracks, and also give me their assessment of this location."

Brightening, Sam smiled and waved at them. They smiled and returned her wave. "That's great! And very kind of them."

"Yeah." Roc slung his rifle across his left shoulder. "I'm taking them around the east side. You doing okay?" He looked over at her. Because the day was warming up, Sam had unwound her muffler and left it hanging around her neck. He noted the warmth lingering in her eyes, and his heart expanded.

"I'm fine. Fine. Go ahead. I'm busy sketching—even Van Gogh would be jealous." She grinned.

Roc motioned toward a stretch of suburb in the distance. "Frank and Jack told me a number of children out there have dysentery. The parents have got all of them at one house that's still standing, trying to keep them warm and do what else they can. When you're done, do you want to go over there and try to help them? We've got *some* medical supplies with us."

"Sure," Sam murmured. "This is only going to take me about ten more minutes and then I'll be ready to go."

Nodding, Roc said, "I'll send Private Lorenzo Gonzalez, my radioman, with you. Don't go anywhere without one of my team escorting you, okay?"

"Sure." She saw the worry banked in his eyes.

"I'll send him over. Will you be taking your team with you?"

"Yes, I will."

Giving her a slight nod, he headed down the hard-packed earth toward the two men. Sam turned and went back to work, her heart focused on Roc and her worry on the sick children.

*February 4: 0830*

Sam walked with Jack Zimmerman, one of the engineers, who had volunteered to lead her and her group to the house where the sick children were being kept. Private Gonzalez, his rifle in his hands, walked alertly down a chewed-up street ahead of them. The leaning sign they passed indicated that the road was called Sunrise Drive. The houses on either side had been nearly all destroyed. This was not a rich neighborhood, Sam noted. Each house was small, most of them made of pastel-colored stucco and brick. The roofs of most houses had been twisted askew and in some cases pitched to the ground; such was the power of the giant quake that had pulverized the whole L.A. basin.

Halfway down the street, Zimmerman halted and pointed toward a half-destroyed redbrick home.

"This is it, Dr. Andrews. The place belongs to Barbara and Dave Platter. They're the only ones in the neighborhood whose house wasn't flattened. I've been through the building and checked it out structurally, and it's safe. All the children are in there. The parents take turns being with them, while the rest of us forage for any food or water we can find for them."

"I see," Sam murmured as she walked up the concrete driveway, which was riddled with cracks.

"Come on," he urged her, "I'll show you in. Barb and Dave will be so happy to see you."

Sam tried to keep her expression neutral as they walked to the back entrance. There was no door left, just an opening where a blanket had been hung. Jack moved the blanket aside and called for Barbara. Entering, he led them through the kitchen. Sam saw that the ceiling was cracked, and plaster dust was everywhere. There was a pitcher of water, covered, on the counter.

In the carpeted hall, which was dirty with footprints of the many who had walked it, Sam had to squint to see. It was very dark because there was no electricity. Jack took her to a room on the right and opened the door, which squeaked in protest. The door stuck and she pushed through it after Jack, her physician's bag in hand.

The odor of illness assailed her nostrils as she entered. Sam moved aside to allow her team to come into the large room, which had a king-size bed in the middle. She counted at least seven children, of various ages between three and eight, huddled beneath the covers. They were trying to stay warm by sleeping together.

"Barb?" Zimmerman called. "We've got medical help. This is Dr. Andrews and her navy team from Camp Reed."

A black-haired woman in her thirties, who'd been sitting near the bed stroking the head of one child, stood up. Her face was pale and pasty looking, her dark eyes widened with the surprise and hope at the announcement.

Jack laughed. "Hey, we got help, Barb! Why don't you come over here and tell Dr. Andrews about all these children and their condition? That way, she and her team can pitch in and help."

Sam gave the woman a gentle smile and held out her gloved hand. "Hi, Barbara. Call me Sam. We're here to do what we can."

Gripping her hand tightly, Barbara sobbed, "Oh, Doctor! This—this is so wonderful! Someone told us earlier that a group of marines went by, but I never dreamed… We were hoping—oh, God, we were hoping for a little more water...." She turned toward the bed and gestured helplessly toward the children, most of whom were still asleep.

"Doctor, they're all dehydrated. All of them have diarrhea.... We do what we can, but it's uncontrollable. I'm so afraid..." She pressed her hand to her mouth and looked up at Sam, tears glimmering in her eyes.

"I understand," Sam told her soothingly, running her hand along the woman's slumped shoulders. That was why the children were huddled beneath the covers for warmth. Dysentery could cause chills. "You can help us as we assess each child. You have their names? Are their parents nearby?"

Nodding jerkily, Barbara looked over at Jack, who stood near the door. "W-will you go find the rest of the parents? Bring them here?"

"Sure, Barb. Not a problem. I'll be back in a jiffy, don't worry."

Sam glanced at Lin, her nurse. She saw the worry in her almond eyes, but like any good medical person, Lin wasn't about to let her worry be seen by Barbara, who was trying to stem her tears. "Lieutenant Shan? Will you start on that side of the bed? Assess each child?" Sam turned to Jones Baker, who had set down his pack. "Jonesy, get the admittance paperwork out and ready to roll on each child, okay?"

"Right away, Doc."

"And Ernie?"

"Yes, ma'am?"

"Come and help me. I'm going to uncover one child at a time. I want you to take their temperature and do all the recording on what I find."

Ernie beamed and quickly dug into her pack. "You bet!"

Sam headed for the first child tucked in the mound of dirty blankets. All she could see was a topknot of uncombed blond hair.

"Jonesy, pull seven IVs from your pack, too," Sam ordered. She tried to keep the grimness from her voice.

"Consider it done!" Jonesy sang out, flashing a brilliant smile.

Sam tucked all her emotional reactions away. Right now they had seven children to try and help. She had worked with her team before in the barrios of Los Angeles, at a small clinic set up for Hispanics who didn't have money for medical help. But this was an entirely different situation. These people had been living in deplorable conditions ever since the quake.

As Sam lifted a little four-year-old girl with limp yellow hair from beneath the covers, she wanted to cry. Without water, the child could not be properly bathed. And without clean water, the child could not be cured. For a moment, Sam wished she was out on the hill with Roc and his team. This was heartbreaking. Shattering. Here they were in the richest country on earth, and children were dying tragically. A part of Sam wished Roc was near. She needed to talk this out with someone, and somehow, because of his past experience, she knew he'd understand.

*February 4: 1300*

The early afternoon sun had warmed the air to nearly sixty degrees. Roc had shed his jacket and helmet, leaving his flak jacket on as he moved across the hill with his team. Jack Zimmerman had come back after leading Sam to the children, and he and Frank Baylor had assisted Roc and his men in assessing the stability of the hill. By 1300, Roc was up on top of the mound, calling Morgan Trayhern via an iridium satellite phone. With the help of Frank and Jack's expertise in civil engineering, Roc was able to tell Morgan that the hill was not only stable, but ready for action.

The blue sky and bright sunshine helped lift Roc's spirits as he got off the phone. His team, as well as the two retired engineers, sat around him sharing MREs—meals ready to eat. The two civilians ate hungrily, and Roc wished he had more food for them, but they needed to ration what little they had. Lifting his head, he looked off across the ruined suburbs. How was Sam? What had they found? He'd worried about her all morning. And if he was honest, he'd have to admit to himself that he wanted to see her.

"Sir?" Corporal Barstow murmured. He sat opposite Roc, eating his MRE.

"Yes?"

"Do you want us to set up camp here for the night or are we going back to the LZ?"

"No, we'll be going back. As soon as we're done here, we'll saddle up and find the doc. Once she's done with her rounds, we'll hightail it back home for the night."

"Yes, sir."

Jack looked up from where he sat on the bare, yellow dry earth, his own MRE balanced on his left knee. "You know, Dr. Andrews is real special, Captain."

"Oh?" Roc stopped eating and focused on the silver-haired engineer.

"Yes, she's something else. She's got that special healer's touch. Now, I've been helping baby-sit those poor kids, who have all been sick for the last week, and they're crying and cranky. Not that I blame them. The moment your doctor came in and started picking up each of those tykes, not one of them cried out or whimpered. It was as if they knew—you know?"

"Knew she was there to help them?" Roc asked.

"Yes, but it was more. I stood there in the doorway watching Dr. Andrews and her team work. They operate like a well-oiled machine. Everyone knew what to do, and in what order to do it. I hung around long enough to see each of those kids get an IV to replace the fluids they've lost."

"Did Dr. Andrews say they were going to be okay?"

"Yes, she was very happy—relieved, I think—that all seven kids are gonna make it with medical help."

"Good," Roc murmured. He finished his MRE and tucked the empty container into a pocket of his field pack.

"She's really special," Zimmerman murmured, resuming eating. "You must be very proud of her."

"We are," Roc said. He knew intuitively that Sam's touch was magical.

"Those kids looked at her like she was an angel come from heaven to heal them. You shoulda seen their faces. You know, they've been so sick their eyes are flat looking. But when Dr. Andrews sat on the bed and drew each child onto her lap, her arms around them, and beamed that wonderful smile of hers...well, let me tell you, Captain, I thought I was in the presence of an angel, too. The way she touched them, held them, hugged them...she's incredible with children. Their eyes shone with love for her."

"Dr. Andrews runs the E.R. of the Camp Reed Hospital," Roc said. "She's had a lot of experience with sick children."

"Well," the engineer said with feeling, "it sure shows. I'll tell you, when this is all over, I'll be writing a letter to my congressman, senators—heck, the president himself—to tell them about Dr. Andrews and her team. If it weren't for you coming here, those children would eventually die. We just don't have enough good water to give them. We've been drinking less and less ourselves so we could give our share to the children." His brows dipped. "But it's unclean water. I spent half my engineering life in Southeast Asia drilling for oil and carving roads outta jungles, and I know what bad water can do to you—in a real hurry. It isn't pretty, and those kids are so tiny that they can't stand to lose as much water as an adult can. That dysentery is nasty stuff."

"It's a killer," Roc agreed. He got up and pulled on his pack. "Okay, men, let's saddle up. With Mr. Zimmerman's help, we're going to find Dr. Andrews."

*February 4: 1330*

Sam was just coming out of the house when she saw Roc and his team walking up the driveway with Jack in the lead. She'd taken off her jacket and removed her outer layers because of the warmth of the day, and her stethoscope still hung around her neck as she eagerly stepped out into the sunshine. Taking a deep breath of fresh, clean air, she smiled at Roc, who was looking at her intently as he stepped carefully up the driveway. Sam felt all her worry melt away as he approached. Even though he had shaved early that morning, his face was already darkening with a beard, giving him the lethal look of a warrior.

"Hi, stranger," she greeted him cheerily as she moved down the driveway.

"Hi, yourself." Roc stopped and rested the butt of his rifle on his left hip as he looked past her toward her medical team, who were gathering outside the house. "Everything okay?" He hated sounding official and clipped, but under the circumstances, military decorum had to be followed.

"Just fine."

"Good news on the kids?"

Nodding, Sam slid her fingers under the straps of her pack. "Very good. We've got them on IVs. They are all responding well."

"What about water for them?"

She gave him a wicked grin. "You'll probably croak, but my team gave them all the water we had." She patted her pack. "Now it's much lighter, and I won't mind carrying it so much."

Grinning, Roc nodded as he watched a number of parents trail out the blanketed doorway of the brick house. "We're only three miles away from HQ. I think my men and I have enough water to share with you black-shoe navy types if you get thirsty on the way home." "Black shoe" was a name for the shore-based personnel.

Rising to his teasing, Sam laughed. "Black shoe" was a derogatory term. "That is very gentlemanly of you, Captain."

"Thank you, ma'am. If nothing else, marines are heroic."

Sam laughed softly. She saw Roc's gaze flit from person to person and then back to her. He was alert, almost edgy. "You guys are certainly heroes in our eyes."

"Compliments will get you a drink of water whenever you want it," he murmured with a smile. Just then the breeze lifted a few strands of Sam's red hair, and for a moment Roc wanted to reach out and tuck those errant locks back into place. But he stopped himself.

"Will we be coming back this way tomorrow?" Sam asked him in a lowered tone.

"No." He saw her frown. "The next medevac site is to be established west of here. Why? You worried about the kids and ongoing treatment?"

"Yes...I am. There's one child who should be airlifted out of here, to the hospital, Roc. She's only seven years old, and in the worst shape of the seven."

"I just talked to Morgan Trayhern. We've got a go on setting up this first medevac site. He's swinging into action. There's supposed to be two navy Super Stallion helos in here tomorrow morning. A Navy SeaBee team is coming in to erect foundations, platforms and tents for the medevac model."

"Oh," Sam whispered, "that's great. I still need to see these kids tomorrow, Roc. Somehow." She opened her hands in a pleading gesture.

Shrugging, Roc said, "We can't be all places at once. There're too few of us and too many of them. I know you care, but right now your mission is to search out three suitable spots for medevacs."

Frustrated, Sam nodded. "Yeah, okay, I hear you, but I don't like what I'm hearing."

"Look," Roc murmured quietly, "maybe if we get done with the second area early tomorrow, we can walk back here and check in on them. No promises, though."

"Good," Sam exclaimed in relief. "Let me tell Barbara. I need to leave her with instructions in case we can't make it back tomorrow."

"Hey," Roc warned her darkly, "don't make any promises to this woman. Diablo's around somewhere. If you come back here, it'll be with me and my team. You're not to go anywhere by yourself, understand?"

Nodding, Sam said, "Yeah, I understand."

As she went back to the house, Roc stood there, frowning. He knew this would happen. Sam and her team were helpers and healers. Seeing the devastation had made the doctor far more aware of how badly needed her services were out here. Sam would want to come back no matter how late it was tomorrow night, how tired she was or how exhausted his team became from their reconnaissance duties. *Damn.*

Rubbing his chin, he waited patiently, his rifle on his hip, as Sam talked with Barbara. Turning to his sergeant, he ordered, "Buck, have everyone leave their MREs and all their water, except for a quart of it per person, with these people."

Simmons grinned hugely. "Yes, sir."

Roc saw the delight and gratitude on the faces of the parents as his men shrugged out of their heavy packs and began to hand over food and water to them. Maybe, if Sam realized these people and their children would have supplies for a day or two, she'd be less likely to worry about them or bolt back here even if she was dead on her feet.

It wouldn't matter how generous they were; the food and water wouldn't last long. Roc knew that at least fifty people had banded together here to try and help one another survive. Still, he absorbed the delight on Sam's face as she hugged Barbara and then walked back to where he stood.

"You really *are* a hero, Captain. Thanks for sharing your food and water with them. They are so desperate...."

Giving her a look filled with warning, Roc muttered, "I'm doing this because I don't think we'll be able to get back here tomorrow, Doctor. You're going to have to pace yourself. You have only so much energy and drive in a twenty-four-hour period. I'm not going to let you spread yourself too thin, nor am I willing to put my men at risk because you want to help the world twenty-four hours a day."

Scowling at him, she said nothing.

He saw her chin jut out in defiance. That hurt. Didn't she have the sense to know she could wear herself out? No one could work twenty-four hours a day. In his business, getting a good night's sleep meant being better prepared for the enemy the next day. Sighing, Roc supposed he couldn't blame Sam for not understanding, but he sensed their different points of view could cause friction, enough to explode into a confrontation between them as this mission continued.

The thought made Roc unhappy. A confrontation with Sam was the last thing he wanted. Recalling Jack's glowing report of her healing abilities, he smiled to himself. She was so damned headstrong, opinionated and spontaneous—qualities he'd never experienced in a woman. In his heart, he pined for a few private moments with Sam Andrews. Maybe he'd get them on the way back to the LZ. More than anything, Roc wanted to know about the person, the woman who stood at his side, her eyes glowing with hope, her lips breathlessly parted as she watched his men give their food and water to those who needed it even more than they did.

# *Chapter 8*

*February 5: 0030*

Sam couldn't wait any longer. Glancing at her watch, she realized it was past midnight already. Dressed warmly, she stole quietly, a pack on her back. Settling the navy knit cap on her head, she absently touched her jeans and moved uncomfortably in her Kevlar vest.

The children were on her mind. Especially the little seven-year-old, Ani, who had been in the worst condition. Gulping, Sam blinked rapidly as she tried to get her bearings. The chugging sounds of several gas-fed generators rumbled in the background. Above her, the sky was clouded over and threatening rain. Pulling her jacket collar around her neck against the inconstant wind, she made her way across the broken parking lot of the shopping mall, stumbling as she went.

Oh, she knew there were marine guards about, but Sam was betting that, under the circumstances, most of them were pulling duty over at the distribution center, where the food and water was kept.

She stumbled several more times as she left the dimly illuminated tent city behind. Finding the street they'd taken earlier, Sam started along. She didn't have a flashlight, and three miles in pitch darkness was going to be rough. Accordingly, she'd climbed into her Levi's, put on her leather hiking boots and thrown on a heavy wool sweater instead of her uniform.

Breathing through her mouth, she ran haphazardly, stumbling often. As the night closed around her, she halted, looking back. The small landing zone looked like a bright, welcoming haven in the blackness. Heart squeezing, Sam turned.

Abruptly, a scream lodged in her throat as a shape, silent and large, appeared out of the night and in front of her. Sam pressed her hand to her mouth, her eyes huge for a moment, and then her shock turned to surprise.

"Roc! What are you doing out here?"

"I could ask the same of you, good doctor."

He looked at the illuminated dials on his thick, hairy wrist. "It's 0030. You're supposed to be in bed." He looked down at her. Pushing his night vision goggles up on his helmet, he managed a thin smile. Sam's hair beneath the cap was in disarray, the collar of her jacket drawn up over the Kevlar vest she wore beneath it and kept in place with a dark blue muffler. She was beautiful in her own special way, and despite the situation, his heart picked up its pace.

"Well..." Sam hedged, running her fingers nervously through her unruly hair, "I wasn't tired...."

"Let me guess," Roc said, scratching his jaw, which was in dire need of a shave. "You were worried about Ani. She was the worst of the seven kids you worked on. And now you're going back to check on her?"

"For a marine, you're pretty smart, Captain." Sam wondered if he'd allow her to pass. He stood there, rifle in hand and a slight, sour smile on his shadowed face.

"Marines come that way, Doctor."

"Oh, please...look, I need to go there. Now. We've got to check out that next area tomorrow morning and—"

"And you were going to spend an hour tramping out to see Ani, and then what? Walk back?"

"Well—yes. Have you got a better plan?"

He grinned slightly. "Doctor, you're like an errant child, given to the whim of the moment." His smile disappeared when he saw in Sam's eyes her burning desire to get to the child.

"I'll take that as a compliment. Fair enough?" Sam felt a sense of urgency and moved restlessly from side to side. But Roc was a large, well-built man, even more imposing in his night gear and helmet.

"You know Diablo's out here, don't you?" he demanded in a low tone.

"Is that what you were doing? Nosing around?"

"Yes, I was."

"I figured the members of Diablo would be like most everyone else—in bed, asleep. They have to sleep sometime."

"So do you, and look what you're doing. You

don't think that gang doesn't have scouts out at night, checking into things? We'd be stupid to think they were all in bed sleeping."

Sam's nostrils flared. "Let me by, Roc. I'm going to see that little girl. I've got seven more IVs in my pack. All those kids are going to need another round of fluids to snap them out of it. That's the least we can do for them."

Shaking his head, Roc muttered, "I don't know whether to drag you kicking and screaming back to your tent or let you pass."

"You'd better choose the latter, because I will not go quietly. I'll wake up everyone. They'll blame you for it."

Lips twisting, Roc turned and looked down the dark street in front of them. Without night vision goggles, it would be nearly impossible to get anywhere without a lot of stumbling and tripping. "Okay, I'll take you. This one time," he warned her, shoving his face into hers, until their noses were only inches apart. He saw she wasn't the least intimidated. Her jaw was set, her eyes hard with determination to do exactly what she wanted to do.

"Thanks…that's nice of you." And it was. She watched as Roc settled the goggles back over his eyes. The instrument looked almost like a pair of binoculars, but she knew it gave him the distinct ability to see clearly in the darkness. When she felt his left hand curl around her right arm and bring her alongside him, relief flooded through her.

"It's going to be rough going," he warned as they began to walk. "I can see where to place my feet, you can't. Put your arm around my waist and hold on. That way, if you stumble, you're less likely to fall. I can't have our only E.R. doctor with a dislocated knee or broken ankle, can I?''

Sam laughed a little breathlessly. Roc was purposely cutting his long-legged stride down to match hers. ''No, you can't. And thanks for doing this.''

''You owe me, Doctor. Big time. And I intend to collect when the time's right.''

A warm sensation moved through her heart as Roc turned and spoke those words in a low, husky tone near her ear. She felt the moistness of his breath as she slid her arm around his narrow waist. He wrapped his arm around her shoulders and drew her closer. Ordinarily, Sam would have balked at such an intimate move. Under the circumstances, she realized that Roc was doing the most sensible thing in dangerous night conditions.

''You're turning out to be more of a hero, Captain.''

''In your eyes?''

''Yes.''

''Is this like winning the blue ribbon at the county fair?''

Squelching a laugh, Sam stumbled and tripped. Her boot had struck a fair-size chunk of asphalt she hadn't seen. In a heartbeat, she felt Roc's arm tighten around her shoulders. As she started to fall, he lifted her off her feet and then set her back down on smoother ground in one easy, effortless motion. Amazed at his strength, she gasped, clinging to him for support.

''Remind me to get some of those night goggles next time I think about doing this.''

Roc liked the closeness the unexpected situation put them in. ''Remind me to hog-tie you to your cot tomorrow night so we can both get a decent night's sleep, because we sure as hell aren't going to get one tonight."

Laughing breathlessly, Sam fell into step with him again. "I'd apologize, but I'm not sorry, Roc."

"Yeah, I know you aren't, and I'm not asking for an apology."

"You know why I'm doing this. You're a paramedic. You know how much difference an IV of fluids can make. Especially for a child."

"Samantha Andrews, you've got the biggest heart and the smallest brain of anyone I've ever met."

She heard the humor in his growl. "Brainless under the circumstances? Going out in the middle of the night in a dangerous place alone and without escort? That kind of brainless?"

Chuckling, he nodded. "Bingo."

"Do you really think Diablo's around?"

"Yes, I do. It's just a question of where. Quinn got a late-evening report of looting along the area 5 and 6 boundary. I think they're a good four miles to the south of us. Tonight, anyway. If we're lucky. That doesn't mean some members aren't around here. We really don't have any idea of the size of their force."

"So, what were you doing so far away from our tent city, when you ran into me?"

"Reconnoitering. Doing what I do best." He liked the way Sam fit against him. She was a trooper; he'd give her that. And he couldn't really blame her for wanting to see those seven kids again. If the truth be known, he'd wondered about them off and on all day. And he knew Ani, the little blond-haired girl, was in need of more medical care than just one infusion of fluids.

"Aren't you tired? Your men are all snoring next door to me."

Chuckling, Roc kept his hand firmly on her shoulder. "Yeah, but I'm in charge of security, so I was checking out the area."

A few drops of rain began to fall. Sam groaned. "Darn. I didn't bring any rain gear."

"We're halfway there," Roc stated. "Let's pick up the pace?"

Sam nodded. "Let's go for it. It's chilly out. I'm not real happy about being cold *and* wet...."

For the next mile and a half, Sam trotted awkwardly at his side. She was soaked to the skin by the time they made it to Barbara's house. It was easy to find the place, because a campfire next door acted as a beacon, despite the rain. The fire had been built under the sheltering eaves of the neighboring house, where a jutting corner of the fallen roof could protect it from the elements, and people huddled around it.

Roc guided her to the dry area, out of the drumming rain. He explained why they were there to the man whose duty it was to keep the fire going all night. The man, who introduced himself as Al, quickly went next door and woke up Barbara. She appeared within minutes, her eyes swollen with sleep, her hair uncombed.

Sam smiled and gripped her outstretched hands.

"Oh, I'm so *glad* you came back!" Barbara cried.

"How's Ani?" Sam asked at once, urgency in her tone. Her hair was damp, with droplets of rain dripping off the ends. Wiping her face, she blinked her eyes to clear them.

"Better...much better. The other kids are really

coming around. The antibiotics are helping so much, Dr. Andrews. Do you want to see them?"

"Yes, can we? I know it's late, but it's the only time I could spare from my other duties."

Smiling with gratitude, Barbara motioned for them to follow her. "I'll have Al make you some hot tea. You're soaked. Bless you for coming...."

*February 5: 0245*

Roc had put the finishing touches on his small, one-man tent when he heard Sam and Barbara speaking outside the door of the house. The rain was splattering down and he knew it would be a cold, damp night. Moving toward the house, he could see the two women standing at the door, talking. Sam had her arms wrapped around her body. She was shivering.

As he approached, Roc nodded to Barbara. "We're going to make camp here tonight," he told the women. "We'll leave early tomorrow morning."

Sam's eyes widened. "Camp?"

Barbara waved good-night to them. "I wish we could be of help, Captain, but we all sleep in one room, and it's crowded with fifteen people in it. It's the only room in our house that can stand the aftershocks."

"We understand," Roc said. "Good night." He reached out, wrapped his fingers around Sam's arm and gently drew her forward. They were alone now except for Al, who stood guard next door, tending the fire.

"Come on," Roc told her, leading her down a stretch of slippery yellow Bermuda grass toward the tent. "You need to get out of those wet clothes and into some dry ones."

Gasping, Sam pulled out of his grip. "You want me to spend the night in that tent? With you?"

"Sure."

"It's...so small, Roc...." And she began to panic. It had never entered Sam's mind that he might have a tent. Or that she'd be sharing it with him.

It was beginning to rain in earnest, and Roc wasn't about to stand out here arguing with her. Leaning down, he unzipped the flap and opened it. "Climb in, Sam. We'll argue inside where it's dry, okay?"

Gulping, she looked back at the house. The rain was splattering coldly across her face. Chilled to the bone, she got down on her hands and knees and quickly crawled into the cozy space. Inside, she could barely turn around. Her damp hands met the dry warmth of a wool blanket Roc had spread out on the floor.

"Move to one side," he ordered, "I'm coming in...."

Crouching in the corner on her knees, her arms around herself, Sam watched him enter and zip the door behind him. Roc's bulk filled up the tent completely. Unsure what to do, Sam simply sat there, her teeth chattering.

"Give me a second," he told her as he took off his helmet and laid it in one corner. Moving his M-16 to the side where he intended to sleep, and making sure it was locked and loaded, Roc shrugged out of his heavy, wet jacket and stuffed it into another corner. Beneath the coat, he was dry and warm.

"Okay, come here." He reached in Sam's general

direction. His hand connected with her left shoulder and a tangle of damp hair. He removed her cap.

"Let's undress you, shall we? I've zipped two goose-down sleeping bags together. Once we get you out of your wet gear, I want you to snuggle down into them. Understand?"

Sam nodded. Turning, she tried to unzip her soaked jacket. Her fingers wouldn't work, but Roc's did, with ruthless, swift efficiency.

"How're the kids?" he asked as he stripped her out of the jacket. He coaxed the Kevlar vest off her.

"F-fine."

"Ani?" He pushed the jacket and vest into the corner of the tent with his. Running his hands across her shoulders, he found that her sweater was damp, as well. "This has to go, too."

"Ani needed a second IV, but she was the only one. She's much better." Sam hesitated, but knowing Roc was right, she pulled the sweater over her head. All she was wearing beneath it was a thin, white silk camisole. It, at least, was dry. The cold air hit her. Moaning, Sam quickly sat down, unlaced her hiking boots and pushed them off. Next she tackled her damp Levi's, which came off stubbornly. Roc's hands were warm and dry as he finally guided her into the sleeping bag.

"I'm glad she's okay," he said. Making sure Sam was snuggled into the dry bag, he took off his own boots and pants. Dressed only in his green T-shirt and boxer shorts, Roc eased himself down into the bag next to her.

"Cold?" he asked.

"Yeah, freezing, as a matter of fact. This bag feels so good." Sam didn't care how intimate they would have to be. She needed something to take the chill out of her. Roc's body was massive, warm and strong. Automatically, she moved those scant inches, to press the front of her body to his.

"I'm so c-cold...." Sam chattered, burying her head against his neck, beneath his jaw. When his arms went around her shoulders and drew her tightly against him, she sighed. "You're so warm!"

"I was wearing rain gear," he said. "I came prepared. You didn't check the latest weather conditions before you left. That's why I packed two sleeping bags. I figured you might want one, too." Rolling her against him, he pulled the sleeping bag over her shoulder and tucked it in so no cold air could enter. Sam was shaking. "Lie flat against me," he said. "I'll try and warm you up." With one hand, he began to rub her shoulders, back and hips to create more circulation. Her flesh was cold to the touch.

Tiredness stole over Sam as she lay there, trusting and limp, in his arms. Roc was solid, just as his name implied. There wasn't an ounce of fat on his body. She tangled her legs with his. Even her feet were cold. His were like warm heaters in comparison.

The dampness of her hair against his shoulder, the lilac scent of it, drifted up to Roc's nostrils as he lay on his right side with Sam pressed against him. Her arm was wrapped around his waist, and he smiled to himself. He liked having her against him. In fact, he was having one helluva time keeping his mind above his waist. She was soft and firm in all the right places. Wishing they had some light so he could see her face, Roc peered into the darkness. Still, she was warm and in his arms, something he'd been thinking a lot about today.

"Better?" he whispered against her ear. Strands of her drying hair tickled his nose.

"Umm...this is wonderful. *You're* wonderful.... You should get a medal for going above and beyond the call of duty...."

Chuckling, Roc continued to run his hand across her hip and firm, long thigh to warm her up. Little by little, Sam was relaxing, her teeth chattering less. "Don't let it be said that marines haven't, yet again, saved the navy's butt."

Exhaustion pulled at Sam. She closed her eyes. "I surrender to the obvious power of the Marine Corps. I'm waving a white flag of truce. You know what, Roc?" Her words were slurring.

Easing his hand back up her long spine, across the soft silk of her camisole, he whispered, "What?"

"You're one of a kind...."

"Thanks, I think..."

"I'm so tired. I'm really warming up now, thanks to you...."

"Good." Her voice was becoming wispy and faint. Roc knew how tired she was. So was he. Feeling how warm her flesh was becoming, he stopped his ministrations and laid his head on the makeshift pillow of clothing he'd created earlier, near Sam's. She had snuggled deeply into his arms.

The splatter of raindrops on the tent continued unabated. Lucky for them, the bottom of the tent was waterproof, or they'd be lying in puddles.

As he closed his eyes, his arms wrapped tenderly around Sam, Roc sighed. It was a sigh of contentment, he realized as the feeling washed through him—something he'd rarely felt in the last couple of years. But, as Roc felt Sam drift off to sleep, her body releasing the last of the tension it had carried, he felt strong and good.

The sudden desire to kiss Sam was nearly his undoing. That lilac fragrance coupled with her special womanly scent had made him hard. Roc was alarmed at his reaction and wondered if Sam was aware of his arousal. Barely breathing, he waited. No, she was asleep. Dead to the world, judging by her soft, slow breath against his neck. Good. He'd dodged the bullet on this one. It would have been embarrassing to her and to him. Roc wasn't at all sure Sam even liked him. Oh, she tolerated him for many reasons. But that was a far cry from wanting intimacy.

As he lay there, his eyes closed, the rain music to his ears and the feel of Sam's heart beating gently against his hairy chest, a balm to his soul, the world felt more right to him than Roc could ever recall. What *was* it about Sam Andrews that drew him? She was the diametric opposite of all other females he'd been involved with in the past. Roc could count the ways she was different. For one thing, she had the crazy bravery to go out in the dead of night in an area that was like Dodge City before law and order had tamed it. She obviously cared deeply about children. Even to the point of risking her own neck.

Roc didn't know how she would have gotten here without his help. And now, as she lay sleeping in his arms like an innocent, trusting child, he felt good about himself. Thank goodness he'd been wearing his combat pack, which had everything he'd needed for roughing it. All she'd had in her pack were IVs and some food and water. She hadn't counted on rain.

And Diablo was out there, prowling around. Roc

could feel them. No, he'd have to watch her in the future. Clearly, her heart led, her head followed.

Just as he was starting to drop off to sleep, he felt the earth shiver. Tensing, Roc waited. Another shiver: aftershocks. Luckily, he had put the tent up on a slight slope, away from all structures. Although aftershocks were happening less and less, many buildings were being weakened more by each one, and eventually would collapse. And any fool dumb enough to be sleeping inside, could die.

They were living in a dangerous, unstable time, Roc decided. Yet as the rain drummed down around them, he felt happy. Happier than he had any reason to be.

# *Chapter 9*

*February 5: 0500*

As Sam slept, she felt incredibly secure and loved. Arms, strong and protective, were wrapped around her. The face of her fiancé, Captain Brad Holter, hovered in her mind's eyes. He was smiling that dimpled, elfin smile that always reached in and touched her heart. How many times, after they had spent their passion, their hearts thundering in unison in the aftermath, had she lain like this with him? He would gently tease her, kiss her brow, her nose and the tip of her chin, and proclaim that her freckles were as Irish as he was. She would laugh and drown in his sea-green eyes. Oh, how Sam missed him. When his Marine Cobra helicopter had crashed, in a senseless accident, she'd felt as if a part of her had died with him.

Now these arms around her, warm and secure, brought her alive once more. Watching Brad's narrow, smiling face disappear, she moaned. Something was different. Out of place, but not in a bad way. Sam moved slightly and burrowed her head in the crook of the man's neck. She felt his arm tighten slightly around her, as if to tell her everything was all right, and to slide back into that abyss of deep, healing sleep.

Something *was* different. But wonderful. As Sam nuzzled her face against that warm neck, she inhaled a very male scent, and her heart skittered with joy. How long had it been since she'd been held like this? Held and comforted against the woes, the tribulations and traumas she faced daily as a doctor? Sam recalled somewhere in the depths of her mind how much she had looked forward to seeing Brad after a hard day at the hospital. Just walking into his arms and being held had helped her shed that tremendous emotional load she often carried. Being held dissolved her anxiety for the patients she cared for. Sam never found it easy to walk away from her job, and Brad had seemed to sense that.

He would sit with her on the couch, cuddling her in his arms, and talk her down. An Irishman and a born storyteller, he'd weave one humorous yarn after another, until Sam forgot about what she'd gone through in the E.R. that day. Laughter was a great healer, Sam had discovered.

She felt strong lips press softly against her brow and follow her hairline in a series of gentle kisses. Her own lips parting, Sam sighed deeply. Oh, to be loved once again! She'd entirely given up on that possibility. Sam knew she was a strong woman and that few men would ever be interested in a relationship with her, because she demanded equality. That was only fair, in her world. She was not some passive thing, nor did she hold that men were always right and women wrong. No, both were equal partners, bringing weaknesses and strengths to their relationship. Brad had honored her, respected her, as she had him.

As that male mouth trailed across the top of her head, dropping small, lingering kisses here and there, her scalp tingled deliciously. Brad had never done that, but she was so lost in the feelings wrapping around her, the love, the care and sense of overwhelming protection, that Sam didn't stop to question who was doing it. Sleep was slowly fragmenting and dissolving. Nostrils flaring, she inhaled that scent deeply into her body. It was a wonderful male fragrance, stirring her womanly yearnings and causing her breasts to tighten with anticipation, pressed as they were against his chest.

And then she felt fingertips, featherlight, sliding across her unruly hair to her right shoulder and caressing it. His touch was so tentative that it caught Sam's wandering attention as she lay there, her head pressed against his shoulder, a drowsy smile pulling at her lips.

His mouth settled near her temple, his moist breath moved like a warming stream across her cheek, as gently as a butterfly. Again the lingering, tentative exploration of his lips against her cheek made her sigh. This time Sam moved her head. She wanted to kiss him in return.

Looking up through her lashes, she saw a face very close to her own in the grayness of the coming dawn.

Only it wasn't Brad's face. It was… She blinked. His eyes were a stormy blue, narrowed and intense. His hair was dark and short and in need of combing. His mouth…it was the mouth of Captain Roc Gunnison hovering above hers, merely inches away! But despite her shock, the look in his eyes invited her. This wasn't the hard marine she'd seen before.

More than anything, Sam slowly realized, his face was open and vulnerable. Gone was the tension that made him seem unreadable. His brow was smooth and no longer scrunched in thought. The slashes around his mouth were not as deep. She smiled softly as she slowly focused on his mouth, inches above her own.

"You have a wonderful mouth when you aren't making it into a thin line," she murmured sleepily. Something instinctive and primal made Sam raise her hand to stroke his full lower lip. Simply allowing herself the luxury of touching him was euphoric. She felt him tense as she grazed her fingers across his mouth in gentle exploration. It was a strong mouth, and she wanted to kiss it. Unwilling to leave the security of Roc's arms, Sam lay there, drowning in the sea-blue of his eyes. Seeing desire burning there made her heart pound with need. Withdrawing her hand from his mouth, she touched his broad, capable shoulder, which was clothed in a dark green cotton T-shirt. Power. The sense of his strength penetrated her heated world, making her yearn for closer contact.

Roc wanted to kiss her, too. She felt his hand range down her arm, and then move back up toward her shoulder in a light caress that spoke volumes to Sam. He might be a hardened warrior, but now she was privileged to see his other side, the man enflaming her senses and turning her heart inside out.

"Kiss me?" she whispered, her voice husky with sleep and need.

Roc lay above her, drinking in her drowsy beauty in the gray dawn light that filtered through the walls of the tent. Sam was incredibly beautiful. She lay like a trusting child in his arms, her hand pressed to his shoulder as she looked up at him with the faith of the world in her large, sleepy eyes. Groaning inwardly, Roc watched as her lips parted in a provocative way that told him she really did want to kiss him. Every cell in his body cried out for more heated contact with her. He'd awakened earlier in the throes of a fiery dream where he was making hot, passionate love with Sam. It had brought him out of a deep sleep into a full and painful arousal.

Roc knew he shouldn't have eased onto his side and kissed her brow or that thick, silky hair. He knew better, but he couldn't help himself. He had been alone for so long, having given up on being able to ever find a woman who could meet and match him, heart and soul. Intuitively, he knew Samantha Andrews could do that—and more. She was a courageous being, all heart, all passion, and God help him, that drew Roc to her like nothing ever had in his entire life.

Lifting his hand, he followed the line of her jaw to her stubborn chin. "When you were coming out of sleep, Sam, you called for someone named Brad...."

She sighed and closed her eyes. "Oh..." she whispered apologetically "...he was my fiancé...." Lifting her lashes, she saw Roc's eyes narrow. "Brad died in a helicopter crash at Camp Reed. It was a stupid crash, not his fault, but he didn't make it.... That was two years ago. I'm so sorry...."

Seeing Roc's eyes widen for a moment, Sam slid her fingers from his shoulder down his heavily muscled arm. Wherever she touched him, she felt him tense. "I...well, to tell you the truth, Roc, I haven't been with a man since Brad died. There just aren't that many that aren't totally intimidated by me."

Digesting her husky words, Roc allowed his hand to rest once again on her chin. "I'm sorry you lost him...." And he was. Even now, in her drowsy green eyes, he could see how much she missed him. "He must have been one hell of a man to get your attention." Roc's mouth curved ruefully. How he himself wanted her attention! It scared him. It thrilled him. He wasn't sure what to do with that realization. When he'd kissed her brow, she'd moaned softly and pressed against him, wanting more. And how much he wanted to give her! Roc found himself reeling from it all. Everything in this moment was magical. Unreal. How badly he wanted it to be real as he absorbed the languorous look in Sam's forest-green gaze, clinging to his. She still wanted him to kiss her. He saw it in her eyes—the yearning, the need.

But was it for him or for Brad? Roc wasn't sure. Giving her a sad smile, he grazed the freckles covering her right cheek with his index finger.

"If I kiss you, Sam, I won't stop.... You're the kind of woman who grabs a man, and he wants to take you all the way. I'm not sure if you see me or Brad right now. Maybe it's the time...the place." Roc lifted his head and looked around the quiet tent. The rain had stopped sometime in the night. "We're in the middle of a terrible trauma. People do funny things when they're under this kind of stress...."

Roc couldn't help himself, he kept stroking her rosy cheek. He felt her fingers tighten in the cotton material of his T-shirt as he spoke those low, husky words to her. Their lips were inches apart...mere inches. Every cell in his body pushed him to lean over and make that delicious-looking mouth of hers his own. Make Sam his...in all ways. His lower body was aching and on fire.

The cold reality—that she had spoken Brad's name while coming awake—made Sam wince inwardly. She saw the sadness in Roc's face. Yes, he wanted to kiss her...and she wanted to kiss him. Yet his words had been tinged with regret. Heart thrashing with continued need of him, Sam watched as his dark brows moved downward. He was sad, too, thinking that she wanted to be kissing Brad and not him.

Snuggling her head against his arm, she nuzzled his shoulder and pressed her mouth to it. Looking back up at him, she clung to his gaze.

"I just kissed you," Sam whispered unsteadily. "You. Okay?"

Roc nodded, unsure of where to go next. Swallowing hard, he said in a low, rasping tone, "Wrong place, wrong time, Sam. I'm sorry. More sorry than you'll ever know..." And he was. His heart ached with need of her. He was so hungry to explore her, to know more about her—the woman, not the doctor. Dr. Sam Andrews was open and relaxed with him for the first time. His heart was pounding like a drum in his chest and he wondered if she could hear it. When she gave him that soft, understanding smile and he felt her hand leave his chest and trail along his jaw,

Roc almost lost the massive control he had over himself.

"The bad part of being an adult is knowing when it is the wrong time and place," Sam admitted. His face was dark with stubble and it lent him a dangerously male look. "I don't like being an adult all the time, Roc."

He laughed in a low tone. "Neither do I, sweetheart, but right now, time's running out on us and we gotta get dressed and get back to HQ We're due to lead that second reconnaissance mission to find another medevac site with our teams in exactly two hours."

Instead of getting up immediately, Sam relaxed even more. Absorbing the feel of his calloused hand as it rested on her cheek, she turned her head and pressed a kiss into his palm. Instantly, she felt him tense. A groan rumbled through his chest. Her heart soared with the knowledge that she could touch him so easily, and she felt euphoric as she gazed up into his darkened, narrowed eyes.

Then she sighed.

"You're right. I hate to admit it, but you're right, Roc."

Easing his hand from her jaw, Roc sat up, the sleeping bag folding down around his torso. The tent was cool and damp. "Maybe, if we can steal some time, we can talk more?" His mind said talk. His body screamed to make love to her.

Sam shoved herself into a sitting position. The tent was so small that they couldn't move without touching one another. "Yes, I'd like that...." And she would. Running her fingers through her uncombed hair, Sam realized that he was weighing her words heavily. Right now, time was their enemy. She wanted badly to tell Roc about Brad, and what he'd meant to her. She knew it would help Roc understand her and her past.

Reaching out and stroking his darkly haired arm, Sam whispered, "Thank you...."

Roc halted in the middle of reaching for his pack, wildly aware of her hand on his arm. He gave her a startled look. "For what?"

"For keeping me warm, safe and cared for. I really needed exactly what you gifted me with."

Roc felt her hand fall away, and cried inwardly for the loss of contact with her. But he understood why she'd let go. Grabbing the pack from the end of the tent, he dragged it up between them. As he opened it, he said, "My men call me a mother hen. They say I protect my own." Lifting out a clean, dry set of desert cammos, he handed them to Sam. "Here, put these on for the trip back to HQ. At least you'll be dry, even if they hang on you a little." He managed a slight grin.

Touched, Sam took his uniform. "Thanks..." She'd never realized how thoughtful Roc was until now. Her own clothes were bunched up in a wet knot near her feet, in a corner of the tent.

Together, they shimmied into their clothing, elbows and knees often touching. Despite the circumstances, Sam enjoyed the whole process. As she fumbled with the buttons, Roc turned, his hands covering her fingers.

"Here, let me...." he said, moving her hands aside. The intimacy of buttoning his jacket over her body was delicious. Heady.

"You really are a mother hen," she laughed softly.

"I can just see you with your own children, making sure they have their coats buttoned, their rubber boots on, their hats on their heads before they go out the door in the rain."

The thought was provocative. Roc lifted his head after he finished buttoning the jacket. Again, inches separated them. How badly he wanted to slide his hands across her flushed cheeks, hold her head gently as he brought his mouth down upon those soft, parted lips, which were just begging to be worshiped by him.

It took everything Roc had as a man to force himself to move away from her. "Yeah, I'm more like a mommy than a daddy at times with my men. It just comes naturally," Roc groused good-naturedly, shrugging into his own jacket and quickly buttoning it up.

"I've seen the way your men idolize you. They really like you. They believe in you. In what you have to say." She struggled into the long pants and then rolled up the cuffs. Wanting to say, *I felt like you would protect me in every way you could, too....* Sam bit down on her lower lip, halting the flow of words. Never had she seen such care radiating from another person as it had from Roc toward her. It left her shaky. Needy. Hungry. For him. Not for Brad. For Roc Gunnison, the man.

"Part mother figure, part father figure," Roc replied. He rescued her boots from the bottom of the tent as she slid out of the warm folds of their mutual sleeping bag and sat on top. "My men fear me," he joked. That wasn't true, of course.

"Thanks," Sam replied, taking her nearly dry leather boots. Shoving her warm feet inside them, she laughed a little breathlessly. "You know what, Roc?

You put on this huge warrior mask that no one can penetrate. The big baddie on the block.'' Lifting her head, she turned and gazed at him, her lips pulling upward. ''But now I know different. I *understand* why your men idolize you the way I've seen them do. You do care. You care with your heart...your soul...for them.''

Roc grunted and put his second boot on. He got to his knees, his shoulders brushing the roof of the tent as he hauled his web belt around his narrow waist.

''Nah, good doctor. You're being an idealist now. I'm a marine. That says it all.'' He flashed her an intimate look as he hooked up the belt. Lastly, he picked up his rifle.

Chortling under her breath, her heart racing because she saw the teasing glimmer in his eyes now, Sam hurried to pull on her protective flak vest. She knew she should wear it inside the jacket, but under the circumstances, she didn't bother. She would make a quick change back at HQ into her navy uniform, and she'd put the vest under her coat at that time.

''You don't fool me, Captain Gunnison,'' she whispered pointedly, donning her still damp, dark blue cap. ''Okay, let's roll. I'm ready when you are.''

Nodding, Roc unzipped the tent and crawled out of it. The sky above was starting to clear. In the east a gray light edged the horizon, illuminating the massive destruction all around them. But nothing could disturb the euphoria he was presently experiencing as Sam grabbed his hand and he helped her stand. Reluctantly, he allowed her fingers to slip from his. The lilac fragrance of her hair remained with him and he inhaled it like a starving man. Trying to gently tuck their unexpected intimacy away, Roc switched to his marine mode: total alertness. Swinging around, he noted that the suburban neighborhood was quiet. It was barely 0515, and most people were still asleep. At the top of the grassy knoll, he saw a woman standing with her hands in the pockets of her jacket, near the fire. He lifted his hand in a silent greeting and she smiled and nodded.

"I'm leaving this tent here," he told Sam. "Just in case we need to swing back this way for some reason or another."

"I think Ani will be okay…but it's nice of you to leave it. They can use the extra shelter." Giving him a grateful look, Sam put her empty backpack on with Roc's help. She absorbed each of his touches like a thief. Smoothing the straps across her shoulders, Sam watched as he hefted his own pack.

Shifting it to get it situated on his shoulders, Roc smiled down at her. "Can't fool you for a second, can I, Doc?"

"You're an open book to me now, Captain. Your secret is out."

Wanting to reach out and touch her cheek, scattered with those girlish freckles, Roc stopped himself. He knew the woman tending the fire was watching. In public, they couldn't indulge in intimate gestures; it just wasn't done. Instead, he gripped his M-16 and placed it on his left shoulder.

"Uh-oh," he teased, as he gestured for Sam to follow him down the damp grass toward the rubble-strewn street, "I'm in trouble."

"Yes," she agreed, laughing quietly as she hurried to catch up with him, "and like a superhero, I have X-ray vision. You're an open book to me now. I've seen the *real* Roc Gunnison."

It felt good to laugh together. Sam walked proudly, her shoulders squared, her stride sure and confident as they moved to the center of the street. Everything was quiet now; dawn was one of Roc's favorite times of day. He watched Sam's thick red curls slide across her shoulders as they walked, and saw a smile play on her full lips. They walked close enough to one another that occasionally their hands brushed.

"This is like a moment out of time," Roc confided to her as they hiked swiftly back toward headquarters.

"What is?" Sam glanced up at him. Looking at him in his helmet, goggles on top and chin strap buckled, she saw his power and danger as a marine. Less than an hour earlier, however, she'd been privileged to meet his vulnerable, gentler side—the man who had almost kissed her and stolen her wildly pounding heart.

"Us. Now. Moments stolen out of time," he answered in a husky voice.

Oh, how Sam wanted to kiss Roc! Even now that that perfect male mouth was flatter, tightened somewhat as he focused on the business at hand. She wanted to help him relax his lips totally.

"Moments out of time," Sam murmured. "Yes, it was...."

"I'm not sorry it happened," Roc told her in a dark tone. He kept swiveling his head and looking around. Diablo could show up anywhere, at any time. He instinctively felt that the survivalist group were nocturnal, like animals that foraged at night and also at dusk and dawn. During the day, they probably rested and slept, heading out on their hunting trips to steal food, water and medicine after dark, when people were most vulnerable. Now was a dangerous time to be up and walking around, in his opinion.

Looking over at Sam, at her bright face and wide green eyes, he couldn't fault her for not being on guard. She was a doctor. A person who thought the best of people, not the worst. That was his job.

Still, Roc sponged in her spontaneity and clung to that joy she was sharing with him.

"I'm not, either, Roc. Not sorry it happened."

"Really?" He gazed into her eyes, remembering Brad, her fiancé.

Losing her smile, Sam said, "Really. I'm scared, Roc…scared in a way I've never been before, so give me some time, will you?" Reaching over, she briefly touched his hard, calloused hand. There was no one up and around to see them in the misty dawn light. "I'm not sorry for what happened. I never expected it…. I'm just not the kind of woman who attracts men, you know? I'm aware of that. And that's okay." Sam released his fingers. "I'm scared for a lot of reasons," she added. "We need to talk more…and often, if you want. There's so much you don't know about me and vice versa."

Nodding, Roc murmured, "We've got duties right now, Samantha. Maybe tonight, when things quiet down, we can spend a few minutes doing just that."

She searched his face. "You mean that?" So many men were afraid of her because she was a strong woman. Was Roc truly different?

"Yeah, I mean it."

# *Chapter 10*

*February 5: 1230*

The noonday sun felt warm and good to Sam as she sat with her team in the middle of what they chose as their next medevac site. There had been four Little League baseball diamonds where they sat cross-legged on the short, yellow grass. The earthquake had knocked down all the fences, and cracks had appeared in the ground along one side, where nearby suburban housing had been totaled.

Sam ate hungrily from her MRE package. Lin, Jonesy and Ernie sat nearby wolfing down their food, as well. The day was beautiful to Sam in more ways than one. In the distance, she saw Roc with his team. They were measuring off the area, noting any potential engineering difficulties—doing the legwork to get the information to Morgan as soon as possible. Sam felt a little guilty that she was eating and they weren't. She knew that Roc wanted these medevac stations up and functional as quickly as possible.

"Beautiful day," Lin said, sitting down opposite Sam.

"Yes." Sam looked around. The local residents had seen them coming. Curious and full of hope, a crowd of at least fifty people had gathered as she and her colleagues walked into the area. When Roc told them a medevac station was going in, there were cheers and tears of relief.

"We're going to set up a clinic over there?" Lin asked, pointing to the area the Recon team was now working along.

"We will."

"Glad we brought extra IVs," Jonesy exclaimed, wiping his mouth with a paper napkin and stuffing it back into the plastic bag his meal had been packed in.

"Looks like we're going to need them," Sam agreed quietly. Her heart was centered on Roc, on the memory of their incredibly intimate night together. But the pleasure waned as she remembered her duty. Her head was whirling with logistics on how best to set up the clinic.

"There are a lot more elderly people in this area," Ernie said, getting up and putting her canteen back in her pack. "The other neighborhood had a lot of kids. Here, it's an older group."

"Nice people, though," Lin said.

"They're all nice," Sam murmured. She wiped her mouth with her napkin and got up. "They're all starving. I feel like hell sitting here and eating when all they've got are crumbs."

Lin grimaced. "Isn't *that* the truth. I gave away the extra MREs I brought, Doctor."

"We all have," Jonesy said. Dusting off his pants, he lifted his arms above his head and stretched. "I heard from Captain Gunnison that a Super Stallion's comin' in here later today, Dr. Andrews. Is that true?"

Nodding, Sam smiled. "Yeah, one's coming in. Morgan is really hauling ass on this project now. Roc—I mean, Captain Gunnison—told me earlier that another Sea Stallion is arriving at 1400 over at Landing Zone Charlie, our first medevac area. They'll have a full complement of medical personnel, equipment and drugs to off-load. A Navy SeaBee team coming with them will erect the tents and get things moving over there."

Rubbing his hands together, Jonesy grinned. "Dude, that's awesome! I love how the military can do this. We're a lot more efficient than the Federal Emergency Management Agency."

Snorting softly, Sam stuffed her empty MRE pouch into her pack. "Without roads, FEMA is stuck with the military to do the job."

"Hey," Lin said, scrambling to her feet, "I heard at the chow hall last night that they've got a lot of bulldozers on the northern edge of the basin. They're supposed to be carving a whole bunch of new roads out of the old ones. They'll be dirt roads, of course, but at least vehicles with food, medicine and water can start getting in here."

"About time," Sam said. She gazed again across the baseball fields to Roc and his team. They were down on their hands and knees, measuring a crevice. Her body responded hotly in memory of his burning gaze, his fingers grazing her cheek, and the hard masculinity of his body against hers. Taking a deep, unsteady breath, Sam figured she was not only sleep deprived, but shaken emotionally by the unexpected night with him.

''Dude,'' Jonesy exclaimed, ''things are a-lookin' up for these poor folks.'' He hefted his pack and placed it on his shoulders.

''About time,'' Ernie sniffed. ''I'm ready, Doctor.''

Sam threw her own pack back on and looked at her team. ''Ready?''

''Ready, ready now!'' Ernie called out.

Sam grinned. Ernie's brother was in the Air Force—a gunnery sergeant who flew in B-52 bombers. ''Ready, ready now'' was an Air Force saying. ''Okay, team, let's rock 'n' roll.''

*February 5: 1700*

Roc looked at his watch. Dusk was falling, and they had to get back to HQ. Walking three miles in the dark was not a good idea. He gave orders for his team to prepare to leave Landing Zone Delta, their second medevac facility. From where he stood in the center of the baseball fields, he could see Sam and her unit also closing down for the night.

He wondered if she was as tired as he was. In another way, he was wide-awake, like a thrilled teenager who was riding a high. All day he'd thought of her. Of their night together. Of their talk. Why hadn't he kissed her? It was stupid not to have, he realized now. His feelings had been hurt because she'd murmured her dead fiancé's name as she woke up. Roc realized that of course she would do that. Grief took a long time to get through; he knew that from hard experience.

They'd been so busy today that he rarely had a moment to look around for Sam, much less talk to her. He was feeling raw and exhausted from loss of sleep, and knew she must be, too. A few times he'd caught her looking in his direction as he worked with his team out on the baseball diamonds. If he wasn't wrong, Roc thought he'd seen longing in her face, as if she wanted to talk to him.

Maybe on the way back they might grab a few precious moments together, he mused as he saw Sam coming toward him, her team in tow.

*February 5: 1730*

Sam's heart lifted magically as she drew up to where Roc was standing, the butt of his M-16 on his left hip, his right hand on the top of his pistol holster. His implacable expression never changed, but as she drew closer, his blue eyes thawed with a silent welcome. That made her feel happier than she had in the last two years.

"Ready to head home?" he asked.

"More than ready," Sam murmured.

Roc motioned to her team members. "Okay, fall in between my men, keep the usual distance and we'll get this show on the road. Doctor? We'll hang back at the rear like we always do."

Everyone knew the drill. A minute later, with Sergeant Simmons in the lead, they were moving at a steady pace toward HQ. Sam waited at the rear, standing a few feet away from Roc. The sky above was turning a delicious peach color with yellow striations, the filmy white clouds a darker apricot hue.

"How are you doing?" he murmured as he waited for the last member of her team to get out of earshot.

"Dead on my feet. You?" She gazed up at him and saw the hard line of his mouth starting to relax. Thrilled, she realized Roc was opening up to her once more.

"The same." Hungrily, he looked down at her shadowed face. There were slight circles beneath her shining green eyes. Sam's hair was unruly as always beneath the dark blue baseball cap she wore, which had USN Hospital Camp Reed embroidered with yellow thread across it. The day was warm, in the sixties, and she was in her white lab coat, the flak jacket beneath it, a stethoscope hanging around her neck. Her navy-blue slacks were stained and dirty.

"We did a lot of good things today," Sam observed as Roc gestured for her to begin walking. They fell into step, their hands brushing together from time to time. Sam absorbed each fleeting touch and realized that was what she needed most. Somehow, he steadied her—in ways she'd never experienced before.

"Yeah, we did. I called in the numbers to Morgan. He's got the whole West Coast navy hog-tied into getting these medevac units in here and operational, as fast as they can push them through. The man doesn't take no for an answer."

"That's good," Sam said, lifting the baseball cap from her head and running her fingers through her hair. "Because people are dying, Roc."

He heard the heaviness in her tone as she resettled the cap on her head.

"Pretty bad, huh?"

Grimacing, Sam whispered, "Yes. We've got three elderly folks who aren't going to make it through the night. I did what I could for them, Roc. It's so sad.... I mean, these are *our* people. We're the richest, most powerful nation on the face of this earth and we can't get in here to help them like we need to."

Reaching out now that the others were walking ahead, their backs to them, Roc gripped her shoulder momentarily and squeezed it. "Hang in there, Sam. You're doing what you can with what you've got. These people got a lot more today than they ever expected, believe me."

"I know." She turned and looked up at him. How badly Sam wanted to simply stop and step into his arms. Judging from the look burning in his shadowed eyes, Roc wanted it, too. When his hand fell away, she felt alone again—the way she always felt.

"It's an adjustment," she admitted. "I'm used to the scrubbed floors of my E.R. I'm used to having everything I need by just asking for it. Here—" she waved her hand in a helpless gesture "—we don't have near enough of anything for these people. It's so heartbreaking...." Her voice cracked and she hung her head, not wanting Roc to see the tears gathering in her eyes.

"You know," he said in a deep, low tone, "I used to think you were a hard-as-nails M.D., but I'm changing my mind hourly about you." Roc couldn't see her face because of her thick hair hiding her profile. "You've sure turned my world upside down, Sam. A couple of times today I saw you working with people who really needed your care. You don't hide a thing, you know. You wear your heart on your sleeve. Sometimes I heard your laughter floating across the field, and it made everyone feel better, me included. I watched very sick people respond to you. You give people hope.''

Reaching out, Roc gripped her hand for a moment. ''I didn't think you felt anything, but I was wrong. Dead wrong. Watching you work yesterday and today...well, it taught me a lot about you.''

Squeezing his fingers, Sam absorbed his touch. ''Everything's so crazy right now, Roc. I feel like I'm in a constant state of trauma and shock myself. First all this—'' Sam lifted her chin and looked up at him ''—and now you.... I never expected last night to happen. It just never crossed my mind....''

Releasing her fingers, Roc nodded. ''Mine, either, if you want the truth. My focus was on keeping you safe, despite your harebrained spontaneous decision to go back and see how those rug rats were doing.'' He saw her smile slightly, saw her eyes mirroring her emotional and physical exhaustion. ''When it started to rain, I knew you were in trouble. You weren't wearing rain gear like I was. Fortunately, my pack is my home, and I had a tent and dry sleeping bags.''

''I never got to tell you how kind and thoughtful that was of you,'' Sam told him. ''I was so surprised when you met me at the door. I was freezing cold. I tried to keep it from Barbara and the kids. And you showed up like a gallant knight to save this harebrained lady from herself.'' She grinned, and felt the warmth of his own smile cascading down upon her.

''I knew you wouldn't make the walk back in that condition,'' he admitted. ''It was the best I could do under the circumstances.''

"Ordinarily, I don't hop in the sack with just any guy."

His smile broadened. "No, believe me, I don't take you for that kind of woman. You'd beat the hell out of the poor bastard who tried that maneuver."

Chuckling, Sam said, "You got that right."

"I didn't know what you'd think," he admitted. The deepening colors of the sunset made her face glow, her freckles stand out across her nose and cheeks. Sam was a breath of clean air to Roc. She had a wonderful simplicity of heart and she obviously loved her work as a medical doctor. Today he'd seen how good she was with her patients, people who desperately needed her touch, her care and warmth. Hell, he needed her himself.

"Oh, about sharing that teeny tent of yours?"

"Yeah…that. It was close quarters. No doubt about it."

"Listen," Sam said, giving him a sincere look, "at that point, I didn't care. I knew you weren't doing this to maneuver me into bed with you. You're a trained paramedic. You assessed my condition accurately—I was beyond chilled. The best way under the circumstances to help me was to peel me out of those wet clothes and get me into something warm and dry. Human body heat is the best way to counteract it. We both know that."

"Good…I'm glad you realize that, Sam, because that was my intention." He gave her a humorous look. "You're the only M.D. we have. I couldn't have you dying on me."

She laughed wryly. "Oh, I doubt I'd have died, but it would have been a miserable trip back to HQ."

They walked in silence for a while, picking their

way along chewed-up streets, through the endless ruined suburbs. Roc stayed alert, his head swiveling from side to side, looking for anything that seemed out of place.

"Have you heard anything about Diablo today?"

"Yeah, they're apparently still ranging along the area 6 border, according to Quinn. They killed two men last night who tried to defend their food store at one house. Quinn sent out two of his men to investigate the situation early this morning. I got a call from him on the radio early this afternoon."

"How sad," Sam murmured. "Why are they killing people? I just don't understand it."

Grimly, Roc looked at her. "Because they enjoy killing, that's why. I'm sure, armed to the teeth as they apparently are, they could just as easily take people's food or water and leave. Their leader likes to kill, and that's what makes him so dangerous."

"We have to go over that way tomorrow, don't we?"

"Yeah, Morgan wants a third medevac station set up on the boundary to serve the southern end of our area, as well as the northern part of area 6. It's a good plan, but I don't like taking you in there. It's a hotspot. And it's going to be dangerous...."

"We'll be okay. We have heroic marines guarding us."

Roc said nothing. He was worried, far more than he was letting on. The thought of a bullet finding Sam made his heart clench like a fist. She was too alive, too beautiful in her own, unique way to be wasted like that. If he was brutally honest about it, he'd have to admit he cared for her far more than he should.

"You know," he began softly, "my mother is the diametric opposite of you."

Sam smiled at him. She hungered for this kind of intimate conversation with him. Her heart soared with anticipation. How badly she wanted to know about Roc, the man. "You sound puzzled about that."

"In a way." He hitched one shoulder upward. To his left, a group of families huddled around a fire, cooking whatever they had found to feed themselves.

"You mentioned she was weak before, that she had depression?"

"Has it even now," he admitted unhappily.

"Does she have a job? Or does she stay at home?"

"When they married, my father made it clear he wanted her at home to take care of him—and me. He made enough money and then some for her to do that. They met in Philadelphia and after they married, he moved to Maine, where he'd been born."

"But did your mom want to stay at home?"

"She had her bridge club, the social circuit, the parties. She was part of the Philadelphia mainline. Blue-blooded, upper crust…whatever you want to call it."

Hearing the distaste in his tone, she said, "It doesn't sound like you wanted that sort of lifestyle." Sam had had no idea that Roc's father was rich.

"I hated it. My uncle practically raised me, up in Maine. Every chance I got, I went to his house and stayed. My mother came from old money. My father was new money. His computer company is called Starling. You've heard of it?"

"Sure I have. Wow. That's really something, Roc. Your dad started it?"

"Yep, Starling Software."

"And you were a little geek?" she teased with a smile.

"Not really. I loved being out-of-doors. My uncle was a hunter and a fisherman. That's what I loved doing most. I didn't like computers."

"Why?"

"I like the quiet of the woods. Instead of the hypocrisy of the social scene, which my mother excelled at, I preferred a babbling brook talking to me."

She saw his lips thin. They'd left the residential section and were making their way down a wide avenue that would eventually lead them to HQ which she could see in the distance.

"So you didn't get along with your mother?"

"I guess not."

"You sound unhappy about that."

"She's weak, Sam. She's a rug that everyone walks on." Roc glanced toward Sam. "Not like you. You wouldn't let anyone roll over you."

"No, not if I could help it," she said, frowning. "Maybe your mother is trapped in a lifestyle she really doesn't want. Did she like the forest, too?"

"Yeah, our house in Maine is her handiwork. Every chance she got, she was out there planting flowers, bushes and trees, to make it look like a greenhouse."

"That's wonderful. She has a connection with the earth, then." Sam gave him a kind look. "It sounds like, in some ways, you really are more like her than your dad. You love nature like she does."

"Yes I do. My dad's a head tripper, and I'm not. I mean, he's a brilliant man and I respect him for that, but I'm nothing like him."

"And you don't like the shadow of your mother's

so-called weakness hanging over you, even though you're like her in some respects?''

Sam saw his eyes flare with surprise and then sadness. ''Bingo. Nobody says you don't shoot from the hip.''

''That's the kind of person I am. What you see is what you get, Roc.''

The corner of his mouth lifted. ''Yeah, that's one of many things that intrigues me about you. You're strong. Independent. Outspoken.''

''Oh, I don't know about 'outspoken,''' Sam countered. ''If a man speaks out, that's fine. But if a woman tells you what's on her mind, then men consider it 'outspoken.' I don't like that double standard. I never stood for it, Roc. I won't now, either.''

''Touché,'' he grumbled. ''You got me by the throat on that one.''

Opening her hands, Sam said, ''Your mom doesn't speak out, right?''

''Right. She's hard-pressed to make any kind of decision. She looks to my dad to do that for her. It's like she hasn't got a life of her own. She's doing what everyone else expects of her, but not what she wants to do.''

''What I hear you saying is that she's trapped and doesn't have the strength to speak up with her own voice and do what she wants in life.''

''Yeah...''

''And it doesn't sit well with you. Why?''

Roc rubbed his chin. ''My dad is like a bulldozer.''

''No kidding...''

Giving her a sharp glance, he asked, ''How would you know that?''

''An educated guess. When a married woman is

mired in deep depression, there's often a man dominating her. In our society, women are taught to be shadows, to be seen and not heard. If she was raised in a blue-blood world, I'm sure all that was conditioned in her from the time she was a little girl. Many times women don't have a clue as to who they really are, what they are capable of doing or how to go about fulfilling their dreams. It sounds like your mother is caught in the web of her family heritage."

"She once told me she was really angry, and I was shocked by that."

"Why?"

"Because I've *never* seen her angry. Not ever."

"Well," Sam said lightly, "in my experience as a doctor, depression is nothing more than a disguise for latent rage that has never been expressed. Many women get trapped like this. They don't know how to voice their anger because their mothers never showed them."

Roc grinned. "Your mother musta taught you."

Sam laughed. "You think?"

"I'll never forget that day in E.R. with you. You were madder than a wet hen standing out in a thunderstorm, as Sergeant Simmons would say. I guess I was shocked by your anger. I didn't expect it."

"Well, you were coming at me full bore, gloves off. Do you think I was going to take your bare-knuckle brawl lying down?" Sam's smile turned to a wolflike grin. Roc had the good grace to smile in response. "Looking back on it now, and knowing you as I do, yeah, I had it coming. In spades. I was way outta line. And—" he gave her a level look "—I was wrong. And I apologize."

It took a real man, in Sam's opinion, to admit a

mistake and to apologize. "I accept your apology, Roc. You're not the ogre I thought you were, either."

He preened a little. "No?"

"No. But you're so full of yourself, Gunnison."

It was his turn to laugh. "I can't help it, good doctor. You just seemed to bring out the best and worst in me."

Sam wanted, at that moment, to stop and throw herself into his arms. For the first time, she'd heard Roc really, truly laugh. It changed his entire face. Before, he'd been so sad and confused when he talked about his mother. Now she could see that marine-officer confidence flooding back into him. He was incredibly handsome, she admitted to herself—and desirable.

For so long, Brad had been the focus of her grieving. Not a day went by in that first year when she didn't long for him, for conversations such as she was having now with Roc. In the second year, her heart began to mend, and days could go by without her thinking of him. And then Roc had crashed into her life. Big. Bad. Bold. And terribly human in a way Sam really didn't think she could ever find in another man.

"We're almost home," he said. The terrain had flattened out, the ruined shopping center off to their left. Roc noticed that a lot more tents were up, and more marines were milling about. "Looks like that Super Stallion delivered us a lot more of everything."

Sam heard the excitement in his voice as he looked toward the growing tent city they called home. Rousing herself out of her reverie, she said, "I don't know about you, but I'm going to fill her tub with hot water and just soak."

"Go for it."

"What about you?"

"I've got to get together with Quinn and go over the day's events. I know he's had his men out scouting for Diablo. I want to see where he's at with it." Scowling, Roc added, "I wouldn't put it past them to attack us."

"They'd be stupid to try. This camp is bristling with marines and firepower now."

Shaking his head, he gave Sam a dark look. "They'd do it just to keep us off balance. No, I don't trust them for a second. And the hair on the back of my neck is crawling."

"What does that mean?" Sam followed him between two rows of tents. In the distance, she saw at least forty more marines in formation, with an officer giving them orders. There were at least twenty more tents set up than there had been this morning. The change was amazing.

Roc halted in front of HQ. "My neck hair stands up when danger is close. I learned a long time ago to pay attention to it."

"Well, come hell or high water, I'm going to find Kerry, get that hot bath and then hit the sack. I'm totaled."

How badly he wanted to reach out and graze her cheek. Roc didn't dare under the circumstances. "Yeah, go get cleaned up, Sleeping Beauty. You deserve that hot bath. Soak for both of us, will you?"

"Will I see you later?" Sam blurted out.

Roc shrugged. "I don't know. I'd like to...but I have to see what's cooking with Diablo." Then he cocked his head and gave her a one-cornered smile.

"Why? Are you telling me you'd like my company later?"

"Well...I was wondering if we could meet at the chow hall, say in an hour?" Sam looked at her watch.

"I'll try, sweetheart. But no promises."

Sam understood. She saw his eyes darken with yearning—for her. Heart thumping in her chest, she forced herself to walk away. Every time she looked at Roc's mouth, she chastised herself for not taking the lead and kissing him this morning. As she walked toward Kerry's tent, Sam felt happier than ever before. Her step was so light that she felt as if she was no longer walking on broken-up asphalt and dirt. Somehow, Roc was opening her heart once more, and it left her thrilled and frightened. Like Brad, he was in the Marine Corps. Roc's job as a Recon made his career even more dangerous than Brad's. And look what had happened to her fiancé....

# *Chapter 11*

"Sam? Sam, wake up...."

Kerry Chelton's voice cut through Sam's dreams, dragging her awake. "Uhh...."

"Hey, you gotta get out of this tub. The water's getting cool." Kerry grabbed the towel hanging on the cot next to the tub. She smiled sympathetically as Sam pushed herself up into a sitting position. Sam must have been so tired that she'd dozed off as soon as she sank into the relaxing hot water.

Sam looked around the washroom, trying to wake up. Gripping the edge of the tub with both hands, she looked up at Kerry, who was grinning.

"What time is it?" Her voice was scratchy.

"Twenty-two hundred hours."

"Oh, dear..." Sam pushed herself to her feet as Kerry brought over the huge green towel for her to wrap up in. Even though there was an electric heater spewing warmth into the tent, the space was still chilly. Climbing out, her feet wetting the unpainted plywood, she muttered, "I fell asleep. I'm sorry...."

"Don't be," Kerry said. "Roc was the one who got worried. I guess you two were gonna meet at the chow tent?"

Rubbing her face and still trying to wake up, Sam groaned. "Oh, jeez...yes, I remember we talked about it."

"You're exhausted," Kerry counseled gently, "so take it easy. I'll be right back. Roc's waiting outside. He was worried about you."

"Tell him I'm sorry, will you?"

Kerry gave her a slight smile. "Oh, I think he's gonna wait for you to come out and tell him yourself."

Quickly drying off, Sam nodded. "Okay. Tell him I'll be there in a minute...."

"You bet." Kerry disappeared outside the tent flap and zipped it back up to keep in the heat.

Muttering to herself, Sam pulled on a clean but wrinkled pair of navy-blue slacks, a light blue, long-sleeved blouse, a dark blue cardigan and then sat down and reached for her boots. After pulling on thick socks, she quickly slid her feet into her boots and tied them up. She had washed her hair, and it was still damp, hanging in thick strands around her face. Roc had gone to meet her at the chow hall, after all. Why had she fallen asleep? Embarrassed, she unzipped the tent and stepped out.

Weak light from bulbs powered by generators spread across the tent city. Instantly, Sam spotted Roc, who stood nearby. There was worry in his eyes—and welcome. Compressing her lips, Sam hurried down to where he stood. His M-16 was slung over his left shoulder. He never seemed to be without a weapon.

"Roc...I'm so sorry...."

"That's okay, don't worry about it. I wasn't sure I could make it to the chow hall until the last minute, anyway." He smiled. Seeing how drowsy her eyes looked, he added, "That hot bath made you sleepy, didn't it?"

Groaning, Sam nodded. "I was out like a light. I remember washing my hair, lying back and I was gone." She touched her wet hair.

"Come on, I've got a tray of food waiting for you at your tent. I had one of the navy chefs rustle it up and wrap it in foil to keep it warm."

Turning, she fell into step with him. "That was so sweet of you! Thank you..." She noticed more marine guards on sentry duty. With the Super Stallion bringing in thirty-five more marines, the HQ area was now well protected, she thought. "Have you eaten?"

"No. When you didn't show up, I figured you were taking a long, luxurious bath in the washroom tent, so I waited."

"Oh, dear... Well, I muffed that one, didn't I?"

"You only had about three hours of sleep last night," he said wryly. "Why wouldn't you knock off first chance you got?"

"You look chipper."

"Marines are tougher than navy squids."

Chortling, Sam stopped at her tent and unzipped it. "Come on in." She moved into the warm space, glad of the heater inside.

Closing up the tent again, Roc put his rifle down near the entrance.

''Oh!'' Sam gasped as she stood inside the tent beside him.

''Yeah...a real bed.'' It was a twin-size bed furnished with dark green wool blankets and a pillow.

Shocked, Sam saw an aluminum tray sitting on it. She saw a second one nearby. ''Wow...this is great! We had cots before. Come and sit down....'' She wriggled out of her coat and placed it on the dresser opposite.

''I found out from Quinn that a second Super Stallion came in with a load of furniture for the staff here. It included beds. The cots are being sent out to the first medevac site, which is already set up and in operation.''

Pleased, Sam sat down and picked up her tray. Removing the foil, she saw aluminum flatware. When Roc sat down nearby, she smiled at him. ''This is like Christmas. And hot food...'' She dug hungrily into the fragrant beef stew.

Roc smiled and uncovered his own tray, which he set on his lap. All was right with Sam. They were alone. He was exhausted, but just being with her made him feel energized and happy. They ate in a companionable silence. Roc had also brought coffee in a thermos and poured them each a cup after their meal.

Sam sighed and put her tray down on the plywood floor near her feet. ''Thanks, Roc. You are taking such great care of me...not that I deserve it. I really intended to head over to the chow hall.''

''This is better,'' he told her, sipping his coffee.

Sam held the white ceramic mug between her fingers, relishing the warmth. Then she sighed and met his dark blue eyes. "You know," she began haltingly, "I come from a very different life than you did."

"Tell me about it?" As tired as he was, Roc was starving for intimate conversation with Sam. He saw the dark smudges beneath her beautiful, wide eyes. There was a special bond between them, more and more evident every time they were together. He'd tried to explain it away with logic, but had failed. It defied logic. His heart, however, was wide-open toward Sam, and his feelings for her growing more fervent by the moment. At his age, he knew better than to act on them. Sam wasn't the kind of woman who could be pushed around, cajoled or forced into intimacy with a man. No, she had to have trust in him, Roc knew. Trust took time. He at least wanted her to know that he cared for her, and he was looking for ways to communicate that to her. Judging from the grateful expression on her face when she'd seen the tray of food in her tent, she had gotten the message loud and clear.

"My dad died when I was nine. He drove trucks, the big eighteen-wheelers, for a living." She grimaced and set her coffee cup on her knees, gazing at the opposite wall. "He was the greatest, Roc. He always told me I could be whatever I wanted to be."

"I'm sorry you lost him so young. He sounds like the kind of dad I wished I had."

Nodding, Sam whispered, "My dad loved me just the way I was. Maybe that's why I grew up so cocky and confident. I always believed I could be a doctor." She tilted her head and held Roc's warm, narrowed gaze. She enjoyed having this time alone with him. "My mother was a registered nurse. I was an only kid, too. From the time I could remember, I wanted to help heal people. My mother let me read some of her old college textbooks when I was around eight years old.'' Sam laughed. ''Not that I understood physiology or anatomy, but it fed my hunger to be a doctor.''

''And what did your dad think about that?''

''He thought it was great. He'd be gone a week at a time, but when he got back, on weekends usually, he'd take me hiking, which I dearly love to do. My mother would come, too, and she'd bring a botanical field guide with her. We'd spend a day out in the hills and mountains of Montana, near Whitefish, looking for medicinal herbs. When we'd find one, my mom would sit us down and read from the biology book about it, and then tell us what prescription drug used today had been derived from that plant.''

''Sounds like you had a lot of great support,'' Roc murmured. He saw the pain and sadness in Sam's eyes when she spoke of her father. It was easy to tell she'd had a happy childhood, one where both parents loved and cared for her, unlike his. Roc wasn't jealous, however. He could see the strength of Sam's family in her. Her gutsy, confident attitude toward life made perfect sense to him now.

''When my dad died unexpectedly,'' Sam confided, looking down at her cup of coffee in her hands, ''I felt destroyed. My mom loved him so much…and so did I. For a couple of years, Roc, I was a mess. I was angry. I was angry at him for leaving us. I was angry at being abandoned.'' Her lips quirked. ''I didn't do well in school.''

''But you moved on? You're strong, Sam. I see it in you, in so many ways.''

Nodding, she choked out, ''Strength created by

hardship. Without my father's income, we went downhill fast. The savings they'd put away for my college fund—for premed—had to be tapped or my mother would have had to put us on welfare. That was something she refused to do."

"So, how did you get to medical school? Scholarships?"

Sam made a strangled sound. "No…my grades weren't good enough. I had taken an after-school job to help make ends meet, just to keep our heads above water, so I didn't study like I needed to."

"That's rough," Roc said as he watched her face darken with memory.

"It was awful, but I was determined to make it into premed. Once I graduated from high school, my SAT scores enabled me to squeeze in at Ohio State University. I worked as a waitress at a local restaurant and studied my head off the rest of the time. I shared a house with six other girls who were going there, so my rent was low. Of course, I shared an attic with one of them, and we slept on the floor, but for us at that time, it was like an adventure." She smiled briefly.

"Hardship all the way," Roc murmured, recalling how easily he'd entered Annapolis. He'd never had to scramble or work hard to achieve the goals he'd wanted, as she had. Regarding her with new respect, he met and held her soft green gaze. "You're a fighter."

"Yes, in case you hadn't guessed that by now."

"Equal to a marine."

"Why, thank you! What a great compliment! No marine would say something like that lightly." She laughed ironically.

Roc set his tray near his feet. "So you made it through four years of premed?"

"Yes. I managed to get a straight 4.0 average."

He was really impressed. "Holding down a job?"

"Sure. If you want something, Roc, you go after it. I was taught to hang on for dear life. Kind of like a pit bull who's grabbing on to something and never lets go."

"And you took your medical degree at Ohio State, as well?"

"Yes. And then I joined the navy, where I did my residency. After that, my first assignment was out here at Camp Reed."

"You weren't assigned head of E.R. right away, though."

Shaking her head, she finished her coffee and set the cup on the dresser. Taking her comb, she sat back down and began to untangle her hair. "No, I wasn't. I worked my way up to the position."

"In a hurry," Roc said. As a paramedic, he knew a lot about the medical service. Sam was very young to have been given a position of such heavy responsibility.

"You're wondering how I managed to do it?" She laughed and continued to smooth out the snarls in her hair. In the shadowy light provided by the single lightbulb strung up at the end of the tent, she saw a hunger and yearning in Roc's eyes. He watched her every movement as she tamed her damp hair into some semblance of order. Heart beating a little harder, Sam felt buoyed and scared simultaneously.

"Yeah."

"As I said before, I'm a triple type A," she said.

"I worked two eight-hour shifts for two years straight."

Blinking, Roc stared at her, his lips parting. "You're kidding me, aren't you?" He knew what raw strength, resolve and discipline it would take to do something like that. That meant Sam had no life other than her medical world, the E.R. "Why were you so driven?"

She shrugged. "What else was there for me to do?"

"Well, for starters, how about a personal life?"

She heard the irony in his voice. And saw the disbelief in his eyes.

Resting the comb in her lap, Sam sighed. "Look at this face, will you? I'm not exactly a movie star. In fact, I know I'm very plain. I had plenty of reality checks with guys as I went through college and my residency. I heard the message loud and clear, Roc—a strong, confident woman wasn't what men wanted." She grimaced and began combing her hair once more. "I wasn't simpering and I wasn't pliant. I didn't roll over when they wanted me to. So I learned early on that I wasn't very marketable—not that I cared—as a woman and possible marriage partner. Besides, all these guys wanted was to dive into bed for one-night stands, and I wasn't made that way. My father romanced my mother for two years before she agreed to marry him. He loved her so much. More important, Roc, he respected her. They were the best of friends. I grew up in a family where the man and woman were equals. I swore I would have the same thing or I'd never get married."

"And you're not going to settle for less," Roc

stated. He could see the resolve in Sam's eyes, and her fire and mettle.

''Right. Nor equate sex with love. I knew what love was because of my parents.'' She snorted softly and stood up. Placing the comb on the dresser, she turned and looked down at him. ''When I met Brad, he treated me the way I wanted to be treated.''

''He respected you.''

''Yes. And he became my best friend.'' She touched her freckled cheeks and smiled sadly. ''He liked me just the way I was. I'm no raving beauty....''

''But he saw your beauty.''

Roc's voice was low. Intimate. Sam stood there, caressed by his words. The yearning in his eyes was unmistakable. Fear walked over her beating heart and stole away some of the euphoria that automatically built when Roc was near her.

''Y-yes, he did.'' Sam patted her heart. ''He saw my inner beauty, and he liked my fire and spirit.''

''I do, too. You have a big heart, Sam. I saw it plenty of times in the past few days.'' Giving her an intent look, he rasped, ''You're one of a kind, Samantha Andrews. And I'm glad as hell I know you. You're teaching me a lot about relationships.''

Caught off guard by his growling tone, plus his look of undeniable respect, she raised her brows. ''Healthy relationships,'' she corrected.

Roc smiled wistfully. He knew he had to leave. God knew he didn't want to, but he could see the exhaustion in Sam's face. After a hot meal, she'd get very sleepy, very fast, he knew. ''Listen,'' he said apologetically, ''I gotta go or I'm going to keel over.''

"I know the feeling...." Sam's heart cried out in protest, but she couldn't voice it. She was too scared. There was so much she wanted to say to Roc, to share with him, but it all stuck in her throat as he rose and went over to claim his rifle. Then he turned and gave her a wink.

"See you tomorrow at 0530 at HQ? We've got the third medevac site to check out."

Lifting her hand, she whispered, "Yes...0530. Good night, Roc, and thanks—for everything. You really are a white knight in my eyes."

Roc felt prickles of awareness all along his spine at her unexpectedly fervent praise. Her voice was off-key and he saw she meant every word. Instantly, joy suffused his heart, filling him with a giddy, reeling sensation. No woman had ever made him feel like this. Not ever. Looking at her across the tent, her hair lying like a red-and-gold cape about her proud shoulders, he smiled gently. "I've graduated from mother hen to knight, eh?"

Chuckling, Sam said, "Yes, most definitely."

"Well, I just hope I don't fall off my white horse and dent my armor."

She felt as if he were embracing her with his stormy gaze. The feeling was wonderful, heated, and she hungrily absorbed the look he gave her. It was unmistakable—a blend of respect, desire and need. Lips tingling, Sam wished once again that she'd taken the lead and kissed him that morning, while they were in the tent together.

"You won't, don't worry," she said softly.

"See you tomorrow, sweetheart," he whispered, raising his hand in farewell.

*Sweetheart...* The word held such promise. And

evoked so much fear. Sam stood there, frozen, as he left, zipping up the door of the tent behind him. Alone once more, she looked around. Without Roc's magnetic and powerful presence, she felt less than whole. Was this how her mother felt about her father? How Sam wished she had a phone right now so she could talk to her mom about Roc Gunnison.

Moving to the end of the tent, Sam reached up and extinguished the light, leaving the tent in semidarkness. She could still make out the shape of her new bed, however—a real bed! Pulling down the heavy covers, Sam saw that someone had put real sheets on it for her. She made a mental note to thank whoever had taken the time. She had a sneaking suspicion it had been Kerry.

Sam slowly undressed, folding her clothes and setting them on top of the dresser, then slid beneath the covers. The bed, the sheets, the blankets—it all felt wonderful. What an unexpected luxury!

Still, as her lashes shuttered closed on her freckled cheeks, she felt guilty. Out there, all around her, millions of people had no beds to sleep on. Most were chilled and cold, while she slept comfortably in a warm, heated tent. Life wasn't fair, Sam knew that.

Her last thoughts as she spiraled down into a deep, healing sleep were of Roc. His face. That hard mask that fell away when they were alone, revealing the man beneath. Tonight's conversation, the personal discoveries they'd shared with one another, had been good. Sam couldn't understand why she'd revealed all she had. She was frightened of ever loving another marine, especially one in a very dangerous occupation. She drifted off to sleep with that quandary racing around in her head.

The one thing she did know was that she eagerly looked forward to every day with Roc. It was a time of discovery. Sharing. Laughter. He made her laugh! He wasn't afraid of her at all. He liked her and she knew it. And yet Sam also knew that every day out here was filled with potential danger. Life was precious. And it could be cut short. The thought made her yearn more than ever for Roc's touch.

# *Chapter 12*

*February 6: 0700*

"Well? What do you think?" Will this make a good Landing Zone Echo?" Roc halted at Sam's shoulder as they stood near the boundary of areas 5 and 6. He was tense, for he'd heard grim reports from a team of marines scouting the area who had talked to citizens on this very border hours earlier. The Diablos had looted one of the camps, killing a man who had put up resistance, and stealing their whole supply of food.

Sam looked around. "Looks okay to me." Today, Roc had ordered more marines to come with them—an entire squad of ten men. It felt like an army to Sam, but she understood his worry. The strain showed in his hard face this morning, as the sun edged the horizon.

It was less chilly today, and Sam was glad. The sky above was a clear, undiluted blue. They stood in what used to be a large metropolitan park. Many of the trees had been uprooted, and the grassy lawns and playing fields looked more like plowed agricultural land due to damage from the earthquake.

"Looks fine on first inspection," Sam added. Though she craved being close to him, Sam knew that under the circumstances they must appear as two officers, trained professionals, not as a man and a woman who liked one another.

Nodding, Roc assessed the row of ruined houses on the other side of the rectangular space, where area 6 began. People were already gathering to gawk at them. Soon, he knew, they would be crossing the field to ask what was going on, and if they had any food or water.

"I want you to stick with me like glue today," he warned Sam in a low tone.

Hearing the worry in his voice, she looked up—and nearly drowned in his dark, intense gaze. Today, more than ever, she was seeing his hunter-warrior side. Roc had been all business with his team, terse and precise. He knew what he was doing, and she was glad he was seasoned in combat. Lieutenant Grayson was leading the other squad, and Sam felt good about that because he, too, was experienced in fighting.

"I will," she promised.

"I don't feel good about this place…." he muttered, holding his rifle in both hands as he surveyed the area again.

"Is the hair on your neck standing up?"

"Yes."

Grimacing, Sam nodded. "I don't know what to look out for, Roc."

"That's why you're going to stick to me like a Siamese twin. I want you to stay on my left side always. Don't walk in front of or behind me. Let me be your shield today. No argument about this, all right?" He drilled her with a look Sam wouldn't fight.

Seeing her green eyes widen with a flicker of fear, Roc felt badly for scaring Sam. But under the circumstances, she needed to be scared. To remain alert. It was the only way to keep her on her toes, so that if something did happen, she'd react appropriately.

"I kinda like that idea," Sam teased, a slight smile curving her mouth. Instantly, she saw his eyes thaw, and then that rakish smile that melted her heart appeared for just a moment before his face hardened again.

"If I tell you to hit the deck, you do it. Understand? Don't ask me where or why. Just do it."

"I will, Roc—I mean, Captain." Darn, she was slipping already. In the field, with people around, she needed to call him by his title, not his name. They were standing apart from the rest of the team, so she was fairly sure no one had overheard them.

"Good." He turned to Simmons, who was standing a short way off.

"Sergeant, take your men and stop all those civilians from coming over here. Tell them they're to consider the whole park area off-limits. We've had Diablo through here recently. Make the folks understand that if we need to have a firefight with any gang members, we don't want civilians getting caught in the line of fire."

Buck nodded. "Yes, sir!" he looked at his expectant team and said, "Let's go, men."

Roc saw Grayson coming his way with his squad. The young lieutenant's face was grim and tense. He, too, was carrying his rifle in a ready position.

"Lieutenant?"

"Yes, sir?"

"Take half your squad and deploy them along the area 6 boundary, over there." Roc pointed in that direction. "You and whoever you choose will work with me and Dr. Andrews as we measure and assess this place. I want to get in and out of here as soon as possible."

Quinn nodded. "Yes, sir. I understand, Captain."

Roc turned to Sam. For once she was behaving herself and doing exactly as he'd asked. If he moved, she remained on the "safe" side of him, away from area 6, where trouble had spilled over last night. Giving her a cursory glance, he noted her beautiful red hair tumbling around her shoulders from beneath her cap. The collar of her pea coat was turned up to protect her from the chill, but he could see her ever-present stethoscope hanging down inside. How badly he wanted to kiss her. He hadn't slept much last night, even though he had been dead tired. That intimate conversation they'd shared in her tent had left him wide-awake and half-aroused.

The urge to reach out, slide his fingers along her clean, stubborn jawline, lean down and brush her lips with his made him groan inwardly. He had to focus on the mission. On the very real dangers that surrounded them.

"I'm ready," Sam told him, and she held up the clipboard and pen in her gloved hands.

Nodding, he looked over at Quinn, who had ordered five of his men to begin patrolling the area 6 suburb adjacent to the park. Roc saw his own men stopping civilians along the boundary, turning them back. Today, Roc didn't want mingling. Diablo wouldn't care if they shot civilians while trying to get to the military, he knew. Their leader couldn't care less who died. Roc didn't want anyone injured or killed on his watch.

''Okay, let's spread out and get this done. I want out of here as soon as possible,'' he ordered everyone, including her team, who would help with the measuring, and collating of information.

For the next two hours, Sam worked at Roc's side. She and Lin would measure one side of the rectangular field, record the figures, then look for cracks in the ground. Roc hovered nearby, keeping in front of Sam to protect her from a possible sniper's bullet. He was putting his own life on the line. Sam's heart swelled with gratitude—and with something else she refused to name.

The sun rose higher in the wintry sky, warming the earth. Eventually, Sam took off her pea coat and set it down with her pack, near the center of the field. So did Lin and the others. Sam was grateful when her fingers finally began to thaw. Stuffing her gloves in the pockets of her dark blue slacks, she worked quickly with Lin, completing their side of the rectangle.

Sometimes, down on her hands and knees as she measured a crevice with Lin, Sam would glance up. Roc stood above them, his legs slightly spread for balance, his rifle raised, on guard. He would call back to HQ once every thirty minutes to get updated reports on any Diablo movements. From what she could overhear, there were none. With the small radio attached to the left epaulet of his jacket, he was in constant touch with the roving squad of marines as well as his Recon team. Nothing seemed out of place.

But something nagged at Sam as she walked to the last fissure they planned to measure. She and Lin held a cloth measuring tape strung out between them. Roc was up ahead, shielding them. What was the feeling? Sam turned toward her left, area 5 territory. There was suburban housing, much of it in shambles, less than a quarter of a mile away. Frowning, she scanned the flattened buildings.

Remembering what Roc had told her—*look for what is out of place and there you'll find the enemy*—Sam blinked several times. What was wrong? What wasn't quite right with the scene before her? Slowing a bit, she turned toward the east.

Suddenly a sharp *crack!* rent the air.

In the same instant, she saw Roc freeze. And then he turned, roaring, *"Get down!"*

Sam hesitated fractionally. And then, everything changed to a slow-motion film before her eyes. She heard another sharp, echoing sound originating from that eastern suburb, but saw nothing, no shooter. As the retort split the air around them, Roc instantly cringed, whirled toward it, and was locking and loading his rifle as he lunged for the ground. His face was harsh, his eyes slits. As Sam heard him yell at them to get down, she saw terror in his eyes—for her and Lin.

Only split seconds had past, but those moments seemed strung out endlessly. Somewhere in time, Sam started to throw herself toward the earth, too.

It was then she felt a hot, stinging sensation in her upper left arm. As she fell belly first on the chewed-up ground, her hands covering her head, she heard the sharp, resounding *crack, crack, crack* as Roc fired toward where the shots had originated.

An instant later, Sam's face was pushed into the ground as Roc leaped over her, kneeling in front of her to protect her. She noted the smell of the earth as she tried to breathe through flaring nostrils.

More gunfire erupted, coming from that same direction.

*Oh, God…* Sam tried to nestle even closer to the ground. She wanted to disappear into it! Hearing the throaty, barking reports of other M-16s in action, Sam shut her eyes tightly. Fear shot through her.

Suddenly, the earth near her erupted in geysers. She lifted her head, amazed. What was doing that?

"Get up, Sam! Lin! Run toward the center!" Roc roared at them. He remained on his belly, his legs spread, firing rapidly toward the shooter hidden among the houses. It was one of the Diablos, he had no doubt. The sniper had them nailed down, and if Sam and Lin stayed, they'd be killed.

"Run!" he yelled at them, lifting his head from his rifle scope momentarily. It was then he saw Sam's arm. Eyes wide, he stared at her light blue, long-sleeved blouse, the entire left side of which was soaked in bright red blood. Sam didn't seem to realize it as she quickly scrambled to her feet and took off running with Lin, but she'd been hit. *Oh, God…no…*

Rage surged through him. Roc had to stay where he was, for the shooter was returning fire. Once again the ground around him spat upward in geysers, bullets biting angrily into the soil near where he lay. He knew he was a target. Repeatedly, with cool precision, he fired round after round. Roc wanted the sniper to zero in on him, not the two women escaping across the field to safety.

Controlling his breathing, he focused his rage. Sam was hit. How bad? Oh, God, how bad? She seemed oblivious to it. *Probably in shock. She's too scared to even know she got hit.*

Roc's mind churned like a rapidly firing machine gun. In seconds he was on the radio with his team, ordering them to flank the position. Instantly, he saw marines running east, toward where the shooter was hiding. At the same time, he ordered Quinn to get the medical team together in the center of the field, and to call in a Huey. They had casualties. They would have to get out of here and back to HQ as quickly as possible.

Having no idea how badly Sam was wounded, Roc didn't want to take any chances. This morning, before they'd left, Morgan had managed to get them a Huey helicopter on standby for emergencies. Roc thanked the man for his foresight.

Trying to focus on the sniper, Roc ran through his first clip of ammo. With quick precision, he grabbed another from his belt by rolling over on his side and jerking it out of his pocket. In seconds, he'd rammed the clip into his rifle and returned to a prone position. More geysers shot up around him. That was good.

Sweat ran down his temples. Blinking rapidly, Roc kept slowly panning the scope of his rifle right to left in order to try and find the son of a bitch.

*There!* Roc held his breath. He saw his men hightailing it to the right. Seeing the flash of sunlight on a rifle barrel, the figure of a man peeking around the edge of one of the walls left standing on a house, Roc grinned.

"You're gonna die, you bastard," he rasped, and pulled the trigger. His rifle bucked against his shoulder. Satisfaction soared through him. He saw the man fly backward, the rifle flipping up and out of his hands.

*Good!* Instantly, Roc was on his feet and running, heading directly for that area. Sprinting hard, he reached the house before his team arrived. He could hear the wail of frightened children nearby. On guard, his weapon raised, he moved along the side of the house where the sniper had been crouching. Roc took no chances, because he could have wounded the enemy, not killed him outright. The thug could be waiting with a pistol in hand to kill him or whoever was stupid enough to come around the corner of the house too quickly.

Breathing through his mouth to keep silent, Roc crouched down and crept along the perimeter. He heard adult voices nearby, urgently trying to shush the crying children, though he was unable to see them. Kneeling down, only two feet from the corner where the sniper had been, Roc saw the rifle. It was an
M-16, military issue. Recalling that the Diablos had, early on, killed two marine helicopter pilots and stolen the entire cargo out of the bird, he knew that this must be one of the slain marines' rifles.

Gripping his weapon, Roc listened for any movement from the enemy. Then, taking a deep breath, he swung around the corner, his rifle raised.

His breath exploded from his body and relief shot through him as he came out of his crouched, ready position. A man, in his thirties, lay dead—sprawled out on the yellow grass, his arms flung above his head. The bullet had got him in the head.

No satisfaction flowed through Roc as he quickly made sure there were no other weapons on the man. Killing a human being always twisted his gut.

His team came jogging tensely around the corner. Straightening up, Roc shifted his rifle to his left hand.

"Sergeant, frisk this son of a bitch and see if you can find any papers, any ID on him." As Roc stepped away, he saw the frightened faces of a few people peeking out of nearby windows.

"The rest of you stay on guard," he ordered them tightly. "I'll go inside this other house and see if these civilians know anything."

"Yes, sir," Buck said, kneeling over the body.

Roc's mind gyrated. His heart slammed into his ribs as he walked up to the house, which was partially destroyed. Sam. Was she okay? Breathing hard, sweat running down his face and his rib cage, Roc put in a call to Grayson.

"Red Badger two, do you read? This is Red Badger one. Over." Roc clicked off the button on his shoulder unit and waited impatiently.

"Badger two here. Over."

"Give me a report on Dr. Andrews. She was hit. What's her condition? Over." Waiting for news made Roc's gut tighten painfully. As he walked up to the door, an older man—in his fifties, with graying hair—opened it. He looked frightened and relieved.

"Any more of them around?" Roc demanded.

"I don't know, sir.... Thank God you got him. He was stealing our food, sir...." The man closed his eyes and sagged against the doorjamb.

"Red Badger One, Dr. Andrews has an upper arm

wound. Her people are taking care of her right now. The bird is on the way.''

''Red Badger Two, is she all right?'' Roc couldn't help the strain he heard in his own voice.

''Roger, I think so. I'm talking to Dr. Andrews right now and she says to tell you it's only a flesh wound. She says there's a lot of blood, but it's only a crease, and for you not to be worried. Over.''

Relief shuddered through him. Roc compressed his mouth. He looked up at the man, whose face was white with terror as he stared past him toward the Diablo gang member lying ten feet away. ''That's good to hear.''

''The bird is coming in now, Red Badger One. Do you want me to board the medical team and wait for you?''

''Negative, Red Badger Two. I want you to get the doctor to HQ for treatment immediately. Send the entire medical team back. Then come here with your squad. Over.''

''Roger. The bird is coming in now.... Over and out.''

Roc could hear the heavy whapping sounds of a Huey as it approached, landing a half mile away. His gaze cut to his men, who were going through every pocket of the Diablo sniper. Turning, he looked up at the older man.

''Tell me what else you saw,'' Roc demanded.

''Sir, he was alone as far as we could tell. He had one of the children as hostage earlier. He put a gun to her head and said if we didn't give him all the food and water we had, he was going to kill her.''

''That pistol?'' he demanded, holding it up for the man to see.

"Y-yes, that one." The man visibly tried to collect himself. "Thank you…so much! We thought we were alone. We didn't know you'd arrived."

Nodding, Roc noticed a stuffed pillowcase lying alongside the wall. "Is that your food, sir?"

"Yes, it is."

"Go get it," he ordered.

The man managed a tight, grateful smile and hurried off to retrieve the goods.

Turning, Roc saw Lieutenant Grayson and his squad approaching at a fast trot, and he heard the Huey taking off. From this angle, he could see the dark green bird as it gained altitude. Swallowing hard, he tried to gather himself emotionally. Sam had been hit, but it was only a flesh wound. She'd know. She wouldn't lie to him, would she? To stop him from worrying? Roc closed his eyes for a moment, and all he could see was her entire upper arm bathed in bright red blood. She'd acted as if she wasn't even aware of being wounded. He knew flesh wounds could bleed like a stuck hog. They could appear a lot worse than they really were. God, he hoped that was the case.

Opening his eyes, he saw Quinn rushing up to him, his face tense and sweaty.

The first thing the lieutenant said was, "Sir, Dr. Andrews said for you not to worry, that she was fine. She said to tell you it's only a scratch." He managed a slight smile. "She asked that you come and see her when we get back to HQ."

Nodding, Roc rubbed his jaw. A wild range of feelings reeled through him, some of relief, others worry. And some…some were feelings so raw and beautiful that they staggered him, took his voice away for a second before he could respond to Quinn's words.

"Thanks, Lieutenant Grayson. I'll do that." Roc searched the marine's glistening features. "Are you *sure* she's okay?"

Grayson nodded. "She said you'd question me about that. Yes, sir, she's fine, Captain. I promise. I'm not a trained paramedic like you, but I saw Nurse Lin cut off the doctor's sleeve and wash away the blood. The bullet creased her upper arm, is all, from what I could tell. It didn't go into the muscle, just grazed the skin, is all."

More relief zigzagged through Roc. He gripped his rifle more tightly for a moment. "Very good, Lieutenant. Thanks..." And he began to give orders for the rest of the marines to disperse and begin a block-by-block search for other Diablos in the area. He knew from previous reports that they usually worked in teams of two. There might very well be another one around, and if there was, he wanted the bastard.

As he carried out his duties, Roc's heart centered on Sam. Right now, the *last* place he wanted to be was here, but he knew his responsibility was to the people, to protect them. It would be hours before he could get back to HQ and see Sam. God help him, the *only* place he wanted to be right now was at her side, holding her, keeping her safe. He knew Sam would be terribly shaken by this event. No one ever thought about getting hit by a bullet, even people in the military. Roc knew it was going to shatter Sam emotionally. She was a casualty now. And she knew some human being hated her enough to try and kill her on sight.

Roc wanted to be at her side to hold her, to comfort her, to let her talk it out. He wanted to let her know he was there for her.

# *Chapter 13*

*February 6: 1800*

Anxiety ate at Roc as he off-loaded his men from the Huey near sunset. Kerry Chelton was standing just outside the range of the marine helicopter's whirling blades, her hands raised to protect her eyes from the swirling, billowing clouds of yellow dust kicked up into the air. She was standing with her feet planted well apart to take the buffeting wind from the blades. Grimly, Roc ran at a crouch until he was well beyond the reach of the spinning blades, then headed directly for her.

His men hurriedly caught up with him. When Sergeant Simmons came alongside, Roc shouted above the whining engine, "Buck, get the men settled in for the night."

"Yes, sir!" Simmons raised his hand and the men

immediately peeled off and trotted toward the tent city in the distance.

Behind him, the Huey took off again, heading back to the same area to pick up the rest of the marines waiting on the field. Pinning his gaze on Kerry, Roc stepped up to her.

"Quinn's comin' in on the second flight," he told her, noting the worry in her eyes.

Dropping her hands from her face, Kerry nodded. "I know the chopper isn't big enough to carry you all back here in one load. Thanks for letting me know, Roc."

He turned and fell in step with her. There was still anxiety in her face. "What's up?" It wasn't like Kerry to meet him at the chopper pad.

"It's Sam," she admitted. "I'm worried about her, Roc."

Alarm gutted him. He slowed momentarily. "Is she all right? I thought she had only a flesh wound."

Raising her hand, Kerry smiled sadly. "Oh, she's fine that way. I'm sorry, I didn't mean to scare you. No, she's okay. I got her into the tub in the washroom tent to take a long, hot soak, I washed her hair and then bundled her off to her tent to lie down and rest."

"Then what's wrong?" Roc tightened his grip on the M-16 he carried in his left hand. The day was dying, the western horizon a blood-red ribbon. It had been a bloody day in many ways.

"Well," Kerry hedged, giving him a sad look, "you and I are law enforcement and military. And I'm sure you can remember the first time you saw combat?"

"Yeah," he answered gruffly, "in Somalia. It sucked."

"And I got my hands bloodied in south Los Angeles in a shootout with gang members a couple of years ago," Kerry related quietly. "Do you remember how you felt after that first time, Roc? Seeing death? Seeing people you cared for hurt or killed?"

Shrugging, he said, "Yeah, I was an emotional mess for a couple days after that. It's called shock, Kerry."

She grinned and nodded. "Yes, but it's more than shock. Have you ever been wounded?"

He shook his head. "No, but I know you have."

Touching her leg, which was still healing from a bullet she'd taken during an earlier confrontation with Diablo, Kerry nodded. "Yes, and that's why I wanted to talk with you, Roc. Being in law enforcement and the military, we have to entertain the possibility that someday maybe, we'll be shot at, even hit. Right?"

"Right."

"But even when it happens, I can tell you, you aren't prepared for it." She managed a weak smile. Pushing her fingers through her hair, she continued, "If it weren't for Quinn being at my side, holding me, just letting me talk and cry, I think I'd still be a wreck from that experience. He made the difference."

"I suspected you two had a personal relationship going." Roc gave her an understanding smile. He saw Kerry's eyes beam with undisguised happiness.

"We're in love, Roc. We try to keep that a secret, but I see it didn't slip past you." Her mouth twitched with humor.

"It's the way I catch you looking at one another sometimes, when you don't think anyone else is watching."

Grinning, Kerry reached out and touched his right

arm. ''You're a good man, Roc. I knew that the first time I spotted you. You have a good heart.''

''Okay, so where are you going with all this praise and insight?'' he teased.

''It's about Sam. She's wounded emotionally from this experience, Roc. She needs someone.... I tried to get her to open up to me, but she won't do it. She's hiding behind that intellectual doctor's facade, but I know she's not as confident as she's pretending to be. I've been shot. I know how it feels. I know how I felt inside. I was a mess. I was hemorrhaging emotionally, even though no one else saw it or knew it.''

''Except Quinn.''

''Yes. Because he loved me, he saw it.''

Grimly, Roc halted in front of HQ. There was so much to do! But his heart—his whole focus, if he was honest—was pinned on Sam, not his work.

''I'll call Morgan Trayhern and give him a verbal report,'' he said, talking more to himself than to Kerry. ''I'm supposed to write up a report and send it, but that can wait.''

''And you'll go see Sam? Right away, then?''

Hearing the concern in Kerry's voice, Roc nodded. ''Yeah, I will, but I don't know how much good I can do, Kerry.''

She laughed softly. ''Oh, I think a lot more than either of you realize right now, Roc.'' Gripping his hand, she squeezed it briefly. ''Thanks...''

*February 6: 1930*

When Roc called to her, Sam jumped. She had been sitting on her bed, staring at the comb in her hands. Her hair was damp, snarled and tangled from being washed. To her consternation, she found it almost impossible to lift her arm and maneuver the comb through the knotted strands. The pain was too great.

Getting to her feet, which were bare and cold on the plyboard floor, she called, "Come in...." She pulled the fleecy U.S. Navy blue robe, which was two sizes too large for her and hung to her ankles, around herself. Her heart picked up in beat as her gaze fastened on the opening and she saw Roc step through the flap. He was here. And he was safe.

Standing there, Sam felt a wave of emotions beginning to engulf her. She had been so worried about Roc out there after she'd left. Worse, she'd learned on the flight back to HQ that he and his team had met more resistance from the Diablos, that a firefight had broken out in earnest. She had sat there fighting back tears of helplessness in that helicopter, her arms around her waist, staring down at the deck, wondering if he was going to be killed as Brad had been.

As Roc stepped into the tent now, her heart flew open. Sam stood there absorbing his scowling, worried face, which was dirty and stained with dried sweat. He turned and shut the flaps.

"Y-you're okay?"

Sam heard the wobble in his strained tone. He turned and took off his helmet, propping his M-16 in the corner, out of the way.

"Yeah, I am." Sam was standing in the middle of the tent, her face white and taut. Seeing the shadows in her huge green eyes, the way her lips were contorted with pain and anxiety, Roc felt his heart tearing open. She was suffering so much!

She watched as he shed his outer gear and threw it

on the bed. Hungrily, she absorbed each of his movements. The flak jacket was ripped open from its Velcro closings, and dropped on the floor. As he turned, Sam saw that his olive-green T-shirt was soaked with sweat and clung to his powerful body.

"I'm taking this off," he told her, holding her uncertain gaze. As he stripped off the T-shirt and bared his upper body, he added, "I smell. I need a shower and a shave, Sam, but right now, something more important has come up. You."

He stood facing her, naked from the waist up. Then he leaned down, unlaced his dusty boots and pushed them off his feet. Placing the boots beneath the bed, and wearing only his cammo pants, Roc straightened and walked to within two feet of where she was standing.

Lifting his right hand, he held it out to her. "Come here, sweetheart. Let me hold you. Please?"

His words cut through her agitation, penetrating her wildly spinning emotional state. Tears welled in Sam's eyes no matter how much she tried to stop them. Roc's face, once so hard and unreadable, was alive with compassion—for her. She stared in disbelief at his proffered hand. It was a large, square hand, the fingers long and strong looking, and covered with many small scars. There were thick callouses on the palm. And he was extending that powerful hand to her....

Gulping, she tried to take a breath. "Oh, Roc..."

He didn't wait. "Come here...." he rasped, stepping forward and sweeping Sam into his arms. In one motion, he brought her to the bed, urging her to lie down on her right side because her left arm had been injured. Lying beside her, their bodies touching solidly at hips and knees, Roc slid one arm beneath her neck and brought her fully against him.

A rush of air flowed out between her parted lips, and she began to sob. Burying her head in the crook of his shoulder, his flesh warm and solid against her face, she felt a tremor run violently through her. It was an earthquake of emotions that she was trying desperately to avoid, to suppress as she always could before.

But something was different this time. The bullet wound had shattered her well-ordered world. And somehow Roc knew it as he gathered her tightly against him. He was so warm and strong and protective. It was all Sam could do to slide her arm tentatively around his torso, bury her face against his hard jaw and try to breathe.

"It's going to be all right," Roc rasped against her ear, kissing her damp, snarled hair. "You're going to be all right, sweetheart. You survived. You lived. You didn't die. I know how scared you're feeling right now...I know how your gut is twisted up inside...but it's going to be okay. I promise you, with time, it will be okay and you'll stop feeling like this...."

The trembling touch of his fingers grazing her hair made Sam sob even harder.

"Let it out, sweetheart, let it out. Cry. I'll just hold you." Roc shut his eyes tightly, his jaw resting against her hair. Slowly, he began to rock Sam in his arms. With each gentle motion, her arm tightened around his torso a little more. He felt Sam fighting it. "This isn't the time to be strong, Sam. I'm here. Cry on my shoulder. You're safe with me.... I'll protect you...." And Roc pressed kiss after kiss against her brow, her hairline and temple to urge her to release the poisonous trauma that she held within her.

As his mouth caressed her, Sam lost control of her virulent, flailing emotions, which were shrieking for release. The sobs that tore from her contorted mouth now sounded like those of a wounded animal. Instantly, Roc's arms tightened around her. He cradled her gently. His heart was pounding beneath her breasts; she could feel it. She felt the rise and fall of his massive, hairy chest and tried to synchronize her breathing with his. Right now, he was truly like a rock, incredibly stable. She was like a rocket going off, directionless and in desperate need of help and stability.

"It's going to be all right," Roc crooned, pressing a kiss near her ear as she continued to cry in earnest. Feeling the wet warmth of her tears falling on his shoulder and then running down his chest, Roc sensed his heart opening as it never had before. Knowing Sam as he did, he knew the fact that she was able to trust him enough to cry in his arms was a treasure of incredible magnitude.

Running his hand down her strong, supple spine, which he could feel beneath the fleecy robe she wore, he smiled softly against her temple. In this raw moment of life, all he wanted was to give her solace, the sense that she was loved no matter how badly she was hurting.

When Roc realized he'd admitted to himself that he loved Sam, he opened his eyes. Continuing to rock her and hold her, he observed that somehow this fiery woman with the heart and courage of a lion had not only opened his heart, but held it in her healer's hands. He wasn't sure right now what to do with that revelation. Sam getting wounded had changed his world in a heartbeat. As he lay there with her, their bodies pressed protectively against one another, Roc also knew that his world was changed forever. And although he was scared, he wasn't running from it.

Caressing Sam's tangled, damp hair, Roc pressed small kisses to her hairline and temple. Little by little, her sobs were lessening, the tremors that had wracked her body were now almost gone. He was amazed at how one human's touch could heal another's hurt. It was a miracle. She was his miracle. They had met one another in a world plunged into chaos. They had to live moment by moment, never sure of what the next second might bring. Never sure if they'd take another breath because their lives were on the line.

Sam lifted her hand and pulled away from him just enough to try and wipe the tears from her eyes. Roc raised up on his left elbow and eased her onto her back.

"Here, let me do that for you." Carefully he wiped away the remnants of her tears. Looking down at her, at those green eyes huge with pain and hope, he smiled. Her lips, so soft and vulnerable, beckoned to him. Curving his fingers into her hair and tilting her face, he leaned down…down to kiss her.

As his mouth grazed her wet, parted lips, Sam shut her eyes. Seconds later, she arched against him, her hand ranging along his muscular arm, fingers sliding up his thickly corded neck and burrowing into his short hair. His own touch was tentative. Worshipful. A moan broke from her as he caressed her, making her feel fragile and feminine. The intense care, the love that was expressed in his kiss broke every barrier Sam had ever hidden behind. Roc's breath was moist and warm as he took the kiss deeper. With each movement of his lips, he let her know just how much she meant to him. Lost in the heat and splendor of his mouth sliding wetly against her own, Sam felt her world explode in shards of splintered sunlight as he caressed her and loved her with his male strength and his male gentleness.

Unable to get enough of him, she responded hungrily, her mouth devouring his, their breaths mingling, their hearts thundering against one another. Seconds spun together as a lightning storm of need was unleashed deep within her. The heated knot in her lower body grew into an ache that took her by surprise. No man had ever kissed her as Roc was kissing her now. As she grasped the tense muscles of his sweaty shoulder, she could feel him holding back, keeping himself in check for her sake. Even in the midst of her spinning, elated senses, Sam remembered that she didn't want a one-night stand. Roc was respecting her decision, she realized, as his mouth took her lips in a final, powerful surge that could only be translated as love. *Love.*

Nothing else mattered to Sam right now. As his mouth cherished hers, she surrendered totally to Roc. Sam had never done that before in her life. Except for her parents and her fiancé, she had never completely trusted anyone outside of herself. Now she did. She trusted Roc with her life. And her heart, her soul and her body were shimmering with a desire to forge a fiery union with him.

That realization struck Sam as his mouth eased regretfully from hers. When she lifted her lashes, still wet with tears, and met and melted beneath his stormy gaze, she knew. She knew she loved Roc.

How it had happened, Sam didn't know. When it had happened, she couldn't answer. All she knew as she drowned in his lambent gaze was that she loved this man. This man who had risked his own life to protect her.

Her lips parted, but words wouldn't come. She saw the corners of his mouth pull upward.

"You have the most beautiful smile…." she managed to whisper rawly. "I don't know why you hide it so much…." She lifted her fingers and grazed his lower lip.

"Because," Roc said in a low, husky tone, catching her fingers and kissing them, "I'm a marine, sweetheart. Marines have to be tough most of the time." Holding her hand, he saw her eyes grow velvety with what he clearly saw was love—for him. His chest expanded. The joy that bubbled through him was something he'd never experienced before. "With you, though," Roc continued, pressing her hand against his chest, where his heart lay, "I feel safe. I feel that you'll take me, warts and all, for who I am."

Closing her eyes, Sam concentrated on his voice, which seemed to vibrate through her entire being. Her heart exploded with such happiness she couldn't find words to express it. All she could do was drown in his warmth, feel his heart beating beneath her hand. And most of all, as she opened her eyes again, absorb that masculine smile that was like sunlight lancing through the darkness of her fear.

"I don't know what's happening," Roc slowly admitted to her. "And I don't have words for it, Sam…. All I know is that we share something special…something so powerful, so overwhelming to me, that a minute of my day doesn't go by without me seeing your face, or your smile, or those dancing green eyes of yours, in front of me."

Nodding, Sam moistened her well-kissed lips. She could taste Roc upon them and wanted more. Oh, so much more! Feeling his mouth press against her brow, she trembled with longing and need. In her heart, Sam knew he loved her with a passion that defied any words they might use to describe it. The fierceness of that truth opened her heart even more, and she felt a flush of heat, euphoria and hope envelop her. Plunged into that golden, sparkling flow of sensation, she floated buoyantly, feeling more strong, more sure and hopeful than at any other point in her life. Because of Roc. Because of what he was sharing with her.

All she wanted was to burn in the conflagration of desire that flamed in his eyes. To feel his rough hand surrounding hers, to have his body pressed to hers protectively.... However, Sam was barely aware of a helicopter landing in the distance. Faraway voices intruded into the tent. The noise of life, she realized belatedly.

Opening her lips, Sam managed a slight smile. "I think I'll live now.... The prescription was just what I needed, Roc...thank you..." *Thank you from the bottom of my heart. You love me and I know it now. I absorbed your love into my shattered spirit, and you gave me the miracle of renewed life. You gave me your love....*

Oh, how she wanted to say those words to him, but something stopped her. Her past experience of losing Brad intruded between them, and Sam cried inwardly over that unexpected barrier. It wasn't fair to Roc. It was her hurdle to climb and resolve. He shouldn't be punished for the wounds she had yet to work through.

Roc gave her a very confident male smile. ''So I'm a doctor now. That's nice.''

Hearing his teasing tone, Sam sighed and relaxed fully in his arms. ''You really are exactly what the doctor ordered. How did you know? How did you know I was hurting?''

Roc reached up and gently brushed several strands of hair from her furrowed brow. ''Somalia taught me a lot. It was a nightmare. You didn't know friend from enemy, just like it is here,'' he told her quietly. Grazing her cheek, which now was a dusky-rose color, he added, ''Enemies were hidden among the innocent. We never knew one moment to the next where the next bullet might come from. My Recon team went into one warlord's territory, and we got pinned down. I lost three of my men. Two were wounded, and a third died in my arms on board the Blackhawk that picked us up out of that hell on the way out to sea.'' His mouth flattened in memory. ''Back on board ship, while I waited for my men to get out of surgery, I went off to a room and cried like a baby. I cried for them. I cried for the loss of my sergeant, who'd died in my arms.''

Touched to the point of tears, Sam whispered, ''Who cried for you, Roc?''

He shut his eyes. His heart swelled with such emotion at her softly spoken question. How compassionate and sensitive Sam was. When he felt her fingers trailing along the side of his jaw, he opened his eyes. Hers were swimming with tears once again. Sam was open and completely vulnerable to him now that they'd shared that life-healing kiss. Capturing her hand, he pressed it against his chest, against his heart.

''No one...''

"You appear so hard. So implacable. And yet—" Sam sniffed, her voice wobbling "—you care so fiercely and deeply for those under your command. You're so protective and loving…."

Roc shook his head, unable to speak.

"And you went to see your men after they came out of surgery?"

"Yes…and it was then, in the next several days after that, that I saw how changed they were. One of them, my radioman, broke down one day and cried. I held him. He felt ashamed of crying. You know how marines are about that?"

"Yes," Sam whispered, giving him a gentle look of understanding, "I do."

"Well, it was from Dennis that I found out how getting shot changes you. In so many ways…" Roc looked up at the tent roof for a moment and then back at Sam. "When I got off the helo a little while ago, Kerry was there waiting for me. She had seen you going into the same kind of emotional void most people fall into when they're shot. She had been wounded recently herself, and when she confided to me that you weren't doing well, I knew instantly what the real problem was."

"And so you came over to see me."

"I was going to, anyway, but Kerry's concern for you made me change some plans and get here sooner rather than later." Leaning down, Roc kissed her brow and felt the tension melt away beneath his lips.

Closing her eyes, Sam rested against him. She'd never felt as safe and cared for as she did now. "Kerry's a wonderful person…so insightful. I'm afraid I fought her every inch of the way when she was washing the dirt out my hair after the sniper incident.''

Chuckling, Roc rubbed his jaw against her hair. ''Yeah, she told me you were a little resistant.''

''My training as a medical doctor,'' Sam said, humor in her tone for the first time. Absorbing the feel of his jaw against her temple, she sighed. ''This is wonderful, Roc. You're wonderful. Everything is perfect despite what happened. I was so worried for you out there. On the way back here we heard you got into another firefight.''

''Yeah,'' he groused. Easing back, he tucked in the collar of Sam's robe, which was revealing more of her chest than he knew she'd be comfortable with. Right now, all he wanted was her trust. He didn't want Sam to think he was like men who take what they want from women before running away like thieves in the night.

''We caught one of the Diablo lieutenants. I...killed the guy that shot you. When we got to the house and found his body, some civilians came out of another block of homes and told us there was a second Diablo member nearby. We took off in hot pursuit.'' Scowling, he caressed her brow and cheek. ''What we didn't realize was that it was a trick.''

''A trick?''

''Yeah. The Diablo leader is real smart. He created a diversion with that sniper and then with the lieutenant to get all of us to head off in the wrong direction. I think he intended for the two of them to lay down a field of fire and keep us pinned, but we got the upper hand first.'' Roc couldn't keep the satisfaction from his tone. He saw Sam frown, and fear entered her eyes once more.

''The leader had about ten of his men in another part of area 5, near the border. He was looting a bunch of homes over there and he didn't want us interfering in the operation, so he created this sniper diversion. We fell for it. I won't fall for it again. I'm getting to know how he thinks.''

''But you have a Diablo member in custody?''

''Yeah. We sent him back to Camp Reed for interrogation. Morgan Trayhern was real happy to hear we caught one alive and unwounded. He said he'd be in touch with us.'' Roc gave her a feral smile. ''I'd like to interrogate the bastard myself, but I don't think he'd survive the beating I'd give him for hurting you,'' he added, gently touching her shoulder through the blue robe.

The lethal tone of his voice said a lot to Sam about Roc's ability to protect those he cared for and loved. Loved? She didn't want to look too closely at the new emotion she sensed between them, but she couldn't stop the bubbling feeling of joy that was moving through her as he lay at her side, caring for her, touching her and giving her small kisses meant to heal her shattered spirit.

''I guess it never entered my mind, Roc, that I might get hit by a bullet someday. I know I'm in the military…but it was just so shocking. I'm a doctor. I work in a hospital. I'm not out in the field, not near any action. I didn't even realize my arm had been creased with a bullet until we got to the center of that field to wait for helicopter assistance to get out of there.''

''I didn't think you knew,'' Roc agreed. ''When you got up, I saw the sleeve of your blouse soaked with blood. At that point, I couldn't do or say anything."

"No kidding," Sam whispered. "You were lying down between me and that sniper, protecting me." She gazed up at him in wonder. "What kind of person willingly puts their life ahead of another's?" Shaking her head, she murmured, "You blow me away, Roc. I knew you were a marine and proud of it. And I know marines take care of their own—I'd always heard that."

"But now," he said, his fingers grazing the top of her unruly red hair, "you've experienced the care we extend to our own."

*Our own.* What did he mean by that? Sam gazed at him, the question on her lips. But she couldn't ask it. She was finding out how much of an emotional coward she really was when it came to raw life-and-death situations.

"Y-yes, I have. And I feel wonderful now. I feel as if I'll heal. I was in such inner turmoil, my brain was shorting out. I was having difficulty listening to what people said to me, acting like I was half here and half somewhere else…."

"You were—and still are—in shock, sweetheart. I'll be here for you when you want…if you want?"

Sam saw the question in his narrowing eyes. Did she want Roc to be an intimate part of her life? Where were the boundaries? What were the rules between them? She had no idea. Ordinarily, due to her training, she made black-and-white, logical decisions. Now her heart was begging her to make an emotional decision instead. This wasn't something to think about, but to instinctually react to.

Pressing her hand against his heart, the wiry black

hair there tickling her palm, Sam said in a broken tone, ''Do I want you in my life? Roc, you just *saved* my life. What kind of person would I be to tell you no after you risked your neck for me?''

''Saving you doesn't have a you-owe-me price tag on it,'' Roc countered. ''You owe me nothing, Sam. What we have...it's, well, different from anything I've ever experienced. Maybe the trauma and intensity of this place is part of it, but I don't think so. It's you. I'm drawn to you, for whatever the reasons.'' Holding her troubled gaze, he took the biggest risk he'd ever taken. ''What I'm really asking is if there's a chance for us to build a personal relationship with each other. And I don't want you to answer yes because I laid my life on the line for yours. That's not what this is about.'' Breath held, he watched her eyes. Roc saw fear in them. He saw joy. And anxiety. Her lips compressed, and her gaze skittered to the right, then to the left. His heart was torn up with anguish. Would she say no? Roc knew Sam had that right. Wasn't what they were sharing now, this moment, the best thing that had ever happened to them? He knew it was for him. No woman had ever made him feel this strong, courageous, protective or needed.

Her pulse speeding up, Sam closed her eyes. ''I'm such a coward, Roc,'' she managed to whisper in a raw voice. Opening them, she forced herself to look up at him. His body was warm and solid against hers, like a bulwark. So protective. So loving. ''I'm afraid...so afraid.... Brad was a marine. I lost him in a stupid helicopter malfunction accident. And you...God, you're a Recon. Even a navy squid like me knows that the most dangerous career in the Marine Corps is being a Recon.''

"You're afraid of once again losing someone you might love." It wasn't a question, it was a statement. Roc's heart sank. The pain serrated him, gutted him, and he felt as if he were dying. Sam was in his arms, her hair spread like fire across his arm, soft and springy. Her body, long and firm, pressed against his. Did she know her own courage? Roc didn't think so. He was old enough to understand how frightened Sam was. And he knew now how much she'd loved Brad.

"I guess I've never loved someone to that depth or breadth, Sam, to understand what you're going through. But I respect it." Roc gave her a pain-filled, lopsided smile. "I've seen enough in this world to know you can't hurry a wound to get well before its time. There's a time for healing and for resolving such things. And your fear of losing me stops you from wanting to take that last step toward a personal relationship."

The sadness in his tone made her want to cry once more. "Oh, Roc, I'm sorry…so sorry. I'm a coward at heart, I'm finding out. You're so special, so wonderful to me…. You don't deserve this, you just don't—"

"Shhh," he whispered, placing his fingertip against her lips. "You can't hurry things that matter in life, sweetheart. You matter to me. A lot. I'll just leave it at that, because the last thing I want to do is pressure you. We have time. I'm a patient man." Roc managed a smile he didn't feel. Just seeing Sam's eyes well up with tears rent his heart. "I don't need you to cry over us, too. Okay?"

"C-can we just leave our relationship open for further discussion, Roc?"

"Sure."

"Right now," Sam said unsteadily, "I'm an emotional mess. Tomorrow I'm supposed to go out to the first medevac facility and be thinking clearly. This scratch isn't going to stop me from working at all. Getting shot wasn't part of the agenda."

"And me pressuring you about us is another thing on your plate you didn't want or expect. I understand."

"I really am a coward, Roc. I know that now. You've shown it to me and I don't like it at all. I want to promise you something. I'll work on that aspect of myself. I don't know what the outcome will be, but I want you to know I'll be trying."

Seeing hope flare in his eyes sent Sam's heart skittering with joy once more. How could she possibly turn down this man, who was more heroic than anyone she'd ever known before? Sam decided she was crazy. On a deeper level, she knew it was about losing someone she loved that prevented her from pursuing something more with Roc. Sam couldn't admit she loved him because emotionally, she just didn't have the stamina to deal with his loss, if it came. And in his line of work, especially during this crisis, that could happen in one terrible instant. Sam just wasn't prepared for that possibility, she knew. But so did Roc. She could see his understanding of her clearly in his shadowed blue gaze.

"If I come to you," she whispered, "and I need to be held for just a little while..."

"Just ask. I'll be there for you." Roc meant every word of it with his heart and soul.

"And if you..." Sam touched the hardening line of his mouth with her fingertips "...need to be held, you can come to me. Okay?"

"We'll do what we can for one another when the time comes," Roc agreed quietly. Sam was trying, and that made happiness thrum through him. He saw the grit in her eyes, saw the fear in them and realized that she was a fighter deep down. Hope sprang to life in him, bright and burning. "Time heals all things," Roc told her. "Maybe what we need is time together, with no expectations or pressures on one another. I can live with that. Can you?"

"Yes," Sam quavered. "Yes, I'd like that, Roc."

# *Chapter 14*

*February 7: 1130*

Sam tried to gather her unstable emotions. It was near noon, the sky a bright, pale blue, the sun making the temperature on this early February day climb into the sixties. Clad in her white lab coat, with her stethoscope around her neck, she left the main medevac tent, where the level of noise, the babble of people waiting for treatment, was making her raw and jumpy. She needed a moment alone to get herself together.

Stepping outside, she looked across the hilltop, now dotted with tents. Their first medevac site was up and running. At the other end, as far as possible from the tent city, a Navy Sea Stallion helicopter was being unloaded. Her heart sped up as she spotted Roc at the opening, clipboard in hand. Ammunition resupply for his team as well as the other marines was on this helo, and he had to check over the contents and sign for them.

Moving away from the tents toward the edge of the slope, Sam wrapped her arms around herself and hung her head. Her mind was spinning. She was still in shock over being wounded, and noise bothered her more than usual. Knowing it was a post-traumatic stress disorder symptom, Sam took a walk along the edge of the hill. Below her stretched rows of tightly packed suburban houses, all destroyed.

The wind played gently with her hair. As she lifted her left hand, a twinge of pain stabbed her arm. She'd received ten stitches where the bullet had grazed her. Today, at least, she could lift it, so that was a good sign. Still, as she brushed her hair from her cheek, the pain was a constant reminder that someone out there had enough hatred inside to try and kill her.

Sam knew that Sergeant Simmons was supposed to shadow her every movement. Roc was worried about the Diablos, and he'd ordered his sergeant to be with her at all times. He expected reaction from the gang because one of their main lieutenants had been captured. Well, Sam hated the idea of a bodyguard, so she'd sent the sergeant on a mission to another tent to get more IVs, then had slipped out the rear door of the main tent just to be left alone for a few minutes. Nothing was going to happen here. There were more than a hundred people waiting in line to be taken care of this morning as the medevac opened its doors officially for business to serve the beleaguered community. The people were grateful and anxious, carrying their sick children and babies in their arms, hoping for help.

*Roc...* her heart whispered. Sam faced the sea of

ruined houses as her thoughts gently turned to him once more. A minute didn't go by, since she'd awakened early this morning and started walking with her team the three miles to the medevac site, that she didn't replay some part of Roc's conversation from last night, when he'd held her so protectively in his arms.

Facing northward, feeling the warmth of the sun, Sam closed her eyes and relished the joy moving through her like a river of heat and promise. She loved Roc. It was that simple and that complicated. Why couldn't she get past her fear of losing him? Oh, why was she such an emotional coward? This morning, as she'd walked with him at her shoulder, he'd proved to be a model of restraint. Roc had promised he wouldn't pressure her, and he'd acted as if last night had never happened. Except Sam saw the warmth and welcome in his blue eyes as he met her hesitant gaze. And when in the grayness and chill of the dawn, one corner of his mouth had curved faintly in a smile meant only for her, she had shyly smiled back. In that moment, Sam knew Roc loved her. And she loved him.

In a quandary, Sam headed down the embankment, which was riddled with cracks and crevices from the earthquake. She needed to walk and think. Lin and her team, along with the other medical staff flown in to take care of this site, could handle the patients for fifteen minutes. Reaching the bottom of the hill, near the first row of flattened houses, Sam turned east. She would go around the base of the hill, then back up to the clinic, she decided.

"Hold it!"

Sam froze when she heard the snarling growl of a

man's voice right behind her. Gasping, she started to turn.

Seconds later, a hand gripped her left shoulder, jerking her around. Pain shot through her arm—a pain so intense that Sam's knees nearly buckled. A cry tore from her lips as the barrel of a gun was jammed against her temple.

"Don't move, bitch. You're coming with us. *Now.*"

*February 7: 1230*

"Captain Gunnison! Captain Gunnison!"

Roc had just signed off for the shipment of ammo from the helicopter loadmaster. He turned, hearing Sergeant Simmons's urgent voice raised in alarm. The Recon marine was running toward him, his face etched with worry, his M-16 in his left hand. Intuitively, Roc knew it had to do with Sam. Handing the loadmaster the manifest, he spun on his heel and started toward Simmons. Heart pounding, Roc saw the anguish in the sergeant's eyes as he skidded to a halt.

"What is it, Buck?" he asked grimly.

"Cap'n, Dr. Andrews is *gone!* She asked me to get IVs from another tent next to where she was working...and when I came back, she was gone." Trying to catch his breath, Buck turned and pointed north. "I was lookin' all over for her when a nurse told me she sneaked out for a breath of fresh air. I followed her footsteps, sir." Gulping, Buck grimaced. "Sir, she was by herself. I'm sorry...."

"Well, where is she?" Roc demanded tightly.

"We don't know. I followed her footprints. They

lead over the northern edge of the hill and down to the flats below. There appeared to be a scuffle. Her footprints are mixed with, I'd say, about three men's shoe prints."

"Damn!" Roc snarled, and he tore off at a dead run, the sergeant at his side. Fear ate at Roc as they moved swiftly across the hilltop. When they arrived at the edge, he saw several young boys scrambling up toward them, fear in their faces.

"Hey!" a red-haired twelve-year-old called out to them, "Dr. Andrews has been kidnapped!" He jabbed his finger toward a street that was now empty of people. "They took her thatta away!"

Leaping off the lip, Roc skidded and slid down the slope, dust billowing behind him. Buck wasn't far behind. They headed straight toward the kids, who were clearly frightened.

"Tell me what you saw," he ordered them, wiping his mouth with the back of his hand.

A blond-haired boy with blue eyes, around age thirteen, stepped forward. "Sir, Dr. Andrews took care of me, so I know what she looks like. We were playing with a soccer ball over there, near my parent's house. We saw her walking."

"She was alone?"

"Yes, she was. Like she was thinking a lot about something. She walked down the hill right here, and when she started to go around the hill bottom, these three men leaped out from behind that house over there—" he pointed to one leaning crookedly but still erect, its red roof tilted "—and grabbed her."

"Who were they?"

"I dunno. I bet Diablos, though, sir."

Roc cursed softly. ''Did you recognize any of them? Can you be sure they were Diablos?''

The blond-haired boy shrugged. ''They were carrying rifles, sir.''

''And what about Dr. Andrews? Did they hurt her?''

''She put up an awful fight. The man with the black hair, the tallest of them, hit her in the arm, and we saw blood all over her sleeve. She went down on her knees, but they forced her back up to her feet. They took her this way, down Mount Baldy Street, sir.''

''And then where?''

''I don't know,'' the kid said worriedly. ''It looked like they turned left at the end of it, onto Holyoke Avenue.''

''How long ago?'' Buck demanded tightly.

''Gosh, not more than a few minutes ago...''

Roc turned and pressed the radio attached to the epaulet of his jacket. The Sea Stallion was preparing to lift off. Radioing the pilot, he asked him to fly in that direction to try and locate the Diablos and Sam. Though his heart was shredding with fear, Roc forced all his emotions away. He had to think clearly! Next, he placed a call to his team to meet him immediately.

Lifting his head, he saw another group of kids appearing at the end of Mount Baldy Street. They were running as hard as they could toward them. If he read the expressions on their faces correctly, they'd probably seen Sam and the gang members. Hope threaded through him as he heard the marine helicopter wind up for takeoff. Maybe, just maybe, with the help of the pilots and these kids running toward them, they could find the Diablos—and Sam—before it was too late.

* * *

''Now, honey, you're gonna go in there and treat my little girl, Jolie, and my wife, Nannette. You understand?''

Sam stood between two armed Diablo guards, both of whom were glaring down at her. She was gasping for breath after the brutal run they'd dragged her on. One of the men, tall and red-haired, gripped her left arm so tightly that the pain was nonstop. Trying to fight off her captors, Sam had instantly torn all the stitches closing her wound, and it had begun to bleed profusely once again. Glaring up at the leader, a man named Steve—who towered over her, his pistol pointed at her forehead—she felt faint with pain. She heard his men also call him Snake. It was a worthy name for him as far as she was concerned.

Rage surged through her as she met his narrowed black gaze. ''You have no right kidnapping me, you—''

''Shut up, bitch.'' Steve scowled, breathing hard from their run. He jabbed the barrel against her temple once again. ''You have no rights. You work for that lousy government that we don't recognize. You're our prisoner. You're also a doctor. We need you to work on *our* people. Now—'' he smiled a little as he wiped his sweaty brow ''—you can either do that or I'll put a bullet through your head here and now.''

They stood in a littered, dirty room inside a house that was leaning to one side due to the damage from the quake. Sam had no idea where they were; they'd been running for what seemed an hour. She'd lost all sense of direction because the men had taken her down a jigsaw puzzle of streets and avenues and alleys. Several times they'd hid in destroyed homes as a marine helicopter buzzed low overhead. Once the helo flew by, the men would yank her out of the house and continue their broken run for an unknown destination.

Breathing hard, Sam glared at Steve. "I'm a doctor. I'll treat anyone who is sick. You didn't have to ask at gunpoint."

Removing the gun, he smiled more broadly. "That's better, bitch. Joey? Take the doc to the bedroom." His dark gaze swung back to Sam. "You either save 'em or yore dead. Hear?"

Trying to steady her breathing, Sam nodded and pushed her hair out of her eyes.

"Good girl."

Joey, the red-haired guard, yanked her to the right.

"Ow!" Sam jerked her arm free. "Dammit! That hurts!"

Steve laughed. "Joey, take her to my family. Tom? You keep guard on the door. Joey, you make sure she has what she needs to treat 'em, hear?"

"Yes, sir, I will," Joey promised solemnly.

Pressing her hand over her bleeding arm, Sam followed them down the darkened hall. Gazing around furtively, Sam tried to figure out how to escape. Her legs were wobbly from the long, enforced run. Her breathing was raspy and her lungs were burning from exertion. She knew this situation was all her fault. She should never have left the medevac complex without a guard. Roc wouldn't know where she was. Heart plummeting with regret over her carelessness, Sam followed Joey down a hall littered with broken chunks of drywall that had fallen from the ceiling during the quake.

Once inside the dim room, Sam saw a woman with blond hair in a large queen-size bed, a little girl, dark-haired and about six years old, in her thin arms.

"Nannette, we got ya a doc," Joey said proudly as he pushed Sam inside. "Yore gonna be okay, Nanny. You and yore young'un."

Sam went to the wall of windows on the other side of the bed and yanked the curtains open. Sunlight flooded into the gloomy, stinking room. Turning, she saw the woman blink several times and slowly sit up in bed. She was wearing all her clothes to keep warm, her face drawn and pinched.

"Lord be thanked," Nanny whispered. She smiled unsurely up at Sam. "You a doctor, ma'am?"

Taken off guard by the woman's soft, hesitant voice, Sam tried to put her fear and rage away. Looking at the diminutive woman and the very sick child she held protectively in her arms, compassion flowed through her.

"Yes...yes, I am. My name is Samantha Andrews. I'm a navy doctor." She leaned over and placed her fingers against the child's limp wrist to find a pulse.

"Please," Nanny begged, her voice flooding with tears, "save our little one. She's dying...." The woman sobbed once, then fought to stem her tears.

Sam gently eased the unconscious girl out of her mother's arms. Laying her flat, she placed her stethoscope against the child's thin chest, beneath the blankets she had been swathed in to keep her warm.

"Can you tell me her symptoms?" she asked the woman who knelt over her daughter, wringing her hands.

"Lordy, Dr. Andrews, it happened so fast. I think she drunk some bad water. We don't have much...we're all dying by bits and pieces around here...."

"Bad water? Did she vomit it back up?"

"Yes, she did." Nanny searched Sam's face. "Then she got this awful diarrhea...and, oh, she's been vomiting and having diarrhea for the last day...." Sniffing, she wiped the tears from her wan cheeks with trembling fingers. "And then she just went to sleep like this...."

"Yes, unconscious," Sam murmured. Turning, she looked over at Joey, who stood with his rifle in his arms, watching her intently. "Do you have any medical supplies? Any IVs on hand?" she demanded.

"Shore we do, Doc. Hold on and I'll go get 'em. How many you need?"

Sam turned to Nanny. "Do you have the same symptoms?"

"Lordy, yes, but not as bad as my baby, here."

"Get me two IVs, Joey," she told him.

"You bet, Doc. I'll be right back...."

In that moment, Sam realized that she could leap up, open that sliding glass door and escape to the backyard. Looking through the window, Sam saw an open door in the wooden fence that enclosed the space. She could escape through it and run. Where, she wasn't sure—just away from here. Away from the Diablos.

Yet, as she sat there tensely, her gaze riveted on the glass door, Sam knew she wouldn't run and leave this little girl's life hanging in the balance. Her mission was to sustain life. And even at the cost of her own freedom, Sam couldn't abandon her doctor's vow.

She felt Nanny's cool hand on her own.

"Thank you...thank you for bein' here. I know my husband, Steve, has been lookin' for a medical doctor for some time now...."

Sam met the woman's pale gray eyes, which shimmered with tears. "Your husband kidnapped me. That's not right. We have a medevac station near here. All you had to do was walk in. We'd have treated you there."

The woman hung her head and sniffed. "We're survivalists, Dr. Andrews. Ain't no one gonna take care of us."

Compressing her lips, Sam tried to rein in her anger. "Your husband has murdered a lot of people...."

"We have to eat," Nanny whispered.

Sam realized it was useless trying to persuade the woman otherwise.

Joey returned promptly with the IVs in hand and gave them to Sam with a triumphant look.

"I need antibiotics, too. Do you have any?" Sam demanded as he stood nearby, the rifle pointed in her direction.

"Uh, yeah...we do...."

"Get me whatever you've got, then," Sam growled as she began to hang an IV from the bedpost and prepare the needle to be inserted into the unconscious girl's arm.

"Yeah, you bet. Hang on...." And Joey quickly left the room again. Sam's fingers hesitated in their task. She could escape now. It was a second chance.

One glance down at the unconscious girl, her face looking like porcelain, her hair thin and uncombed, made Sam's heart plummet. There was no way she was going to make this little girl pay with her life for what her father had done to get Sam here. No, she would try to save her....

*February 7: 1300*

"Tie her ankles," Steve ordered Joey with a smirk once he'd forced Sam to sit down in the small bedroom opposite the room where she'd taken care of his wife and child. "Now, yore gonna stay here." Steve added. "Joey will tie up yore legs so you don't get any ideas about runnin' off and leavin' us. I've put out the word that we got a doc on board, and plenty of my people are comin' here for treatment. As soon as they arrive, yore gonna help them, too."

Sam sat in an overstuffed chair littered with plaster that had fallen during the quake. There was a twin bed in one corner and a child's dresser nearby. Joey bound her feet together with some nylon cord, pulling it so tightly Sam was worried about her circulation being cut off.

"Loosen that rope!" she demanded.

Steve scowled. "Doc, you don't have a leg to stand on around here. You get that?" He looked her up and down, a smile playing on his full mouth. "Joey, go easy on the rope. We don't want our doc to lose her legs and not be able to work on our folks."

"Yes, sir," Joey mumbled, kneeling at Sam's feet and reworking the nylon cords around her ankles.

Sam didn't like the look glimmering in Steve's eyes. He was a tall, muscular man, probably in his mid-thirties. He held his M-16 across his barrel chest, with several bandoleers of ammunition crisscrossing beneath it. His hair was long and uncombed, and he had a scraggly beard that was nearly a foot long.

There was dried food stuck in the strands near his thin mouth. Sam shuddered inwardly. The odor around the men was horrific. They hadn't bathed in weeks, she was sure. It made her nauseous to breathe in his scent.

"You thirsty or hungry?" Steve demanded.

"I could use some water."

"Joey, go fetch the doc some good water from our other supply out in the backyard," he ordered. "And not the stuff that made my wife and child sick."

Leaping to his feet, Joey grabbed his rifle. "Yes, sir!"

Alone with the Diablo leader, Sam tensed. He stood near the door, a lazy smile crossing his lined and weathered face. Sensing his interest in her as a woman, Sam avoided his appraising gaze. Mouth dry, she closed her eyes and tried to steady herself. Oh, God, what was she going to do? By now, Roc must know she was gone. He'd be so upset. And angry that she'd ordered Buck to leave her side. Oh, why hadn't she listened to Roc? He'd felt the Diablos would strike back and he'd been right.

"You know," Steve said, breaking the silence, "yore marines killed one of my best snipers yesterday, and they captured Jessie Lambord, one of my lieutenants. You wouldn't happen to know about that, would you?"

Lips compressed, Sam stubbornly shook her head. She wasn't about to give the bastard any information.

"Why's your arm bleedin' like it is?"

"I cut it the other day," Sam retorted, lifting her chin defiantly and glaring at him.

"What do you know about my man bein' captured?"

"Not a damn thing! I'm a doctor, not a marine!" she snapped angrily.

"Feisty…I like that," Steve murmured. Shifting the rifle to his left hand, he smiled crookedly. "Doc, yore a good-lookin' woman. Now, I ain't had any from my wife for a long time, since she fell sick."

Sam's heart froze. She stared in disbelief at him.

"And, hey," he chortled as the door opened and Joey returned, "you play yore cards right, little lady, and I'll let you stay alive longer than I wuz planning to…."

Gulping, Sam watched as Steve left. Joey, panting, held out a bottle of clear, clean water toward her. Taking it, Sam recognized it as being from a shipment that had been brought in by marine helicopter. The Diablos had obviously stolen the boxes. Twisting off the cap, she drank deeply, with Joey watching her intently.

Her heart thumped wildly in her chest as she finished it off. She handed the empty bottle back to Joey, who took it and left. Silence settled in the cold room and a chill went through her. Wrapping her arms around herself, Sam sat in the chair, her legs bound, feeling scared as never before. Oh, why hadn't she told Roc she loved him? She knew that Steve was a murderer. He would have no problem shooting her if she resisted him. Escape was her only option. Looking around, she saw a small window, but it wasn't big enough to crawl through.

Disheartened, she pressed her hands against her face and tried to think. How could this have happened? It was her own fault. She'd disregarded orders. If Buck had been with her, the likelihood of the Diablos kidnapping her would have been much less.

They'd jumped her because she was alone and unguarded. How stupid she'd been! And now the happiness she'd had with Roc was in serious jeopardy, because of her independent streak.

"I love you, Roc..." she whispered between taut lips. "Please forgive me...forgive me...."

# *Chapter 15*

*February 7: 1450*

Near 1500, Sam was untied and hustled out of her prison room by Joey. Pushing her hard, he growled, ''Git in there and take care of Steve's kin. I'll be awaitin' out here for you. After yore done with them, we're taking you to another house to help our kin.''

Glaring at him, Sam opened the door. She'd been sitting alone for hours. During that time, she'd often heard men's voices, along with the heavy thunking of boots along the carpeted hall. This was a busy place, no doubt about it.

Worried about Jolie's deteriorated condition, Sam hurried into the room. She saw Nannette sitting on the bed, joy on her face as she cradled her daughter in her lap. Jolie was awake, her big, blue eyes watching Sam's progress into the room after she shut the door behind her. Going to the bathroom, she washed her hands in a small basin of water that was waiting for her.

"Look, Doctor! Look. My baby is gonna make it! She just opened her eyes a few minutes ago and called out for me. Ain't that wonderful?" The woman smiled gratefully as Sam moved to the bed after drying her hands on a nearby towel. She checked the girl's IV drip into her slender arm.

"She looks much better," Sam murmured sympathetically. The tears running silently down Nannette's face as she stroked her daughter's hair touched her deeply. Quickly checking the girl's pulse and listening to her heart, Sam eased off the bed.

"She's going to be fine, Nannette. Her pulse is strong now. She's getting the fluids she needs."

"And the antibiotics are workin', Doctor?"

"Yes. She doesn't seem feverish anymore." Sam smiled tenderly down at the thin little girl beneath the mound of blankets.

Sniffing, Nannette said, "I feel much better, too."

Sam nodded and came around to her side of the bed to check the IV hung on the bedpost above her. "That's great." The IV bag was empty, so Sam removed the needle from the woman's arm and quickly put a Band-Aid over the area to prevent bleeding. She had no protective gloves to wear, and that bothered her, but she said nothing.

"Y-you saved our lives, Doctor. I'm so grateful...." She gave Sam a wobbly smile.

Removing the little girl's IV bag, Sam took a second one and put it in place. "You're welcome. I'm going to put Jolie on a second drip." She studied the label. "This one has antibiotics in it, Nannette. Just let her sleep while this flows into her arm. Once it's done, I'll remove it and she should be feeling much better.''

''Bless you, Doctor.''

As Sam stood at the girl's side and gently adjusted the IV drip, she saw that there was now a tall, rough-looking man with black hair outside the sliding glass door, keeping watch. Heart sinking, Sam realized that her hopes of escaping that way were now squashed.

''Is my husband treatin' you right, Doctor?'' Nannette frowned and sniffed.

''No, but that's not your concern,'' Sam said, smiling down at the little girl, who sucked her thumb, her huge blue eyes fixed on her.

''I'm so sorry.... I—I tried to tell him that no one would know me or Jolie, that we could walk to your new medical tent, which is only about four miles from here. But he wouldn't listen....'' Nannette reached out toward Sam's left arm, gazing worriedly at the bloodstained sleeve on her shirt. ''He hurt you....''

''I fought back,'' Sam said, giving her a game smile. ''I don't take kindly to kidnapping.''

Closing her eyes, Nannette whispered, ''I'm so sorry, Doctor. I truly am.... Steve...well, he gets in a rage awful easy.''

Looking at the woman, Sam saw evidence of Steve's anger. Nannette had the remnants of a black eye, a yellow-green bruise on her left cheekbone. Reaching over, she gently touched the woman's injured cheek. ''He hits you, too, doesn't he?''

Shrugging, Nannette bit her lower lip, unable to look at Sam. ''Ohh, you know, Doctor...my Steve means well. It's just that so many people rely on him for food and water and all. He's jumpy, and he's angry at the government. He's got god-awful responsibilities—you know, everyone lookin' to him for everything...."

Straightening, Sam saw the guard move toward the left and disappear from view. He seemed to have heard something. Resting her hand on the bedpost, she looked down at the woman, who was quite obviously an abuse victim. "No one has any excuse to hurt someone with their fists, Nannette. Not ever."

Just at that moment a huge crash sounded outside the bedroom door.

Sam gasped and whirled around. Men's voices called out. Shouts tunneled down the hall. Shots were fired.

"Oh, no!" Nannette screamed. "The feds!" She threw her body over her daughter to protect her.

Caught off guard, Sam hesitated, unsure what to do as more explosions occurred. The room shook, she fell to the floor, covering her head. Seconds later, bullets smashed through the walls of the room. The glass door shattered and blew outward into the yard. Screams and yells joined the staccato noise of M-16s firing, assaulting Sam's sensitive ears. Her mind whirled with questions, confusion. Who was attacking? Marines? Police? A rival gang? She wasn't sure.

The house shook again, this time from a grenade that had gone off. The door to the room blew inward, smashing into what was left of the windows on the other side. Glass spewed everywhere, hundreds of fragments raining down on them. Sam kept her arms over her head, lying flat on her belly, next to the bed. Dust billowed in from the hall. Only it wasn't dust. It was a white, curling, cloudy substance that made Sam choke as soon as she breathed it in. Tear gas!

Immediately her throat burned and tears streamed from her eyes.

"Get out!" Sam screamed as she scrambled to her hands and knees. "Get out! It's tear gas!"

Launching herself to her feet, Sam grabbed the IV and hauled Jolie into her arms. Gasping and choking, blinded by tears streaming from her eyes, she stumbled toward the backyard. The ground was slippery with shattered glass. Nannette was choking, too, but managed to grab on to Sam's lab coat and follow her outside.

Once in the yard, Sam hurried to the fence, where they could breathe clean, fresh air. Laying Jolie down, she held the IV bag high enough so it continued to drip. Nannette fell to her knees beside them, coughing violently and holding her throat with both hands.

Looking up, Sam gasped. That was Sergeant Buck Simmons jerking open the gate to the backyard!

"Buck!" she cried. "Over here!" Sam waved at the Recon marine.

Instantly, Buck changed course.

Sam saw the relief immediately etched on the marine's sweaty face. His green eyes were slits, his M-16 ready to be fired at any enemy he saw.

"Get down, Doc!" he yelled at her. "There's a full assault under way!"

Immediately, Sam flattened, her body as a barrier between the house and the little girl. Nannette screamed and dived down alongside her daughter, her hands over her head.

In minutes, it was all over. Buck hunkered near them, on one knee, his full attention trained on the house at all times. He was providing a barrier between them and the Diablos, Sam realized belatedly.

Sam saw a dark figure move through the bedroom they'd just occupied. It was a marine. As soon as he stepped outside, rifle in hand, Sam gasped. She handed Nanette the IV bag to hold for her daughter.

"Roc!" she cried, scrambling to her feet. "Roc!"

Sam didn't care who saw her at that moment. After the terror of nearly being killed, having Roc appear so miraculously shattered her military restraint.

Roc heard Sam's voice calling his name. When she got up from behind Sergeant Simmons and ran straight toward him, her arms wide, his heart mushroomed with relief. He didn't give a damn about military protocol at that moment, as she flew into his arms.

Taking her full weight, while she wrapped her arms tightly around his neck, Roc took two steps back and clamped his left arm around her body.

"Sam..." he rasped.

Sobbing, Sam whispered, "Oh, Roc...I'm sorry...so sorry. This is all my fault! I was so scared.... I love you so much! I love you!" And she pressed a series of fierce kisses on the hard line of his mouth.

Those precious seconds spun out of time for Roc. Her mouth was soft and hungry against his. Holding her hard against him, he leaned down and savagely returned her kisses. Had he heard right? Had Sam said she loved him? He could barely take it all in. There was too much going on. The Diablos had been routed. Roc and his men had prisoners to take care of.

Tearing his mouth from hers, he looked down into her eyes, which were swimming with tears of relief and joy. "Stay with Buck, sweetheart. I've got to get the prisoners rounded up. A bird is on its way here to take us back to HQ. You okay?''

Sam realized Roc was in charge of this assault. She quickly eased out of his embrace. ''Y-yes, I'm fine. Fine. Go ahead...I know you're needed elsewhere....'' And she touched her lips, which still sang from the cherishing strength of his mouth upon hers.

Giving her a burning, intimate look, Roc said in low, gravelly tone, ''When we get back to HQ, we'll have time, Sam....''

*February 7: 1830*

Sam sat on the edge of her bed in her tent. Her left arm had new stitches in it now, and a new bandage over it. The pain she felt was just deserts, she figured. And small enough payment for being rescued. Darkness ate away at the dusk outside her tent. Dressed in her fleecy robe, fresh from a hot bath, thanks to Kerry, Sam felt a cauldron of emotions that simply wouldn't be tucked away or ignored. Roc had been busy since their return aboard the Sea Stallion helicopter. He and his Recon unit had captured five Diablo members, though not their leader—Steve had escaped. But Roc and his team had put a major dent in the survivalists' camp, capturing four of their lieutenants.

Sam tried to comb her wet hair, but every time she raised her throbbing arm, pain shot through it. As she picked up the towel with her right hand and tried to blot her hair dry, her mind swung to Nannette and Jolie. They, too, had been taken prisoner, but Roc had dealt gently with them. It was as if he knew the wife and child of the leader had nothing to do with the man himself. Right now, both were in a recovery tent nearby, warm, safe and being fed their first hot meal in Lord knew how long.

"Sam? It's Roc. May I come in?"

Heart bounding once, Sam leaped to her feet. "Yes...come in...." She gripped the towel to her breast in anticipation.

Her eyes widened as Roc slipped into her tent and then zipped it shut. He was out of his military gear except for a clean green T-shirt and trousers. His hair was freshly washed, and gleamed in the low light of the single lightbulb. He'd shaved, too. The fact that he'd made an effort to look good before he saw her touched Sam deeply.

"How are you doing?" Roc asked as he turned around. Sam stood there looking like a disheveled, freckle-faced girl, the dark blue towel pressed between her breasts and hanging down to her knees. The light blue robe made her look young and vulnerable. Her red hair was wet, in dire need of being combed and tamed. Seeing her face grow pink, he smiled as he approached her.

"Better," Sam admitted in a husky tone, "now that you're here. You cleaned up, too."

Looking down at himself, he grinned slightly. "Yeah, I thought it would be a good idea. After running four miles between houses and up and down streets, we all got a little funky smelling."

Grinning, Sam gestured to the bed. "Isn't that the truth? Come, sit down."

He saw her comb on the bed. "Looks like you need some help with that red hair of yours." He picked the comb up as she sat down.

"My left arm is hurting too much to raise it," Sam griped.

"Mind if I try, sweetheart?" He stood over her, the comb in his hand.

Shocked but grateful, Sam looked up into his eyes…and saw how they burned with desire. She remembered the words that had flown out of her mouth when they'd met earlier. Nodding slightly, she whispered, "Yes, I'd like that…."

"I'll probably be all thumbs," Roc warned her good-naturedly. How badly Roc wanted to pull her into his arms and hold her. Simply hold her and feel grateful from his soul, that she was alive.

"I trust you, Roc." Her voice broke. "With my life…"

"Now, don't go getting mushy on me," he chided warmly, and lifted the first strand in his hands.

As he moved close, Sam closed her eyes. Roc was incredibly gentle as he awkwardly began to comb through the strands of her tangled hair. Clasping her hands together in her lap, she whispered, "I owe you a huge apology."

"You gave it to me back at the Diablos' headquarters," he growled. "I don't need two."

Shrugging, Sam said, "Well, you're going to get another one whether you want it or not, Captain. I was wrong. I should have listened to you. I guess I really didn't take you seriously. I thought…well, hell, I thought that after that firefight out at the last medevac site, the Diablos would slink off with their tails between their legs and leave us alone, because you'd overpowered them."

The red-gold strands of hair gleamed in his hand as he ran the comb slowly through them. Just listening to Sam's voice made his heart open like a flower to the heat of the sun. "Their leader is wily, Sam. He's crazy like a fox. I knew he'd hit us again."

"Lesson learned," she said, apology in her tone. Scalp tingling pleasantly as he finished combing out her hair, she watched when he put the comb on the dresser and then came and sat down next to her.

"Come here," Roc coaxed as he placed his arm around her. Being careful of her left arm, he laid Sam on her right side. Rearranging her robe so she kept warm, he stretched out against her length, propping himself up on his left elbow to look at her. To absorb her beautiful face into his heart. "There," he murmured. "Better?"

With Roc's hand resting gently on the curve of her hip, she nodded. Drowning in his stormy looking blue eyes, she said, "Much." She took a deep breath, and the words she'd been dying to say for so long tumbled out. "I've changed my mind, Roc."

"Oh? About what?" He grazed her damp hair with his hand. Every time he touched Sam, he saw flecks of gold come to her large, vulnerable-looking green eyes. How badly he wanted to kiss her. To love her and share with her how much she meant to him.

"About us," she managed to answer, looking down. Then she forced herself to gaze back up at him. "I said something out there that I should have told you before, but I was afraid." Compressing her lips, she saw him nod slightly. "The last time we were in here together, I wasn't completely honest with you."

"I know you weren't, sweetheart." Roc gave her a tender smile as her eyes flared with surprise. "You were scared. I knew you liked me—I hoped you loved me or were falling in love with me. But you couldn't admit that because of Brad. You lost one marine. You weren't prepared to maybe lose another. I understood, Sam. Believe me, I did."

Gulping back the tears that created a lump in her throat, Sam reached up regardless of the pain it caused her, and touched his face with her fingertips. "You knew?"

"Sure."

"You're awful confident of yourself."

Grinning, he said, "I love you, Samantha Andrews. Don't ask me when or how it happened. When I first met you six months ago, you were the biggest pain in the rear I'd ever come across. But now—" his smile turned gentle as he brushed several strands of hair away from her cheek "—now you own my heart, my soul, and I'm the happiest marine on the face of this earth."

His words, warm and emotional, blanketed her with happiness. Sam realized in those tender moments that the love she held for Roc was different from what she'd shared with Brad. Deeper and more passionate. Her heart pounded with joy as she cupped his face with her hand.

"You have the courage of ten men, Roc."

"I never gave up, you know? When Diablo kidnapped you, the people of the area helped us locate you." His brows drew down. "If it weren't for them, for the kids and adults who had seen you being dragged along by them, we'd never have found you...."

Closing her eyes, Sam sighed, her hand resting on his chest. "I never expected you to find me. I figured I was a dead person walking."

"Well," Roc teased, lifting her chin and watching her eyes open to touch his soul with joy, "the woman

I love had been taken from me. I'd have moved heaven and hell to find you. We got lucky. So lucky..."

Then his fingers caressed her cheek and he lifted her chin toward his mouth, and Sam realized this was all she wanted and needed right now. "I owe a lot of people for saving my life...and what I owe you, Roc Gunnison, is my heart, my soul. I love you. I love you so much it overwhelms me. It scares me...."

Leaning down, brushing her lips in a featherlight caress, Roc whispered against her mouth, "We need to live each moment as if it were the last, sweetheart. Every heartbeat needs to be enjoyed. Every touch—" he bent down and worshipped her lips, then drew away "—needs to be taken into our hearts and held and remembered."

Lifting her hand, she curved it along his thick neck. "I want to love you, Roc. Love you with everything I have in me to give to you.... I'm afraid, but I'm not going to let it stop me this time. I've learned my lesson...."

"Let's be scared together," Roc said, and slowly disrobed her. Because it was so cool, he stood up and pulled back the covers, allowing Sam to snuggle down between the sheets to get warm. She was incredibly beautiful to him, naked yet vulnerable. He pulled off his T-shirt, got rid of his boots and trousers and slid in beside her. There was such love in Sam's emerald eyes as she came boldly into his arms, pressing the naked length of her body to his. Always being mindful of her injured arm, Roc maneuvered her onto her back.

As he leaned down to worship her parted lips, he caressed her small, firm breast with his hand. Hearing her moan, he closed his eyes and took her mouth more surely. Allowing his touch to range from her taut breasts down her long torso to the flare of her womanly hips, he then trailed his fingers along her sleek, firm thigh. There was such softness and strength in Sam, he realized as he began to slowly map out her body, learn it, absorb it and luxuriate in it.

The courage of her heart, Roc realized humbly, as he felt her hands began to outline his face, neck and shoulders, was awe inspiring. As she kissed him hungrily, teething his lower lip and arching insistently against his hardening body, he reveled in her bravery. Only hours before, Sam hadn't been sure she would live or die. Now they were here, in one another's arms, their bodies, their mouths, clinging together, reveling in life.

And yet, as Roc trailed his fingers upward, opening her long, curved thighs and feeling the honeyed fluid that her body was gifting him with, he knew that life and death were entwined irrevocably. Because of it, he vowed to cherish this time with her—and to love her as fiercely and tenderly as he could. Sharing his love with her was more than just physical, he knew. For right now, this minute, as he carefully maneuvered his weight on top of her, her glorious green eyes shining and her arms moving coaxingly around his shoulders as he gently entered her, life had won over death.

A moan tore from Sam as she felt Roc slide hotly into her wet, awaiting depths. As she twisted her hips upward in joyous welcome, an explosion of sunlight and rainbow of color seemed to cascade through her body. When his arms bracketed her head, his chest against her taut breasts, his hips moving in unison with hers, all her fears dissolved. Lashes closed, Sam clung to him, to his strength, to his tenderness as he slowly moved within her, the exquisite sensations leaving her gasping for more.

The world became a heated mix of smell, taste and touch as she met Roc's mouth, kissed his shoulder and absorbed every pleasure aroused by his damp, tight body moving sinuously against her own. The volcanic eruption of heat, like a jarring earthquake, shattered her inner core, and flung open the doors of her wildly beating heart as never before. When she climaxed, Sam felt Roc's arms tighten around her protectively. Once again, as she nuzzled his jaw, her face pressed against his tense, muscled shoulder, Sam felt his fierce protection blanket her. When he tensed and groaned, she smiled softly and welcomed his life into her body.

As they lay there afterward, caught in the swirling heat and light of their love for one another, Sam felt her incomplete and shattered world become healed and whole once again. Roc's love for her had mended her wounds, her fear. And she loved him fiercely in return, with all her heart.

# *Epilogue*

*March 3: 0900*

"Roc!" Sam called when she saw him up ahead of her, walking down the passageway of the naval hospital at Camp Reed. It was the first time she'd seen him that day and she could tell by the warmth in his eyes as he turned to her, his M-16 slung over his left shoulder and his helmet beneath his left arm, that he was just as glad as she was. Once she reached him and looked up at him, her heart swam with incredible joy. How had two weeks passed so quickly? So wonderfully?

Morgan Trayhern had had them flown in from area 5 for a huge Logistics meeting yesterday, and last night Roc and she had shared a room at the BOQ—Bachelor Officers Quarters—which was an incredible luxury. Her body still throbbed with warmth from the memory of their lovemaking last night. As his gaze focused on her, she saw his blue eyes turn tender.

"Laura Trayhern is leaving in a few minutes," Sam said, looking at her watch. "I'd like to drop in and say goodbye. I was her surgeon when they brought her in here, and we've formed a wonderful friendship. Would you like to join me?"

"Sure," he murmured. Orderlies, nurses, civilians and military personnel coming into the hospital flowed around them nonstop as he and Sam halted at the bank of elevators. Giving her a slight, one-cornered smile, Roc remembered tangling his fingers in that red hair of hers quite recently. Her cheeks were flushed and her eyes were a bright reminder of her love for him.

"You don't mind? I know you wanted to check that shipment going out to area 6 HQ before we took off with it."

"It can wait," he said. "This is more important." Roc understood now, more than ever, how Sam formed relationships with her patients. She never had been a distant, disconnected doctor. Just the opposite. In the past two weeks, they worked all three new medevac stations with Sam assisting the new navy medical teams flown in to run them. Roc had discovered so much more about Sam. About her unflagging spirit and fierce determination to help those who were suffering.

As the elevator doors swung open, they stepped in and the doors closed, cutting them off from the hustle and bustle of the hall. Immediately, Roc grinned down at her. "We're finally alone...."

"Yes, and I'm taking advantage of it!" Sam stretched up and planted a swift, hot kiss on his smiling mouth. As she eased away, her hands still resting on his powerful chest, she whispered, "I love you, Roc Gunnison. Every day is better with you. You make me feel like a giddy teenager!"

Her laughter was sweet. Before he could respond, however, the door started opening. Giving her a wink, he said, "More later, when appropriate, Dr. Andrews."

Chuckling, Sam tossed him a merry look over her shoulder and gestured for him to follow her. That was a pleasure, because Roc enjoyed seeing that loose, wild hair of hers flow like fire across her proud shoulders. Enjoyed watching the gentle sway of her hips, despite the long lab coat she wore. He was getting to know her body well.

How loving Sam was! Now that she'd fully entrusted herself to him, no matter what their dangerous future portended, she held nothing back. The nights spent together in the privacy of her tent at area 5 HQ were a heated, emotional outpouring, soothing their past wounds like a balm and healing them both.

"Laura!" Sam hailed as she opened the door to the private room. "Hi! Roc and I wanted to say goodbye to you before you left." She smiled at her friend.

Roc stepped into the room and nodded toward the blond-haired woman standing by a crib. "Morning, Mrs. Trayhern."

Laura smiled at them. "Hi, Sam. Captain, call me Laura. I'm not much for professional courtesy." Lifting her hand, she gripped Sam's. "I'm so glad you came!"

Just then, Roc heard the door open once more. Twisting his head, he saw Morgan come in. The man's expression had been dark and scowling, but as soon as he entered the room and spotted his wife standing over the crib, Roc saw his face relax and warmth come to his blue eyes. Wasn't that how Sam affected him? he wondered. Just having her nearby made all his worries and consternation dissolve.

As Morgan nodded hello to him and moved to his wife's side, Roc realized that the man loved his wife with a fierceness that he hadn't recognized before. He saw it now, because it matched his love for Sam.

"Well, well," Sam murmured, "look at you, Laura. All decked out and ready to go home to Montana! And you're wearing a movable brace on that ankle. No more crutches. No more wheelchair. I'll bet you're happy about that?"

Laughing, Laura reached up and gave Morgan a kiss on the cheek as he came around to her and settled his hand on the crib, where Baby Jane Fielding—so named when the orphaned child was rescued from the rubble—lay bundled in a pink, fluffy blanket.

"You should know better than anyone," Laura said with a chuckled. "I've been a good girl while here at the hospital, and my physical therapist pronounced me fit and ready for this on-and-off brace." She pointed proudly to her ankle, which was encased in an inflated plastic device that gave her newly healed bone the support it needed.

Chuckling, Sam stood with Roc on the other side of the wooden crib. Gazing down at the baby, Sam said, "Hey, I've heard scuttlebutt down in Maternity. Is it true? You're going to *adopt* this baby girl? That she has no relatives? No one?"

Sighing and smiling, Laura reached over and touched the infant's plump pink cheek. "Yes, it's true."

"We're going to be the proud parents of this little tyke," Morgan murmured, pleased. "She went through the hell of the earthquake with us, was found at the side of her dead mother by a woman marine and her search dog. From that time forward, Laura has been taking care of her, feeding her—''

''Changing her diapers...''

Grinning, Morgan nodded sagely. ''That too... often.''

''Of course,'' Laura told them proudly, ''Morgan has lots of experience in that department. He was a big help with our four other children.''

''Raising a baby is a full-time job, even with two people doing the work.'' Morgan agreed, placing his hand on his wife's shoulder and giving her a loving look.

''I think it's wonderful!'' Sam breathed. ''All the state and federal obstacles have been worked through so she can fly home with you, Laura?''

Groaning, Morgan said, ''All the i's have been dotted and the t's crossed.''

Reaching down, Sam stroked the baby's soft fat cheek. ''Well, she's in the best of hands. You have such love to give her. I hope, someday, she knows just how lucky she is.''

Roc marveled at the look on Sam's face as she caressed the baby's cheek. His body ached with a blinding need to someday give her a child that they would love as fiercely and devotedly as Morgan and Laura did this lucky little baby.

''Have you got a name for her?'' Sam asked, looking up at them.

Laura beamed. ''Yes. In fact, Morgan was able to cobble a family conference call on this so we could all decide on a name together.'' She clapped her hands in joy. ''Aly and Clay are stationed in the middle of the Indian Ocean at a top-secret island facility. Noah and Kit are up in Maine, because he's now the commander of a Coast Guard station, and of course, their parents, Chase and Rachel, are in Florida. And we were able to get our children on the phone, as well. Well, three of them at least. That was a major undertaking in itself!'' Laura laughed.

''It took a bit of a miracle,'' Morgan admitted with a slight smile. ''We weren't able to reach Jason, our oldest son.''

Laura heard the disguised pain in her husband's voice and gently laid her hand on his arm. ''But you tried and that's all you could do. I'm sure when Jason hears about it, he'll approve, darling.''

''I'll bet they were thrilled to hear from you, under the circumstances,'' Sam said enthusiastically.

''You bet.'' Morgan gave his wife an affectionate look. ''The family decided that she should be christened Kamaria Rachel Alyssa Trayhern.''

''Rachel is Morgan's mother's name,'' Laura explained. ''And Alyssa is his sister. Kamaria will be her first name and means 'beautiful like the moon.'''

''I'll bet everyone was pleased,'' Roc murmured.

Laura tucked her arm around her husband's waist. ''Oh, yes. I think everyone was.''

Leaning over the crib, Sam whispered to the infant, ''Well, Kamaria Rachel Alyssa Trayhern, welcome to your brave, bright new world. You've got two of the most wonderful people to love you, watch you grow up strong and confident.''

Roc hated to break the moment, but their time was running out. ''Sam?'' There was regret in his voice as he said it.

''I know...time to go.'' She straightened up.

"We've got lots to do out in the field, thanks to you, Morgan."

Nodding, he said, "No, thanks to you two. Sam, I didn't think you could do it so quickly, but you've given us a plan of action that we can now duplicate in every area of the basin. That was no small task."

Glowing beneath Morgan's praise, she murmured, "Thanks...but I had some great help and support here with Roc and his men. We couldn't have done it without them." She gave him a fond look, not trying to hide her love for him.

Laura glanced at them, and then up at her husband. She nudged him with her elbow. "Morgan, dear...are you seeing to it that Captain Gunnison and Sam will remain together out there in the field? You aren't separating them, are you, dear?"

Morgan grinned uncomfortably. He knew by the tone of his wife's voice what she was up to. Laura was matchmaking. Again. Laura's implication confirmed what he'd suspected: that Sam and Roc had fallen in love. They were a good match for one another. Equals. Strong and sure of themselves as individuals.

As he saw the warmth they felt for one another mirrored in their eyes, he felt Laura nudge him gently in the ribs again in case he didn't get the message the first time.

"Yes, dear, I've made sure that Captain Gunnison is going to shadow Sam's every movement out in the field for a long time to come. With the Diablos' leader still on the loose, Sam is still a target."

Frowning, Sam felt some of her joy dissipate. Turning to Morgan, she asked, "What have you heard from the interrogation of the Diablo lieutenants?"

"They're over at the base brig," Morgan said. "The FBI is taking their statements. And," he scowled, "they aren't talking. None of them. They've all lawyered up, claiming their innocence."

"Survivalists are a group unto themselves," Roc said. "And it looks like they're not going to give up key information, such as where the group's main headquarters is, or anything else."

"No," Morgan sighed, "they aren't. There's nothing else we can do. They don't want any deals. They don't want anything. They hate the federal government and keep repeating to the interrogators that they aren't part of it."

"That's too bad," Sam murmured. "I was so hoping that this could be over. We've got epidemics in full swing now. It's a race against time to get those medevac units up and fully functioning in all these other areas, and we've got to be on guard against the Diablos and their weapons, as well."

"Well," Morgan groused, "I've finally gotten a marine hunter-killer team from Camp Lejeune in North Carolina cut free, and they're flying in. There's a firefighter, a Lieutenant Mandy Wilson, who thinks she knows where one of the gang's staging areas is located. I'm going to hook up the captain and his team with her in hopes of smoking them out and capturing them." Running his hand through his short dark hair, he smiled at his wife. "Now stop looking worried, Laura."

Gently picking up her baby, Laura cradled the infant in her arms. "I just worry for Sam, that's all. I want to make sure she has Roc at her side to continue guarding her...taking care of her...."

Shaking his head, Morgan murmured ruefully,

"Darling, you don't need to worry your beautiful blond head about that. Captain Gunnison is Sam's permanent bodyguard." In more ways than one, if Morgan was any judge of it. The way they looked at one another did his heart good. And he hadn't missed the fact that around Sam's neck was a small gold chain with a very old-looking wedding ring hanging from it. That hadn't been there before, and he had a hunch Roc had given it to her. Since they spent a lot of time out in the field with danger around them, Morgan knew their personal time together was at a bare minimum. The hours Sam worked were horrendous—up to sixteen a day—while she made sure the medevac models were operating properly and at maximum capacity.

"We gotta go," Roc said apologetically, giving Sam a tender look. "Congratulations on the new baby, Laura, sir...." He held his hand across the crib to Morgan, who took it and shook it warmly.

"Thanks, Roc," Laura said, gently swaying with the baby in her arms. "You two stay safe out there, you hear?"

"We will," Sam promised. She quickly moved around the crib and gave Laura and little Kamaria a gentle hug. "I know Morgan is going to miss the daylights out of you."

Groaning, Morgan said, "You don't know the half of it."

Roc opened the door for Sam. He understood Morgan's comment. There wasn't an hour that went by that Roc didn't enjoy having Sam in his company. The idea of her not warming his bed at night seemed like the worst kind of loss. Morgan would remain here, at Camp Reed, and Laura would be flying back to their home in Montana.

"Bye!" Sam called breathlessly as she hurried out the door.

Walking quickly down the passageway toward the elevators once more, Sam gave Roc a brilliant smile filled with love. "Isn't life wonderful? Even out of the worst carnage and disaster, something like this happens. Baby Kamaria gets new, loving parents." She clapped her hands in joy and skipped along for a moment like a child herself.

Chuckling, Roc slowed and hit the button on the elevator. The doors opened and they walked in. Once more they were alone. As the elevator began to move downward, Roc wrapped his arms around Sam and drew her near. Leaning down, he kissed her awaiting, smiling lips.

"We're getting pretty good at finding private moments with one another," he growled, humor in his tone as he grazed her soft, eager lips.

"Mmm...very good, Captain Gunnison." She reached up on tiptoe and met his mouth with undisguised hunger. Then, rocking back in his arms, which held her securely against him, Sam inhaled his very male smell. As they drew apart, she enjoyed the dangerous, glinting quality in his blue eyes. Touching the ring that hung in the hollow of her throat, she whispered, "I love you, Roc. And this ring—your grandmother's wedding ring—it was such a wonderful gift! I'll treasure it always."

Pride flowed through him as the elevator came to a stop. Before the doors opened, he whispered, "That ring shows how serious I am toward you. Right now, our future is nothing but chaos. We're going to make every hour count. We're going to learn more about each other every day.''

Eyes filling with momentary tears of happiness, Sam nodded and blinked them away. ''I've learned my lesson, Roc. I'm committed to you. To us.''

The doors opened and they stepped out. Threading their way through the traffic in the passageway, past Sam's E.R., they moved out into the fresh, chilled morning air. Beyond the hospital, not far away, Roc could see the airport. He spotted the Sea Stallion, which was already warming up, its blades whirling. At the curb, a Humvee waited to take them there. As he stepped out of the crowd, Roc moved close to Sam's side. Leaning over, he whispered to her, ''And I'm committed to you. Forever, sweetheart. Forever...''

* * * * *

*Coming in February 2003 from*
USA TODAY *bestselling author*

*LINDSAY McKENNA*

*A brand-new book in the*
MORGAN'S MERCENARIES:
DESTINY'S WOMEN *saga!*

*HER HEALING TOUCH*

*(Silhouette Special Edition 1519)*
*Turn the page for a sneak preview....*

# *Chapter One*

Angel gulped as she looked up into the craggy features of Burke Gifford as he approached her. Why on earth was she so drawn to him? Was it his cool gray eyes assessing her like a predator might look at a quarry? This man had dynamic charisma, she realized.

He moved like a jaguar, his body lean and tight. He missed nothing with those alert eyes of his. She felt her pulse race erratically. His curiosity made her feel a little too vulnerable at the moment. She hadn't expected to be overwhelmed by this Special Forces guy. But she was. Confused by her feelings, Angel tried to pretend she was at ease and casual.

''Sergeant Paredes? I'm Burke Gifford,'' he said, stopping before her and holding his hand out to her.

''Welcome to the Black Jaguar Squadron,'' Angel replied and proffered her right hand.

His hand was large, with thick calluses on it along

with a lot of scars here and there. She led her much smaller hand into his, hoping he wouldn't give her a bone-crushing shake. He didn't. To her surprise, Gifford monitored the amount of pressure he exerted on her damp fingers. That implied he had some sensitivity. That was good.

"Thanks. This is quite an operation. I'm impressed. I had no idea..." Burke replied, still holding her hand. He liked, too much, the feeling of her strong yet soft hand in his. Her fingers were cool and damp. Was she nervous? Burke perused her upturned face. She was arrestingly attractive in an alluring, exotic way. Sternly, he warned himself he shouldn't care what Angel looked like. He was here on a scouting mission. That was *all.*

Angel nearly jerked her hand out of his. The wild tingles fleeing up her hand jolted her. Surprised her. She saw his straight dark brows gather together over her obvious reaction.

"Thanks, Sergeant." Quickly, Angel tucked her hand into the pocket of her coat, her fingers burning like fire.

Now she was really worried. How was she going to work with this man for the next six weeks when he had such an effect on her?

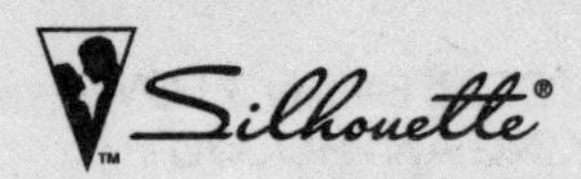


INTIMATE MOMENTS®

# COMING NEXT MONTH

**#1189 SECRETS AND LIES—Maggie Shayne**
*The Oklahoma All-Girl Brands*
Agent Alex Stone's assignment sounded simple: impersonate a missing foreign dignitary who had a habit of hiding out with his new bride. The hard part was working with Melusine Brand, the brash beauty playing his wife. When Alex's perfect plan turned deadly, he found capturing kidnappers easy compared to fighting his feelings for Mel.

**#1190 THE PRINCE'S WEDDING—Justine Davis**
*Romancing the Crown*
Jessica Chambers had no idea the Colorado rancher she fell in love with was actually Prince Lucas Sebastiani of Montebello. For their son's sake, she agreed to marry Lucas and return to his kingdom. As she prepared for her royal wedding, Jessica searched for her former lover in the future king, but was she really willing to wed a virtual stranger?

**#1191 UNDERCOVER M.D.—Marie Ferrarella**
*The Bachelors of Blair Memorial*
A drug ring had infiltrated Blair Memorial Hospital, and it was up to DEA agent Terrance McCall to bring them down. The plan moved smoothly, with Terrance posing as a pediatrician, until he saw Dr. Alix DuCane, the woman he'd walked away from six years ago. Now he had two missions: defeat the drug lords *and* win back the only woman he'd ever loved.

**#1192 ONE TOUGH COWBOY—Sara Orwig**
*Stallion Pass*
Suffering from amnesia, Laurie Smith couldn't remember her own name, but she knew that her car crash was no accident. Someone had run her off the road—someone who was still out there. Handsome cowboy Josh Kellogg promised to protect this beautiful mystery woman from the killer on her trail, but who would protect Laurie's heart from Josh?

**#1193 IN HARM'S WAY—Lyn Stone**
Falling in love with a murder suspect wasn't the smartest move detective Mitch Winton had ever made. But in his heart he knew that Robin Andrews couldn't be responsible for her estranged husband's death. Once Robin became the real killer's new target, Mitch was determined to prove her innocence—and his love. But first he would have to keep them both alive....

**#1194 SERVING UP TROUBLE—Jill Shalvis**
After being rescued from a hostage situation, Angie Rivers was ready for a new life and hoped to start it with Sam O'Brien, the sexy detective who had saved her. Love, however, was the last thing Sam was looking for—or at least that was what he told himself. But when Angie unwittingly walked straight into danger, Sam realized life without Angie wasn't worth living.

SIMCNM1102